EMAIL FROM MARS: OUTBOUND

LON GROVER

*Ad astra per
ardua ad nostra*

ISBN: 1492253944
ISBN-13: 978-1492253945

DEDICATED TO:

Hannah Raymond, my great niece

The first crew to land on Mars has already been born.

TABLE OF CONTENTS

ACKNOWLEDGMENTS

The first person I would like to mention is my wife's aunt, Margean Gladysz, for her gift of providing the inspiration to write. It was the publishing of her adventures (*A Spy On The Bus: Memoir of a Company Rat*) that prompted me to even attempt to write a novel.

When I first came up with the idea for this book, being in the Science Fiction genre, I wanted the science to be as realistic as possible. So, the first person I contacted for technical assistance was Julie Edwards of the Mars Society. I asked if she could put me in touch with anyone that might be willing to answer questions as they arose. Julie proved to be a great contact, as she put me in touch with Brian Enke, the author of *Shadows of Medusa*. Brian's assistance in orbital mechanics proved to be invaluable. Later, Julie was instrumental in putting me in touch with Alan Chen, who contacted Steve Foss, who then contacted Darrel Robertson. The cover art is based on original artwork by my wife, Lou Ann, which also appears within the pages of the book, and porthole photos by Darrel Robertson at the Mars Desert Research Station in Utah. Lou Ann also drew the sketch of the bolo, as well as the one of Earth, Mars, and Luna. Ben Slack finalized construction of the cover by using his computer skills to combine the artwork and add graphics. Thanks, Ben. J. B. Markus generated technical drawings. I think you will find he converted my *pencil on graph-paper* sketches to a usable spacecraft design, quite well. Now, I just need to find someone to build the real thing.

I would like to thank Dr. Geza Nagy of Infrastructure Composites International for answers to questions regarding the Mars Society's Flashline Arctic Research Station Habitat construction, as well as Michelle Webb, Technical Services Representative for the Charlotte Pipe Company, for coming up with the weights and measures for the water pipe-storage concept and helping to establish the feasibility of such a system. Also, Dr. John Lennoff assisted with a bit of material science, in the form of leaded acrylic in place of the leaded polycarbonate, I had envisioned.

Another big thank you goes out to Dr. Robert Zubrin, founder of the Mars Society and author of *The Case for Mars*, *Entering Space*, *Mars On Earth*, *How to Live on Mars*, and several other books. Dr. Zubrin is a wonderfully powerful and inspirational public speaker. When posed with a question about the manufacture of fuel on Mars, he came up with an answer in less than twenty minutes. Thanks again.

As the title implies, email communications are taking the place of postal letter writing. So, to gather inspiration through real-world communications for the book, I emailed a few friends in my social network, explained what I was about to attempt and asked them for input. The basis for one of the characters (Commander Tyler Cody) resulted from the input of Tom Smith. A great deal of input from my wife, Lou Ann Grover, went into the development of the characters of Emma Devlin and Penny Castle (and she promises me that someday she will give me a calendar like Emma sent to Brandon). In the character of Rich Devlin, there is more than a touch of the whimsical nature of my stepson, Jay Ball.

Plot development also got an assist from Lou Ann as well as John Stitzel, one of my co-workers. John suggested the book could use some international intrigue.

Once the base story was written, Lou Ann read through it and found typos and grammatical errors. Along the way, she began making suggestions for things like, 'Sally smiled at Tom.' Changing it to 'Sally smiled warmly at Tom, dimples appearing at the corners of her mouth.' Occasionally, she would pick up an entire paragraph, turn it inside out and shake it, just to get the bugs out. Then, she would highlight the changes she had made so I could view them and either accept or reject the suggested change. Being a man of at least average intelligence, I usually accepted her suggestions. Thus, I give credit and many thanks to her for proofreading and first-round editing. (Thanks bunches, sweetheart.)

As this process went along, I began emailing out copies of chapters to friends, soliciting their opinion of the story. Unfortunately, as we all have real lives to lead, not everyone had time to read through it or just didn't find time to comment. For those that endured the rough draft (rough being the operative word) and provided commentary and constructive input, I wish to thank the following readers, in no particular order: Margean Gladysz, Jay Ball, Mike Coppens, Richard Salassi, Tom Smith, Mary Anne Anderson, Tracy Black Smith, Kerrisha Havens, Ilagene Moss, Andy Weller, and Michelle Jones. Thank you, one and all, for your valuable assistance.

And last, but by no means least, I wish to thank you, the reader. Without your interest, this novel would just be collecting dust. I am sure you will find as much enjoyment in reading this book as I had in the creation and writing. *Ad Astra* (To the stars).

Lon H. Grover

INTRODUCTION

Just a mere 29 years ago, after President George H. W. Bush proposed a manned mission to Mars by 2019 (the 50th anniversary of the Apollo Moon Landing), NASA conducted a study to project a cost estimate. Ninety days later, they came back with a package consisting of ideas from every NASA facility in the country. This scenario required six launches to assemble a spacecraft in Earth orbit and would cost the taxpayers around half a trillion dollars. Congress put a kybosh to that idea on the spot.

Around that same time, Dr. Robert Zubrin and others at Martin Marietta came up with a plan they called *Mars Direct*, which would utilize some of the natural resources found on Mars. The theory was that if you don't have to take the fuel along with you for the return trip, your spacecraft doesn't have to be the size of the Battlestar Gallactica.

By reducing the size of the craft and utilizing a few other specialized modifications, the total cost was $50 billion, one-tenth of the NASA sum. NASA was even impressed with the ideas that the team had devised, but chose to add one more element to the mission scenario (an Earth Return Vehicle parked in Mars Orbit) as well as two additional crewmembers. NASA then called their mission profile *Mars Semi-Direct*.

As outlined in Phase One of the mission, an unmanned and unpressurized workshop was blasted to Mars in 2016, by a SpaceX Falcon Heavy (heavy-lift launch vehicle). Onboard was a fuel processing plant stocked with a few tons of liquid hydrogen, together with foodstuff for the flight that would follow. Along with these was an unpressurized lightweight truck carrying a One Mega Watt Electric Thermonuclear Generator mounted on a winch in the bed. Once on Mars, the truck was off-loaded and driven (remotely from Earth) onto the surface. The truck spooled out a few hundred meters of power cable as it rolled, then dropped the generator into a small crater (which provided shielding) before it was fired up. That generator is now providing the power needed to run the fuel processor.

The fuel processor is designed to produce methane and water, then breaking down the water to make hydrogen and oxygen: the process only produces twice the oxygen as methane. As it is used to oxidize the methane for the return trip to Earth, a lot more oxygen is needed: four and a half to one is the ideal ratio.

Another way to produce oxygen is to distill it directly from carbon dioxide, making one part oxygen and the other part carbon monoxide. Normally, you wouldn't need the carbon monoxide and would discard it back into the atmosphere, but in the spirit of living off the land, one of the mission coordinators came up with a novel use for it: inflating the greenhouse's superstructure. Not the interior where the plants will be located, but the exterior structural envelope of the greenhouse.

Shaped like a Quonset hut, the greenhouse is an arched structure made up of three layers of inflatable, transparent, Mylar tubes. As an air mattress contains tubes running back and forth from head to foot, the tubes of the greenhouse run up from the ground on one side of the canopy, over the open area, and down to the ground on the other side. By inflating these tubes with carbon monoxide, it is a way of using the non-breathable gas and not dumping it back into Mars' atmosphere. Steel cables running over the structure every meter, and anchored on the ends, will keep the building from blowing away in a windstorm.

If the outer layer were to be breached, another layer can be moved into place on the inside and inflated. The breached layer can be left in place for quite a while before needing to be removed, and that can be done in pieces. As long as it lets in the light, keeps in the air, and keeps out the cold, all is well.

Included on that flight was a pressurized rover for

exploring the surface in a shirtsleeve environment, and a SpaceX Dragon, Mars Ascent Vehicle (MAV). Eventually, the crew will use the MAV to leave Mars and rendezvous with the Earth Return Vehicle (ERV).

In 2017, the second unmanned Falcon Heavy deposited the fully fueled, fully stocked ERV into Mars' orbit. The third launch, happening this year, will consist of the manned crew module (the habitat: Bolo One), which is supplied with just enough fuel to last them until they reach Mars. This will be a lengthy expedition. The time line for the journey consists of six-months traveling to Mars, eighteen months spent on the surface, and then a six-month traverse back to Earth: 2 ½ years total. The final launch will occur two weeks after Bolo One lifts off, and will propel an identical workshop/fuel processor to the planet. This is the mission these six brave pioneers have chosen to undertake. And so, here in May of 2018, they are about to make that next giant leap.

Back in July of 2011, at the end of the Space Shuttle era, the Obama Administration was vacillating between the George W. Bush *Return To The Moon* initiative and a manned mission to Mars. Mars appeared to be a much better target, but NASA's timetable for a manned mission was set in the sphere of the 2030s. Then, an association of private investors came forward with a unique proposal. This group, who became known as The Sponsors, would front money for the radically new equipment from SpaceX. The Sponsors devised their plan based on economic analysis from the 1980s, which showed that for every dollar spent on the Apollo Program, seven dollars had been put back into the economy in creation of new products, spin-offs, and jobs. An updated study has now put that figure at more than fourteen dollars per dollar spent.

Based on the *Mars Semi-Direct* scenario, NASA's plan called for five consecutive manned missions over the next ten years. Because the orbits of Earth and Mars are so different, the five missions would consist of different travel times between launch and landing. The first manned mission will launch on May 11, 2018 to take advantage of the perigee, or closest alignment between the planets, for the shortest travel time of six months each way. As the perigee distance changes every two years due to Mars' elliptical orbit of the sun, travel times vary on a fifteen – seventeen year cycle, optimizing again around 2030.

Using economic models of industry, The Sponsors estimated that all five missions could be completed for less than $10 billion. In exchange for their support, The Sponsors would be awarded all patent rights to products developed specifically for the missions, gleaning a 15% return from sales. They would also be granted mineral rights to any and all discoveries on Mars. The Sponsors expect to recover their investment before the fifth mission. *The best way to predict the future is to invent it.* – Alan C. Kay

Chapter 1

Friday, May 11, 2018 (Alanday, Sagittarius 25, 0031)

Captain Steven Thomas and two of the men under his command, Williams and Bentley, were swiftly lowered on ropes from the helicopter, as it hovered almost silently, above the rooftop observation deck of Marina City's southwest tower, in the heart of Chicago. Barely a sliver of a moon would have been visible, had it not been cloaked by an overcast sky, and it was just a bit past 01:00 hours. After touching down and disconnecting their harnesses from the floating ropes, Steve and his Armored Tactical Assault Command (ATAC) team rigged rappelling ropes and prepared to drop over the south side of the tower, overlooking the river, flowing nearly 200 meters below.

Meanwhile, on the twenty-first floor, the lowest of the residential floors, situated directly above the parking decks, Fahid stood up and stretched, as if trying to touch the ceiling with the palms of both hands. "Abu, this movie is very good, but I'm getting exhausted," he yawned. Abu crossed the living room for the door to the balcony, tapping an unlit cigarette on the breach of the Uzi slung around his neck.

"You should get some sleep. Tomorrow, we have a busy day at the Sears Tower. Or, you can take my watch and I'll get a nap," Abu offered. Fahid corrected, "Willis Tower, now." Abu smiled snidely, revealing a gold-capped tooth, "Soon, it won't matter what it is called."

"And, no thank you. You keep your guard duty. I'm just going to get a glass of water and turn in," Fahid replied as he wandered into the kitchen. Abu stepped out onto the balcony, raising the cigarette to his lips. As he lowered his head, bringing the match up to meet the cigarette, a .223 hollow-point went

13

zipping through the top of his forehead, exiting the base of his skull through a hole the size of a golf ball, before shattering the living room window with a loud crash. 'I guess he didn't read the Surgeon General's warning,' the sniper thought as he removed his infrared headgear and prepared to descend from his perch atop the Renaissance Hotel.

In the kitchen, Fahid dropped the glass he had just pulled from the cupboard, grabbed the 9mm Parabellum from the back of his waistband and dashed into the living room. At that same moment, four other cell members, who had been sleeping in the bedroom on the far side of the living room, met him there. As Fahid turned toward the gaping hole that was once the window, Captain Thomas' assault team swung inward and set down over the rail of the balcony. Gunshots exploded with a Pop! Pop! Bang! Pop! Fahid aimed his weapon toward the first two men on his left, fired, and hit them both squarely in their chests. The force of the impact pushed the two back over the rail. The third shot, discharged by Captain Thomas, successfully struck and killed Jamal who, freshly awakened, had brought his gun up to the ready. The fourth shot, issued again by Fahid, sent Captain Thomas flailing backward over the rail, following his teammates.

Fahid and the remaining three terrorists spent the next several minutes scurrying around, gathering the rest of the weapons in the apartment. As they were about to exit the condominium, Ayman al-Masri, the cell leader, turned to Fahid, ordered him to lay low for the next four hours and then meet at the primary cell hide-out, at 9423 South Lafayette, near the 95th St. Greyhound Sub-Station. Fahid repeated the address back to Ayman, to be sure he had heard it correctly, "ninety-four twenty-three South Lafayette. I have it. Salaam."

"Nine four two three South Lafayette, check," Captain Thomas parroted. He and his team were already wringing out their black fatigues in the pick-up boat, slowly and stealthily maneuvering upriver. Their attention was focused on the conversation being picked up by the transmitter Fahid had planted a few hours prior to the firefight, just under the edge of the cocktail table, in the middle of the living room. Fahid had been firing the well-aimed, special low-velocity rounds, designed to leave no more than minor bruising behind the team's flak jackets.

This had been a most successful seven-man operation, including: Captain Steven Thomas, Jake Williams and Howard Bentley, along with the chopper pilot (Charlie Cook), the sniper (Harvey Hawkeye Hawkins), the boat pilot (George Shay), and their comrade under deep cover, Fahid, better known as Jesus Gonzalez. His Hispanic characteristics were ideal to allow him to blend in as a member of the Middle Eastern terrorist cell.

From: Steven Thomas
Subject: Stuck at work
Date: May 11, 2018 6:02 a.m.
To: Dr. Valerie Thomas

_____Communications Lag Time (CLT): Zero, pre-launch, no delay.

Dear sweet Val,

I know you're busy with launch preparations and won't see this right away, but I wanted to let you know how sorry I am that I won't be able to make it to the launch to see you off, as I had hoped. It's a hair past 6 a.m. and I'm still at work. : (Been at it all night, but we're finally wrapping up the loose ends. As usual, I can't go into any detail, but I can say the launch this morning won't be the only story making the 6 o'clock news tonight. LOL

It's been a long night and I've still got a report to write. Hoping to get to bed by about 10 this morning, but if the launch looks like it will get off on schedule, I'll stay up awhile longer to catch it on the tube.

I'm sure going to miss you, babe. Give me till about 10 p.m. and Facetime me if you can. I'll be all rested up by then

15

and look forward to seeing you, sweetheart.

I love you, so much,

Steve

< ≡ ♂ ≡ >

*

(Thursday, July 20, 2017)

Held a little over eleven months earlier, on the 48th anniversary of the first moon landing, was the night of the big press conference to announce the Manned Mars Mission. Launched during the previous year by a Falcon Heavy Rocket, the unmanned Fuel Processor One (FP1), with the Mars Ascent Vehicle (MAV) mounted atop, had already touched down at the designated landing site, in the Avernus Colles region. A systems check showed everything was in good working order. FP1 was now producing methane and oxygen for the crew to use on the surface after they arrive, as well as to fuel the MAV when they are ready to return to Earth.

At the media event that evening, the handpicked crew was being introduced to the world, headed by their Mission Commander, Dr. Tyler R. Cody. Ty, as his friends call him, wasn't even a year old when Neil Armstrong and Edwin 'Buzz' Aldrin, Jr. made the first footprints on the Sea of Tranquility. Now, this sandy haired, 1.7 m, Navy doctor was about to lead a group of top-notch scientists and engineers on the adventure of a lifetime; *the next giant leap*. Although he had made a real career for himself in the Navy, this was the crowning achievement Ty had worked for since his days as an undergrad at Western Michigan University.

How beautiful his wife, Claire, looked sitting down there in the front row, amongst the other wives and husbands of the crew. She was smiling broadly, proud of her husband for being among the best of the very best. Ty couldn't take his eyes off of her. He nearly missed the Master of Ceremonies announcing his name, had it not been for her gaze with sideways head nod, cuing Ty that he should be doing something (besides staring at her as if they'd just met). In the nick of time, he got to his feet, hoping he had not looked too foolish. He approached the podium amidst the thundering standing ovation.

Ty began, "Ladies and gentlemen, distinguished guests, my fellow colleagues, it is my extreme honor to stand before you this evening as the team leader of such a fine group of individuals. Each and every one of them was selected for their expertise in not only one field of study, but two, and in some cases, three or more." He made a sweeping gesture in the direction of Dr. Valerie Thomas, and the room stood to applaud once more. Valerie stood up and nodded to the audience in grateful acceptance, smiling broadly.

Ty continued, "We, the crew of Bolo One, have been honored and blessed to be selected as the first crew to venture beyond Low Earth Orbit and even the Moon, to travel outward to the next planet from the sun, Mars. It is our goal to travel to Mars, study the planet, establish a base of continued exploration, and return safely to our loved ones back here on Earth. A two-and-a-half year roundtrip mission, spent battling the solar radiation of space, the reduced gravity and micro-thin atmosphere of Mars, and the worst of all hazards, the boredom of the six-month transit *there and back again*." He smiled broadly and a roar of applause and laughter erupted from the auditorium. "And so with that, I would like to introduce to you the crew of Bolo One. To my immediate right, my second in command and a wonderful mechanical engineer, as well as a top-notch geologist, ..."

*

Ten months later: Friday, May 11, 2018 (Alanday, Sagittarius 25, 0031)

A distant and disembodied voice came over their headsets, "Launch in one minute... 60... 59... 58..." Preparation is underway for the launch of the first manned mission to Mars. On a mission such as this, it is important to keep the overall spacecraft weight to a minimum. To this end the crew will consist of two medical doctors, two geologists, two horticulturists and two chemists, along with one geochemist and three mechanical engineers. All of these duties will be shared by the six-person crew, each possessing multiple talents.

"57... 56... 55..." Commander Tom, the new mission commander, is a veteran of two Earth orbit and two circum-lunar missions undertaken to work out any bugs in the Artificial Gravity Assist System (AGAS) being used on the Bolo One journey. It was Tom's idea to use a type of clockwork mechanism, able to reel out the tether a little at a time during the trip to whatever length was desired. On the way to Mars, a full one Gee of gravity is preferred to keep the crew strong and healthy. But, after a year and a half at thirty-nine percent of Earth gravity, they will start their trip home at one Martian Gee and gradually build themselves back up to one Earth Gee.

"54... 53... 52..." Commander Tom is a rugged, good-looking six-footer. Prematurely gray at 40, this gives him an aura of experience, marking him as the kind of leader people like to follow. Though happily married to his high school sweetheart, Penny, since '99, he's still a favorite with the ladies at every press conference. Commander Tom holds a doctorate in Mechanical Engineering, as well as almost holding a Masters in Geology (just missing the paperwork).

"51... 50... 49..." As a private corporation, the majority of people involved with these Mars missions are not employed by NASA or any of its sub-contractors. Nevertheless, some of the old traditions are hard to discard. For example, none of the Bolo One crewmembers were ever in the military, but the group leader is still referred to as Commander, much like in the merchant marines. Likewise, the old Mission Control has given way to Mission Support, even as some of the old buildings and systems are still being used under contract. It is clear that the *Corporation* is running the show. Being somewhat casual-minded, Tom is not crazy about being called Commander, but when leadership needs to be asserted it is clear that Commander Tom is in charge.

"48... 47... 46..." Tom's number two, Dr. Valerie Thomas, is a General Practitioner, with training in Psychology, making her the ship's onboard councilor. Valerie is also a certified Master Gardener, her favorite hobby. As a result, Valerie can cultivate and grow many of the specialized herbs and plants needed to concoct some of their medications. In addition to her horticultural skills, she is cross-trained in Physical Therapy, some Eastern medicine, and General Dentistry.

"45... 44... 43..." Valerie honed her horticultural skills aboard the International Space Station (ISS), back in 2011. At that time, Russian cosmonauts and American astronauts were growing crops as a test bed for long-term space missions. Back then, the lack of gravity demanded shoebox sized gardens using Arcillite and grains of clay enriched with time-released nutrients. These minuscule gardens will not be needed on this mission to Mars due to the use of artificial gravity to keep the plants in place during the transit.

"42... 41... 40..." Valerie is a petite, slender lady in her late thirties with medium brown hair, curling softly to her shoulders. She is not what you would call a 'looker', rather plain in fact. Valerie has been married to her second husband (Steve Thomas, a covert ops group leader) for four and a half years. It isn't that she was hard to get along with; she was simply too absorbed in her career to maintain a relationship, until she met Steve.

"39... 38... 37..." The next member of the crew is Dr.

Carl Wilson. He's a short, rather stocky, blonde kid, 24 years of age, and named after the Astronomer / Astrophysicist, Dr. Carl Sagan. Dr. Carl Wilson is the crew's Mechanical Engineer / Geochemist.

"36... 35... 34..." Tom jokes that Carl is as smart as a whip, but not very bright: he still has a lot to learn about life. One of those 'whiz kids' you hear tell about, he received his Masters in Mechanical Engineering at the tender age of eighteen. But, it was the Doctorate in Geochemistry that won him a berth on this first Mars mission. While still in college, Carl met the love of his life, Mary Croft.

"33... 32... 31..." Adding to his impressive resume, is an even more impressive pedigree. Dr. Warner Von Braun was Carl's maternal great-grandfather and, Nazi accusations aside, helped tremendously with mission publicity.

"30... 29... 28..." Dr. Sally Chung, the mission's Chemist / Geologist, is rather attractive, mid-thirties, Asian American who is also well versed in Gemology, having studied for three years in Amsterdam. Sally has two shuttle missions on her resume: the first was a resupply mission to the ISS; the second, a six-month stay conducting crystal growth experiments in Zero Gee.

"27... 26... 25..." Like Tom, she is also married to her high school sweetheart, Robert Hackard, although she has kept her maiden name. Which is a good thing since their marriage has been on shaky ground for quite some time. The mission psychologists might have pulled Sally from this trip had they been able to see over the top of her well-constructed wall of denial.

"24... 23... 22..." Number five, Dr. Jackie Miller, is a Chemist / Physician. She and Valerie will easily be able to switch chairs and work equally well as Dentist, with both having dental cross training. Jackie had applied to the space program less than two years ago at the recommendation of one of her father's friends. He wished to remain anonymous, even to

Jackie, so as not to appear to be playing favorites as he was working as one of the mission planners. Like Carl, this is her first trip into space.

"21... 20... 19..." Jackie was the replacement for Commander Ty Cody (having the same Chemist / Medical training), who had to be pulled from the mission. Strikingly beautiful, Jackie is a twenty-nine year old, light-skinned, African American / Chinese. Taller than average Asians, but quite trim, Jackie looks 'just how a fashion model should.' Her husband of two short years, Mike Miller, is always quick to point this out.

"18... 17... 16..." The last crewmember, Brandon Devlin, is the ship's Mechanical Engineer / Horticulturist. He is married to Emma, the cutest little schoolteacher in Norfolk, Virginia (second time was the charm). Eight years senior to Commander Tom, he is the old man on the ship and I don't mean 'Captain'. His hair is a medium, reddish brown and most of it is still there. All in all, Brandon doesn't think he looks any older than Tom.

"15... 14... 13..." Brandon pulled two six-month tours on the ISS in 2012 and 2014, but has spent most of his career designing this ship. From the water tubes in the outer bulkheads, to the leaded acrylic radiation-shielded storm shelter running through all three decks of the ship, Brandon knows more about Bolo One than most of the team who assembled her. He also designed quite a few of the storage tanks, tables, and chairs, as well as the onboard bunks.

"12... 11... 10..." Brandon met Ty Cody while they were both attending Western Michigan University (WMU). Ty was studying Chemistry while Brandon tackled Mechanical Engineering. Eventually, Ty went off to study medicine at the University of Michigan (U of M), before returning to WMU to become one of the first graduates from its new School of Medicine. He had decided to focus his skills toward General Medicine, which dealt with many disciplines affecting the human body.

"9... 8... 7..." While Ty was off fulfilling his personal goals, Brandon immersed himself in a second discipline: Horticulture. This had always been a favorite hobby and getting his hands dirty enabled him to relax and bleed off stress. This second specialty would also make him more versatile, even if it and Mechanical Engineering didn't seem to go together at first glance.

"6... 5... 4..." From the onset, Commander (Dr.) Tyler R. Cody was a born leader and had been the first choice to head-up the mission. Ty was the only one of the group that actually earned the title of Commander through his service in the U. S. Navy. Through the ROTC Program, he had been able to serve while attending college.

"3... 2... 1..." However, suffering from severe depression after a drunk driver killed his wife, Claire (and nearly took his right leg), Ty was scrubbed from the mission. It is hoped he will return to duty and join the Mission Support Team before the crew reaches Mars.

"0... We have ignition, and liftoff of Bolo One on the first manned mission to the red planet: a two-and-a-half year mission for the six-person crew. Godspeed, Bolo One. Our hopes and dreams go with you."

"Roger that," Commander Tom replied as the Falcon Super Heavy began slowly rumbling skyward. From the crew's vantage point, seven-eighths of the way up the rocket stack and cocooned in their space suits, the roar and vibration of the 36 engines was somewhat muffled. "To get a feel for this," Carl earlier told a group of reporters, "put a plastic five-gallon bucket over your head and stand under water at the base of Niagara Falls. Yeah, it's kind of like that."

In 2002, Elon Musk founded SpaceX and by 2011, they had successfully test-flown the Falcon 1, Falcon 9, and Dragon Spacecraft through orbit and recovery. In 2013, they test-flew the Falcon Heavy, building on the success of these predecessors.

The Falcon 9 had nine engines in a single booster stage, whereas the Falcon Heavy was a set of three such boosters, set side-by-side with the payload mounted atop the center stage. The two outside boosters, cross-feeding propellant to the core booster, would give up a third of their fuel while lifting the payload higher and higher. Once the two outer boosters flamed out, they separated from the core booster and deployed parachutes to fall gracefully into the Atlantic Ocean for recovery and reuse. Meanwhile, the core booster, nearly fully fueled, was still rocketing the payload skyward.

But for the Bolo One mission, even the Falcon Heavy turned out to be inadequate. Thus was born the Falcon Super Heavy, consisting of five Falcon 9 boosters: four arranged in a circle spaced 90° apart, with the fifth one at the center. However, where three boosters are not quite enough to put the craft into orbit, five are actually too many. But this configuration still works as the rocket is launched with the core booster un-fueled. As it lumbers toward the heavens, the four outer boosters lift the empty core booster with its 45 metric ton habitat (the Hab) module. Each of the outer boosters begins cross-feeding the core booster in the same manner as the Falcon Heavy configuration, albeit sending only a quarter of their propellant. Once the outer boosters flame out (first the NS pair and then the EW pair), separate and drop away, the core booster will be at the threshold of space, fully-fueled and ready to fire the craft on a trajectory towards Mars. Far above the bulk of Earth's atmosphere and already moving at nearly 10 km/s, the kick from this single booster will send them on their historic journey.

In the 90's, when Dr. Robert Zubrin presented the *Mars Direct Plan*, he described this launch style as a 'lift and throw'. Since Bolo One's launch lifted off on schedule without any countdown holds, it was not necessary to actually go into orbit of Earth. The launch was a direct throw to Mars.

Although only able to view the ISS on the monitors, the entire crew gave the station a rather non-military single-digit salute in its direction as they passed it by, a good 290 kilometers off the port beam. Ironically, at that moment, a message came over the radio, directly from Leonid Korotaev, a former ISS crewmate of Brandon's, still serving onboard the ISS, "Живите долго и процветать, янки сукины дети. [Live long and prosper, Yankee sons of bitches.]" As many of the U.S. astronauts studied Russian in preparation for duty aboard the ISS, Valerie and Sally both burst out laughing at the missive.

"И то же самое для вас, мой друг. Я жду, чтобы поделиться напитком, когда я вернусь, [And the same to you, my friend. I'll expect to share a drink when I get back.]" Brandon replied to his old friend.

The crew is now on its way to the Red Planet: no turning back, at least not for a while. Barring any major complications, they wouldn't want to anyway. It's not only the glory of being the first humans to travel to Mars, the paycheck will be pretty impressive, too. For each crewmember, a promissory note was deposited into a private account at the First Galactic Savings & Loan (FGS&L) in the sum of $5 million. Added to this amount will be $5,000 for each day they stay on Mars. Since this mission is scheduled to have the crew living on the surface for a year-and-a-half, each crewman could receive an extra $2.75 million for the trip. (Not to mention the royalties from commercial product endorsements and public speaking engagements, once they are back home.)

The crew will reach Mars late in its dust storm season. Among the possible complications cutting their overall surface stay short, would be heavy dust storm activity upon arrival: thereby forcing them to delay landing. In the past, some robotic missions were stalled in orbit for a month or more before they could safely set down. As the $5 million up-front is a nice sum of money, the $5,000 per day is chicken feed by comparison and not worth the risk of a hazardous landing.

FGS&L was conceived by The Sponsors as a bona fide financial institution, with branches in most major cities throughout the United States. Space enthusiasts from around the world have already opened accounts there, just to be a part of it all. Once people start moving to Mars, they will still need an Earth-based bank to tend to their financial needs during the course of transitioning to a Martian life-style. As many colonists might initially work for The Sponsors on Mars, the money they will earn will be deposited into their accounts for times when future supplies will be sent to Mars on their behalf.

*

Now coasting towards Mars, the crew has a bit of work to do. The Hab is positioned in, what most would call, an 'unusual configuration'. When the stack of components was being assembled in the Vertical Assembly Building, the Hab was placed upside down from the way it will rest on the Martian surface. The launch couches (in which the crew is strapped) are bolted to the ceiling so the crew's backs are to the thrust. Behind them are the Falcon 9 core booster, the connecting tether, and their atmospheric drag chutes. Going up the rocket stack are: the landing rocket thrusters to help them touch down softly on Mars; an inflatable combination heat-shield and aero-brake to aid in slowing the craft as it enters the micro-thin Martian atmosphere; and finally, the retro pack of engines to slow Bolo One's orbit allowing them to fall into the atmosphere. This upside-down configuration avoids the need to undock, rotate, and re-dock with the booster. That antiquated maneuver was used by the Apollo Service Module to extract the Lunar Excursion Module from its shroud, back in the late '60s and early '70s. This adaptation is just one step in eliminating un-necessary risk.

After the core booster flames out and the ship is drifting on toward Mars, the crew will un-strap from their seats and experience the full effects of weightlessness. Their launch couches will then be unbolted from the ceiling and stowed away in the EVA Prep Room, until the craft nears their destination. At that time, they will be brought out and attached to the floor, this time, in preparation for landing.

Floating around in the Hab is an exhilarating and potentially unsettling experience. Those who have previously ventured into space are familiar with the effects, but Carl and Jackie are rookies on this trip. Training in the 'Vomit Comet' (NASA's low-Gee aircraft trainer) helps prepare for the event. Valerie was tasked with monitoring the rookies' possible 'stomach discomfort' as the veterans say.

After getting their ship secured and ready, the crew will release the hold down clamps on the booster and begin deploying the tether: the Anti-Gravity Assist System that Tom had been testing as he orbited the moon. The tether will be reeled out fifty meters to start with. Then, the small rockets engines mounted on the sides of the Hab will be fired to get the two pieces rotating around the center of gravity, amid the tether, like a bolo.

Since the tether is attached to the top of the Hab, akin to spinning a rope attached to the handle of a filled bucket, the centrifugal force from the rotation will push the crew toward the floor, thereby simulating gravity. There are two ways to alter the amount of centrifugal force and the resultant level of gravity. One is to change the length of the tether, while keeping the spin rate constant. The other way is to keep the length of the tether the same and alter the rate of the spin. Mission planners believed that a spin rate over two revolutions per minute could cause severe dizziness. To keep the spin rate down around one rpm, the tether needed to be 910 meters from the Hab to the center of gravity. If the Hab and the booster were of the same mass, the center of gravity would be halfway between the two and the tether would then be twice that length. But, if the booster were lighter, this would require the tether to be much longer, as the center point of gravity would be closer to the Hab than to the booster, like the way a teeter-totter's fulcrum can be shifted when one child is heavier than the other.

This variable tether concept will be especially useful on the return trip to Earth. As Mars' gravity is only about 38% that of Earth's, the crew will lose a lot of their physical strength during the 18-month stay on the surface. If they had to make the trip home in Zero Gee, the sudden return to Earth's gravitational strength could very likely prove fatal. Similarly, going from Mars gravity to Earth gravity, rather than a gradual introduction, is not ideal either. But, by starting off at 38% Earth Normal Gravity (ENG) when they leave Mars, and steadily increasing the gravity effect by about 2.5% per week, the crew will be able to build up their musculature to survive the change.

This gradual build-up is reminiscent of the tale of 'the farm boy and the calf'. As the story goes: on the day a new calf was born, the young farm boy picked up the calf and carried it all the way around the barn ten times. He did this five times a day until the calf grew so big he could no longer lift it. By that time, the boy could lift over 135 kilograms (nearly 300 lbs.).

The crewmembers will only need to lift their own weight to move around freely, but the concept is the same. Little-by-little their gravitational weight (centrifugal force) will increase and, presumably, their physical strength. In theory, they could come home from Mars in as good of shape as when they left Earth.

*

"Brandon, how's our electrical power supply holding up?" Tom asked, after about three hours of flight.

"Battery power is reading eighty-one percent," Brandon replied.

"Then let's get those solar panels deployed. When you're ready, fire the bolt for release," Tom ordered. Any time you are working with exploding bolts, the best rule to remember is: the fewer the better. For example, if there are four bolts which all have to explode at the same time to release something, Murphy's Law says one of those bolts will fail. The breakaway shroud surrounding the entire spacecraft, holding the solar panels tightly to the side of the Hab, is hinged on one side and clamped with a single exploding bolt on the other. Behind that bolt is one very strong spring designed to send the shroud flapping away from the Hab, mimicking the wings of a giant seagull.

"Firing bolt," Brandon reported, pressing the proper keystroke sequence. The related indicator light on the panel went green, signifying a successful firing. A mild tremor could be felt, but barely. "Shroud away," he announced. Sally and Jackie approached the nearest porthole to watch it flutter away. Carl was quick to point out that the Hab was still wrapped with solar panels, and the ladies wouldn't be able to see anything until they were completely unfurled.

"OK," Tom laughed. "Then it's time to inflate those struts." As the two solar panels are each the size of the Hab (top to bottom and wrapped tightly around), their total area is just over 488 square meters. Five inflatable tubes run the length of each strut, spaced equidistantly from the top to the bottom. By inflating these struts the way one might blow up an air mattress at the beach, the solar panels unwrap themselves from around the craft and spring straight out from the Hab, like a pair of wings. In the vacuum of space, the contents of a dozen small nitrogen bottles will be all they need to accomplish this task.

"Carl; Jackie; make your way to the deck and prepare for rotation," Tom ordered. "We are ready to release the clamps on the booster." The rest of the crew was already strapped to a wall or seated at the workstations; their feet firmly anchored in the floor-mounted stirrups. Jackie took hold of a chair back and flipped herself over it slowly and gracefully, coming to land gently in the seat as her feet slipped into the stirrups. Carl, on the other hand, pushed off from the ceiling with a little too much enthusiasm and bumped the chair-back hard with his shoulder.

"Ouch!" he yelped and turned a bit red-faced, while righting himself in the seat. Tom looked over to Brandon, flashing a little grin. Brandon just raised an eyebrow and permitted himself a slight smirk in response.

Sally glanced around, checking to see if everyone was in place and in a very businesslike voice reported, "All is secure, Commander."

"Tom," he said. "Just call me Tom. We're merely six people living together for the next two-and-a-half years in a vessel the size of a small yacht. No need to be so formal when we'll all be getting so close, so to speak."

Sally shyly smiled, becoming a bit more relaxed, "We're all ready, Tom."

"That's better," he replied. Then in his best Scottish brogue called out, "Release the Kraken! Er, I mean release the clamps."

Brandon fingers danced quickly across the keyboard, entering the appropriate code. The ship shuddered slightly before jerking hard. "Whoa!! We must have developed a little slack in the tether," he noted.

"That would be my guess," said Tom. "Let's put some tension on it and keep the slack out. We don't want that tether to snap. Power-up spin to five percent and begin the reel-out."

"Powering up to five percent," Brandon reported, while he moved the joystick on his right, ever so slightly, and throttled it up to a setting of 50 meters. In a matter of seconds, the crew began hearing soft sounds throughout the ship, with the ring of an occasional screw or pen or thump of a shoe, slowly falling to the floor.

Tom glanced over at Sally, "I'm glad everything is secure." They all started laughing, as Brandon moused over to the music program, clicking on his preselected cut: the chorus of an early 70's Billy Preston tune.

*

Back on Earth, 6:00 p.m. (seven-and-a-half hours after launch):
"Good evening and welcome to CNN News. As the world intently watched this morning, the first manned mission to Mars got under way, precisely on schedule, at 10:30 a.m. Eastern

Time. The crew of Bolo One reports all is 'Go for Mars' and they have separated from the booster rocket. They are now reeling out the tether, and starting their rotation sequence. This will provide the artificial gravity needed to maintain good muscle strength during the long journey to the Red Planet

"Their mission entails a six-month journey to Mars, with a year-and-a-half stay on the Red Planet's surface. This is followed by a six-month trip back home, an undertaking far exceeding anything humanity has ever attempted. As the gravity of Mars is a third of our own, it is vital that the crew have some form of artificial gravity, especially for the return trip. Without it, the crew of three men and three women would arrive back home too severely weakened to stand and possibly worse, the return could prove to be fatal.

"In other news, on the south side of Chicago this morning, a crack team of U. S. commandos conducted a daring, predawn raid on a suspected al Qaida terrorist cell, taking fourteen suspects into custody and confiscating several hundred pounds of explosives and more than twenty weapons with ammunition." The anchorman paused a moment, hearing something in his ear-bud. "We have breaking news: a related early morning operation provided information leading to another terrorist cell and resulted in the death of two suspected operatives, Abu al-Zawahiri and Jamal al-Masri. No U. S. forces were injured (the bruised ribs under the flack-jackets, as a result of the light-load rounds from Jesus' gun might dispute that, but no *serious* injuries). We will be back in a moment with sports and your weekend forecast, but first a word from First Galactic Savings & Loan: Making your savings astronomical…"

Chapter 2

Thursday, July 20, 2017 (Yuriday, Cancer 46, 0031)

As Ty and Claire left the reception that night and headed for home, a torrential rain was blowing sideways, lashing the car. It was a two-hour drive down from D.C. to Richmond in good weather, but in this storm it would take two-and-a-half, at least. Ty maneuvered his recently acquired sunshine-yellow Mercedes-Benz convertible with the vanity plate ON2MARS, slowly and carefully, not wanting to over drive the range of his headlights.

As fate would have it, about a-mile-and-a-half from home the left front tire suddenly exploded, sounding like a roadside bomb. The Benz veered wildly. Ty wrestled the wheel to keep control and steered the disabled car a short distance to where he could pull over onto the side of the country road. With no streetlight for miles, the pouring rain made the evening appear even darker. As Ty exited the car to change the tire, Claire also climbed out with a large white golf umbrella held over her head and clutching a flashlight to assist him.

A few miles up the road, Dave Weller was on his way home from a friend's bachelor party, his car weaving back-and-forth across the wet pavement and the wipers flapping about at full speed. As he drove, he tapped a cigarette from the fresh pack and lit it, using the car lighter. Normally, it was his practice to use matches, except whenever he was in the car. But, in his advanced state of inebriation, he forgot which he was using and after lighting his cigarette, tossed the car's lighter out the window. As he manually rolled the window back up, it dawned on Dave what he had just done. In disbelief, he stared down at the empty socket where the lighter had been. "Damn!" he thought out loud, "that's the second one this month." Returning his attention to the road, he glanced up and saw Ty and Claire standing behind the open trunk of their car, directly in his path. Dave, with a blood-alcohol level of 0.23, hit the brakes, screamed "Oh, shit!", and yanked his wheel sharply to the left, though much too late. Upon impact, his airbag crushed the glowing ember of his cigarette hard-against his right eyelid.

Hearing the rapidly approaching wet skid, Ty turned to confront the noise and tried to jump out of the way, but only managed to get his left foot high enough to step into the open trunk before the collision. Having swerved left, the right corner of Dave's front bumper hit Ty's rear bumper at an angle, crushing Ty's right leg in the vee of that angle. Losing consciousness, Ty's last image of Claire had been that of an angel, her face illuminated by the bright oncoming headlights, and the metal ribs of the umbrella creating a halo framing her crown, reflecting the light.

Not wanting yet another DWI conviction, Dave fumbled under his seat and pulled out the survival knife that he kept 'for protection'. He quickly hacked away the airbag from the steering wheel, pitching it over his shoulder to the back seat. Throwing the car into reverse, he backed up ten or twelve feet, releasing Ty's leg from the vise-like grip between the bumpers. Dave then peeled out, ignoring the disembodied OnStar voice asking, 'Mr. Weller, we have detected a crash. Are you in need of assistance?' Ty's limp body collapsed into the trunk. Twenty minutes later, the rescue squad located Ty's car after his own OnStar operator received no response.

Another rescue squad had been dispatched to a second scene, located about a mile down the road. That was as far as Dave was able to navigate, after trying to rub the burning sensation from his eye and failing to negotiate a sharp curve in the road. This time, the airbag lying on the floor behind his seat didn't help. The force of the crash caused the already weakened steering wheel to break away in his hands and what was left of the steering column penetrated nearly three inches into Dave's chest cavity. He was pronounced dead at the scene. Coincidentally, his car lay on its roof in Ty and Claire's side yard, after rolling three times.

Ty slowly regained consciousness in the ambulance, rushing toward the hospital. "Where is Claire? Where's my wife? How is she?" he queried, groggily.

With eyes widening, the paramedic exclaimed, "Was someone else with you? We didn't find anyone else at the accident site."

Ty cried, "My wife! Claire was holding the flashlight. You've got to find her! She might be hurt!" He tried to grab the paramedic's arm, but found a splint had immobilized his right hand, with what his medical training told him was a compartment fracture. Instinctively, he had reached out to stop the approaching car and his wrist was crushed.

Trying to calm Ty, the paramedic offered, "We'll have someone look for her right away." He turned to the driver and ordered, "Call dispatch and have them immediately send a search and rescue back there. His wife was with him."

Early the next morning, after the rain had stopped, Claire's body was discovered almost twenty yards into the woods where the collision had thrown her. Her limp body was draped in a tree, with her back arched over a heavy limb. Already lifeless from the crushing blow of Dave's car, she never felt the impact with the limb.

*

May 11, 2018 (Alanday, Sagittarius 25, 0031)

As part of the Mission Support team, Clinical Psychologist Dr. Pamela Willis is tapped surreptitiously into the personal email transmissions to and from the crew. At the first sign of any discord or anxiety, the message in question, along with Dr. Willis' comments, is forwarded to the head of Mission Support, Commander Lewis. He will, in turn, liaise with the onboard psychologist, Dr. Thomas. Each morning Dr. Willis reads through the latest batch of email messages, and either saves them in a special storage system or addresses potential problems. The majority of the messages barely rate a first glance and a negative report is a very rare occurrence, as the crew is composed of well-balanced individuals. Of course, professionalism always prevents details from being divulged to anyone other than Commander Lewis, and then only if it is deemed hazardous or essential to the mission.

Commander Morgan Lewis has been with the Space Program since he graduated the Naval Academy in 1995. Though only approaching his fifty-fifth birthday, he looks much closer to sixty-five, if not seventy. A bottle of scotch with an eight-ounce 'water' glass secreted in his desk drawer, and a carton of unfiltered cigarettes tossed in the back seat of his '07 Impala have that effect on a person. Cmdr. Lewis dresses professionally, but the odor of stale smoke wafts around him, making a first impression many would rather forget.

    From: Richard Devlin
 Subject: Way to go!!!
    Date: May 11, 2018 11:36 a.m.
      To: Brandon Devlin

_____(CLT): 0.13 sec

Dad, YEAH!!!!!!!!!!!!!!!!!!!!!

You made it. Whoo Hoo!! You're actually on your way to Mars. Congrats! Sorry I couldn't be at the launch with Mom to see you off. I'm trying really hard to keep a low profile here at Western and need to keep myself out of the press. There are only three or four people in the entire state of Michigan that even know you're my dad. And, I need to succeed on my own merits, without it being all about 'the son of an astronaut on his way to Mars' and hearing buzz about riding on your coattails. Dad, I can't tell you enough how proud I am of you, and how very proud I am to be your son. I just want to make you proud of me, too, by making it on my own. Well, gotta head to class. If you come across Marvin the Martian, be sure to get his autograph for me. lol

Rich

< ≡ ♂ ≡ >

From: Thomas Castle
Subject: Blast off!
Date: Sagittarius 25, 0031 14:28
To: Penny Castle

_____(CLT): 0.39 sec

Hi Pen,

Like you saw from the ground, the launch went off without a hitch. We've made ready the ship, reeled out the tether, and started our spin to achieve artificial gravity, making it easier to tell up from down. Everything's running like clockwork. (ha, ha) Of course, the clockwork part won't come into play until the return trip, but you get the idea. Valerie and Brandon have turned in for some rest, Carl and Jackie are on duty, and Sally and I are off duty. I wanted to get some Earth photos, but I've shot it so many times from lunar orbit I think I'll wait for a better angle. ;~p From LEO, shooting the Earth and Moon at the same time's hard because the Earth is so damn close. But, just give me a week or two and I should be able to put them both in the same frame, with space between the two. They won't quite be the nature photos you are so good at snapping, but I think you'll like the way they turn out.

As a chemist / geologist, Sally really doesn't have much work to do until we touch down on Mars, nor most of us for that mater. Brandon and Valerie are the masters in hydroponics and we will all get our hands dirty up there, so to speak, once everything is squared away. For now, Sally's headed down to

35

Deck One to check on Jackie and see if she needs any help setting up the Med-lab. Though, on second thought, we really should let the rookies fail on their own, so I can complete their initial evaluations. ;~p I'll then use that to chart their progress over the course of our trip. I'd better let Sally know about that. Be right back...

Ya miss me?

Isn't it great that we're able to stay in contact this way? Valerie told me she remembers when Tim Creamer worked together with flight controllers in setting up an Internet interface from a laptop onboard the ISS to see a desktop computer at Mission Control. Before that, we could send email, just not Internet email, as we know it. Pre-Internet email had to be copied and re-sent by someone at Mission Control.

I think she said it was on January 22, 2010, that Tim sent the first tweet from space, which said, "Hello Twitterverse!" They didn't invent anything new, but those words might rank right up there with "Watson, come in here!" We can still use the Twitters, even though that's for the birds now days. (Speaking of birds, I had to delete all of those Angry Birds games from my laptop. They're too addicting and I don't get any work done. Plus, here I can play Angry Birds Space without my iPad, he he.) Besides, if I do need a distraction for a few minutes, I can always do a Sudoku or play Mahjong. Those are a couple of my favorite apps.

We can also Skype each other for a couple more days. It'll be nice to see your beautiful smile for a while longer. Unfortunately, after that, the time lag will get annoying. The further away we get, the longer it will take for a normal conversation. In a week, it'll be worse than a dial-up connection. (ha, ha) Tomorrow, after I've had some sleep, I'll give you a call to see if you've gotten back home. Otherwise, I'll email ya a 'hello'.

I already have a few dozen e-books downloaded on my beat-up Nook to read. So, I think that's how I'm going to spend my next few hours/weeks/months. Going to clear my mind and relax a bit before rustling up some dinner. While I'm upstairs, on the HP deck, I also have another dozen or so audio-books I can listen to.

Well, that's all for now. When we talk tomorrow, be sure to let me know how everything is going on your end. I know your work is sometimes a real bear. Keep going to the gym and working through the stress. I admire your dedication to your job and know the affection you have for your co-workers. But, while I'm gone don't let the job be your entire life. Got it? As always my love, a penny for your thoughts; the moon and stars for your love. Can't wait to talk to you tomorrow.

1-4-3 always, Your Tom

$< \equiv \male \equiv >$

From: Sally Chung
Subject: We're on our way
Date: Sagittarius 25, 0031 15:32
To: Robert Hackard

_____(CLT): 0.48 sec

Dearest Bobby,

We have left the home world! Everything went just as it should and we're now headed for Mars. It's so exciting! LEO was never like this. I mean, I really enjoyed the experience of spending so much time in zero-g on the ISS. The feeling of flying through the modules was so liberating. But, I'm sure glad we won't have to live that way for the next six months. We had zero-g for a couple of hours today before we got the tether deployed and started rotating the ship. I got a chance to fly around for a while. Now, it's just like being on terra firma. Well, almost.

The only way to tell that we're moving is to look out the window. Seeing the stars rotating past the porthole in this way is a bit disorienting, but that doesn't last long. At least the view is different from that on the ISS. The stars seem to rotate counter-clockwise past the forward window. They would appear to rotate clockwise past the rear window, but we have that side shuttered since it's on the sunny side of the ship. It's a very tranquil, slow rotation, 1 rpm. If we look out the side windows, the stars are going up on one side and down on the other. When you see the stars going up, you get a slight sensation of falling. That takes some getting used to. It's like the optical illusion of standing on the west side of a building when low clouds are moving quickly to the east. If you look up at the edge of the building and see the clouds passing, there's a momentary feeling that the clouds are not moving and the building is falling towards you. It's a very strange sensation.

Anyway, the crew is divided into three work shifts. Carl and Jackie are on duty now. Brandon and Valerie are sleeping (Or, at least trying to). And, Tom and I are off. I'm glad I didn't draw the first sleep shift. With all this excitement I wouldn't be able to shut my eyes. In fact, I hope I'll be able to sleep in about 2 ½ hours, when it's my turn on the bed.

A short while ago, I was giving Jackie a hand with the med-lab unpacking and setting things up, but Tom reminded me that I was on my free time and really didn't have to do anything other than relax. Also, he was observing the work being done by the rookies and wanted a fair evaluation of their performance. I guess that makes sense, but I hope these evaluations are a temporary thing. You know I need to keep myself busy or I'm gonna go bonkers. Even when I'm on duty, I won't have much to do for the next six months. Anyway, like one of those ex-VPs once said, 'a mind is a terrible thing to lose' or something like that. Ha, ha. Once Hydroponics is up and running, we will all have more work to do: tending to the gardens and picking fresh fruits and veggies. Yummy.

Well, it's about time to get a bite to eat and to try and relax a bit before bed. I'll write more, later on. I miss you already.

Love,

Sally

< ≡ ♂ ≡ >

From: Valerie Thomas
Subject: Mars bound
Date: Sagittarius 25, 0031 19:15
To: Steven Thomas

_____(CLT): 0.80 sec

Well Honey, we're on our way to Mars. As you can see in the date line, we've already tried to adapt to the Martian calendar. That'll take some getting used to. I totally understand your not being able to come to the launch. Some of us have to work for a living and get the job done. I saw the CNN Internet feed of this morning's events. Such is the price of freedom, I guess.

When you finally manage to get back home from being on the road, you'll find a pleasant surprise on the Blu-ray player. Grab yourself a good bottle of wine, then sit back and enjoy the show. But, make sure to draw the shades first. Don't want to startle or embarrass the neighbors. (wink) Let's save the Skype for then.

I love you very much,

Val

< ≡ ♂ ≡ >

While Carl was on duty at the console and babysitting the monitors, Jackie went about making the science lab comfortable and, more importantly, usable. The primary workspace on Deck One is where the launch couches had been attached to the ceiling and where they will be attached to the floor for the landing. Kneeling on the floor not more than three feet behind Carl's chair, she assembled one of the two workbenches, placing it lengthwise across the space, and setting stools in appropriate locations. In this configuration, a person using the workbench could look beyond his own work to view the console monitors. This well-equipped lab has plenty of room and Jackie has been truly inspired, coming up with a novel use for the extra space. "Hey Carl, what would you think of one of the portable tables being used for card games, setting it up over here?" she queried, motioning toward the wall just inward from one of the airlocks.

"Sure, as long as it's outside of the lab area, maybe between the secondary control console and the EVA prep room," Carl replied, nodding in agreement as he scoped out the locale. "That would be a good spot for a poker table, unless you think it would go better upstairs?"

Jackie pondered a moment and said, "There's no room on the hydroponic deck for something like that; and a rowdy poker game might disturb someone trying to sleep on the mid-deck. I think here would be the best choice of the three."

"Yeah," he reasoned. "And the head is right over there and snacks are just at the top of the ladder. I'd say go for it." He gave her a big grin and began contemplating where to find the makings for suitable poker chips or maybe settling for some faceless app.

Besides the lab area, the remainder of the first deck consists of a control console, secondary control station, full bathroom with laundry facilities, two airlocks, and the connecting EVA prep room.

As with any airlock, before opening the opposing hatch a properly suited person must enter, seal the airlock, and depressurize the space (or pressurize, depending on which direction they are heading). The pressure suits are stored in the EVA prep room, and the user suits-up in there. Before donning the outfit, a trip to the bathroom is recommended for short-duration outings.

For longer forays away from the Hab, there is a selection of diapers, collection devices, and undergarments for each crewmember – individually labeled by name, of course. And as someone will usually point out, while you are suiting up: whatever you do in the suit stays with you in the suit. Upon returning to the Hab, one might want to shower after being cooped up in the suit for a time, as sweat, body odors, and 'other' odors tend to build up in the enclosed space. If two people have been out on an EVA, there is a second full bath with shower, on the berthing deck, one level up.

Elsewhere, there are two more hatches providing an exit outside of the Hab. The first is located in the floor of the first deck, just behind the ladder. This one requires closing off all deck admission to the ladder-well, thereby creating an airlock in the ladder-well, itself.

The remaining hatch is atop the Hab and is also accessed by sealing off all three deck-hatches and decompressing the ladder-well. To reach this hatch, the suited crewmember would climb a stationary, rung-style ladder from the third deck. Because the Hab was wrapped with solar panels before liftoff, this was the crew's entry point, through an opening in the coupling between the Hab and the booster. Once inside, the opening was sealed from the outside, in much the same way as the Space Shuttles or the old Mercury, Gemini, and Apollo capsules.

It is hoped that no one will need to use this hatch until they set foot on Mars, or to use any of the hatches, for that matter. There are a couple of good reasons: (1) a space walk would mean something has probably been damaged and must be repaired; (2) each suit weighs nearly 45 kg and is cumbersome, making climbing the ladder and maneuvering through the hatch a chore to be avoided. Due to the reduced gravity on the planet's surface, the suit will weigh less than 17 kg and can be easily maneuvered. At that point, any one of the crew will gladly scale the ladder to hoist their two flags.

The two flag display is a unique combo. First, the tri-color Martian flag, with 'its colors of red, green, and blue as the primary components of light, and thus symbolizing light, enlightenment, and reason', wrote Dr. Robert Zubrin, as well as its association with the Kim Stanley Robinson epic future trilogy, *Red Mars, Green Mars, Blue Mars*. Second, the American flag representing their homeland. In reverse of their standard order on Earth, the Martian flag will rise first and take the top spot. One day on the red planet, the flags of each newly emerging nation shall be flown in honor of their perspective immigrants.

The galley is situated in the ladder-well on the middle (berthing) deck. At first, this might seem like an odd place, but the location was actually well thought out. With the ten-foot diameter ladder-well performing secondary duty as a solar flare shelter, a few minutes advance warning allows the entire crew to gather and be protected from the harmful radiation of a major solar flare. On average, flares occur about once per year, can be very intense, and may also last several days. It's a great port in a storm.

While working out safety designs for the craft, Brandon had determined that if you're going to be cooped up for several days, a location near the galley and its food supply would be ideal. Safely situated in the ladder-well with access to three decks, even with the hatches sealing off the rest of the ship, there is plenty of room for six people to do almost anything, except perhaps shower. An emergency toilet is stowed beneath the stairs on the first deck, and although it hooks into the ship's waste system when needed, this toilet does not provide for the same level of privacy as the others. Also stored here are six old-fashioned rope-and-canvas hammocks. By stringing these hammocks up in pairs on each deck, everyone has a place to sleep. Though fairly cramped, the crew could ride out a solar flare storm for a month in relative comfort.

*

20:00 - Brandon jerked awake in bed, dutifully opening his lids in response to the clanging alarm. Message received: one hour before going on duty. No snooze button, no music, nobody nagging him to get up – accountable for his own actions. Long ago in college, after slumbering through a crucial exam, Brandon made a pledge to never oversleep again. Employing an old-fashioned windup clock (instead of a battery powered model – batteries having the bad habit of dying just when they are needed the most), he placed it atop a shelf on the opposite side of the room. To quiet the din, it is necessary to get out of bed, cross the room, and shut off the alarm. The premise: if you're awake enough to handle that task, you're darn good and awake. "Time to make the doughnuts," he muttered, with a yawn.

Throwing on a few clothes, he stepped out of the room. His first stop was the head, followed by a side trip to the galley, grabbing a cup of hot coffee, and sipping it on the way back to the room to check his email inbox in private. Having already read the message from his son, he replied,

    From: Brandon Devlin
 Subject: Pride
    Date: Sagittarius 25, 0031 20:28
      To: Richard Devlin

_____(CLT): 0.90 sec

Dear Son,

You have already made me as proud as a father can be. It's still hard to wrap my brain around the thought of you attending university classes. It seems like I only graduated a few years ago, myself (rather than decades).

Your mother and I firmly believe that having you, as our son, has been the most rewarding experience of our lives. Don't ever forget that. And yes, I do understand about you wanting to stand on your own two feet. That's another thing about you that fills me with pride. Some kids would rather take the easy way and ride on the coattails of their parents. But, your ethics and drive set you a breed apart from the norm, and you have the potential to lead the first manned mission to Io, Europa, or Triton, or places not yet even discovered. Between us guys, I know I'm not always around for much face-to-face time with you, but all your mom and I ask from you, is to always do your very best, complete your own work, never cheat, and always be ready to do a little extra when it is asked of you.

I'll let you in on a little secret. My grades weren't always the greatest in a couple of my classes. But, when there was a chance to earn additional credit toward a higher grade, I went for it, and managed to keep a 3.86 GPA throughout my college years. Extra credit and a little hard work can make up for being an average student. LOL

The only other thing we ask of you is to never do anything to make us less than proud. That's about all there is to it. Be sure to keep in touch, especially with your mom. She's gonna be especially lonely with both of us away right now. Call her when you can. Don't try to ring me up, though. The charges would be astronomical! Ha, ha.

I don't say it enough, but I love you son.

A proud dad

< ≡ ♂ ≡ >

As a high school student, Brandon had been somewhat lazy. He barely graduated with the minimum required credits. He even joked about it saying that he wasn't a dropout, but a 'drop-in'. Occasionally, he would drop in to attend a class, if the mood hit him. In his senior year, Brandon developed an interest in space technology and became a member of the National Space Society, which advocated *a space faring civilization in our lifetime*. This was the spur Brandon needed to help him get his act together. He began reading everything he could get his hands on regarding the space program and space technology. That's when he decided he had to be a part of it all, no matter what it took.

There were several bad study habits to overcome, but his intelligence and ability to learn were not lacking. He hadn't been a slow student, just an undisciplined one. Brandon firmly set his mind to the task, becoming unstoppable as he started taking classes at the community college, in the evening after school. He considered going for a GED, but there were only a few more months until graduation and he had the minimum number of credits needed. Once his study habits were corrected and he had proven himself capable of getting through the basics at the community college level, it came down to proving himself to the university admissions board. He was able to transfer to Western Michigan University, eventually graduating with honors.

From: Brandon Devlin
Subject: Hi
Date: Sagittarius 25, 0031 20:36
To: Emma Devlin

_____(CLT): 0.90 sec

Hi M,

     I just got up, 8 p.m. (20:00 military time, as we use it on the ship), about to start my shift. Luck of the draw, I guess (being one of the first two having to try to sleep right after acquiring artificial gravity). I don't think I slept more than three hours, too much excitement going on. After a couple of days, I'm sure things will settle down and we'll fall into our routines.

     Surprisingly, the movement of the ship isn't as much of a factor as we thought it might be. Just like being on board the ISS, we really can't feel it moving, but if we look out the window, there is either an Earthrise or Moonrise every minute. That'll change too, the further away we get from Earth. Of course, the big difference between this and being on board the ISS is the artificial gravity. We didn't feel the movement on the ISS because we weren't touching the floor or anything.

     I have to say, you were right again; me and my big mouth. LOL I was the cause of today's sleep deprivation, since I'm the one that came up with the bright idea to stuff those other four staterooms with supplies. But, such is the life of a spacecraft designer, eh? As Elton John sang, 'It's just my job five days a week.' Ha, ha. Except, en route to Mars, it's my job seven days a week... but, if you take a look at the date header, we've started using my version of the Martian calendar, so it's now my job eight days a week.

     Well, I'm going to get a bite to eat before I start my shift. I'll write more, later.

Love from me to you,

Brandon

PS, missing you already. HOLLAND

< ≡ ♂ ≡ >

Elton also wrote, '…It's lonely out in space…'

    From: Jackie Miller
  Subject: Lift off
    Date: Sagittarius 25, 0031 20:31
      To: Michael Miller

_____(CLT): 0.90 sec

Mike, my love,

Lift off was smooth as silk, though noisy. It's now been just over 12 hours and my ears are still ringing. Carl and I had the first watch and we got off duty about an hour ago. While setting up the lab, I had a brainstorm – there was plenty of room, so why not have a special place for relaxing over a game of cards. Carl loved the idea and assisted in the creation. During free time, like now, we have an area with a table where we can cheat at cards, play rowdy board games, or even construct a jigsaw puzzle and work on personal projects.

It's hard to imagine that we are going to be traveling through space for 6 months before setting foot on solid ground again (and that being on another planet). Then, after 18 months on the surface, it's another 6-month trip back. The hardest part will be fighting off the boredom and working through missing you.

I wish I could have smuggled you aboard in my luggage. I know we wouldn't get bored, because you really know how to keep my attention, if you know what I mean. And it's not like you'd be missed at work for a few days or so. (LOL) Oh well. I suppose I'll just have to stare lustfully at your photos and rely on battery power. Sure hope I brought along rechargeable batteries. ;) On that subject, you'll find some racy pictures I slipped under the t-shirts in your top drawer. They might help you entertain yourself while I'm away. (ROFLMAO) Well, I've got a lot to tell you, but I'm not going to do it all at once. There will be a very long 2 ½ years to relay what's going on here. Perhaps these little notes might get transcribed into a book, someday (after a lot of 'editing', that is). So I'll send more, very soon.

Missing you so much and my love always,

Jackie

< ≡ ♂ ≡ >

(Note from Dr. Willis to Commander Lewis: Miller appears to be showing signs of separation issues, already. I will watch for acting out with other crew.).

Chapter 3

Sunday, May 13, 2018 (Johnday, Sagittarius 27, 0031)

From: Mike Miller
Subject: Missin' ya so much
Date: May 13, 2018 4:30 p.m.
To: Dr. Jacquelyn Miller

_____(CLT): 4.66 sec

Jackie,

I'm already missin' ya so much, babe, that it hurts. I'm gonna go CRAZY while you're gone. I'll be dreamin' of that long slender booty of yours and have to change the sheets every morning. Wink. I'm just keeping it warm for you, babe. Here all by myself and wanting nobody else around but you.

Missin' ya an' takin' care of bizness,

Mike

PS, Thanks for the pix. I love 'em.

< ≡ ♂ ≡ >

With a big sigh, Mike clicked off of the email screen, shut his laptop and abandoned the thug-persona that always made Jackie laugh and, more often than not, led to a pleasurable romp in their big California king-sized waterbed. Mike makes his living as a drug dealer and spends much of his time on the streets. At least, that's the family joke. He is really a traveling sales representative for Pfizer Pharmaceuticals. He and Jackie met, while she was interning at Bethesda's National Naval Medical Center, outside of Washington, D.C., and he was there drumming up business.

One glimpse of Jackie's well-toned, tall, slender body and fashion model beauty, and Mike was hooked. She received her tall frame from her African-American father and her smooth complexion and almond eyes from her Chinese mother.

Born in China during her father's term of appointment as a U.S. Envoy of China, to her Chinese physician mother, Jackie is blessed with dual citizenship. This allowed her to live in either country. She lived in China until age seven, when the family moved to the U.S. At fifteen, she had been a gymnast in the 2004 Olympics, but her entire team was disqualified due to 'doping' allegations against their trainer.

Although she was innocent, the brush of accusation had smeared Jackie and her teammates. After the heartbreak and trauma of not being allowed to complete the competition in '04, Jackie's parents applauded her decision to stay with family friends near Beijing to continue her training.

During the three-and-a-half years prior to the '08 games, Jackie was granted permission to train with the Chinese gymnasts. As a dual citizen, Jackie became a member of the Chinese delegation, taking two Gold and two Silver medals in gymnastics, her specialty being the Uneven Bars.

Athletically, Mike is no slouch, either. With a whip-thin physique, at 6'1" and 185 pounds, he had played college basketball and still enjoyed running whenever he could find the time. Although five years her senior, he didn't look anywhere near his actual years. Mike was often carded at the bars, well into his late twenties. Mike and Jackie dated for nearly eight months before he confessed his true age. When he finally did, she asked to inspect his driver's license before she would believe his story. And that, of course, was a tremendous boost to his male ego.

Mike likes working as a traveling sales representative and visiting different parts of the country. He says the biggest perk is being able to occasionally slip away from his job for several days. No one would miss him being gone, as they might if working with him in an office. He could disappear for a long and romantic weekend with Jackie, anytime he wants, with no one the wiser.

    From:Emma Devlin
Subject: Hello
   Date: May 13, 2018 7: 31p.m.
    To: Brandon Devlin

_____(CLT): 4.92 sec

Hello, Sweetheart,

    It is wonderful to hear from you. It already seems like you've been gone for weeks, but it's only been two days. I arrived home from the launch this afternoon, it's back to school tomorrow. I'm glad things are going so well and I can relate to the excitement. I wouldn't be able to sleep with all that is going on up there, either.

    Last week, one of the children in my class asked if you were going to live on Mars and meet little green men. He's the funny one in the class (kind of reminds me of you). How to use the bathroom was also a big concern. So, you can see that the youngsters are very curious. I'm going to write down some of their questions and send them to you. It would be wonderful if you would send back answers. Receiving mail from space would be thrilling to them and generate many follow-up questions. I'm sure they'll want to know more about the rover and your Martian calendar, as well as any little green men you happen to stumble upon. Who knows, perhaps we'll be educating future astronauts. Wouldn't that be something!

I'm overjoyed for you and looking forward to hearing about the fantastic achievements to come from this mission. I miss you terribly and am especially lonely after dinner. This was the time we shared and chatted about our day. There will be much to talk about when you return home and are in my arms. That is, after we get reacquainted. They say absence makes the heart grow fonder, and I am especially fond of you.

Today, on our special day, I am missing you more than ever. Over the years, we've managed to celebrate most of our anniversaries together. Many couples in the space program haven't had that luxury, so I feel blessed. Of all your anniversary gifts, those most dear to me have been in verse. So, in celebration I have composed a poem for you. It's an unusual form called a tanka and I hope you like it. A tanka is kind of like a haiku but adds 2 more lines of 7 syllables each. Happy Anniversary to my husband: my only love.

Cherish

This day comes each year
My heart was captivated
By your wit and charm
Joyful tears spilling as I
Tenderly cherish your love

Forever yours,

Emma

< ≡ ♂ ≡ >

Chapter 4

Sunday, May 13, 2018 (Johnday, Sagittarius 27, 0031)

The six staterooms on the Mid-Deck are quite
comfortable when compared to berthing accommodations aboard
a submarine, or even an aircraft carrier for that matter. Each one
is furnished with a bed having the most durable (and
comfortable) twin extra-long mattress money can buy, a desk
with chair, and three personal storage compartments. Minus a
sink, these are better than officers' quarters aboard most large
ships. The rooms are paired together, so that the room on the
left's bunk is placed below the room on the right's bunk.

The three storage compartments are arranged
horizontally and separate the top and bottom bunks, putting these
cubbyholes at about chest level. They take up the space (head to
foot) of the bunks and about half their width. The bunks also fill
the space from one wall to the other, thus dividing one room

from the other, providing the much-sought privacy during the two-and-a-half year mission.

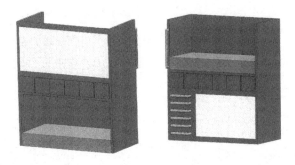

     In an effort to transport as many supplies as possible, in the smallest space possible, Brandon came up with the novel idea of Space Utilization Through Divisional Shifts. By dividing the crew's work schedule into three eight-hour shifts (two people on duty, two off duty, and two sleeping), four of the staterooms will be empty at any one time. Instead of leaving these spaces empty, they will utilize the four staterooms as in-transit storage for a variety of items such as inflatable Mars greenhouses, tie-down stakes, spare parts, etc. All of this equipment will be off-loaded upon arrival. During the six-month journey to Mars, the crew will only use two staterooms. Each person will have their own pillow and sleep sack to place on top of the mattress. This provides a sense of sleeping in their own bed, instead of 'hot-bunking' as is done on many navy ships. Once they have settled in on the planet's surface, all six staterooms will be available. Then they will all have their own personal, but more importantly, private quarters. This Mars-transit sleep strategy freed up nearly 54 cubic meters of storage space. To put it another way, less spacecraft equals less fuel used at launch.

*

21:00 - It was time for Valerie and Brandon to go on duty, with Tom and Sally heading for their respective staterooms and sacking out. Jackie and Carl are coming off duty and now have some time to grab a snack, relax, read, or be shutterbugs while Earth and Luna slowly rotates past the port and starboard portholes. It's called free time, so what they decide to do is up to them. However, the view of the two familiar heavenly bodies is changing rapidly. Already, it is necessary to look toward the rear of the craft to see them, as Bolo One corkscrews its way through space.

Brandon takes the first watch at the flight control console on the bridge, as Valerie heads up to the Hydroponics Station on the third deck. She will trade places with him in four hours. There really isn't a whole lot to do on the bridge or much one *can* do if something were to cross their path unexpectedly. The early warning system would sound the alarm via an ear piercing, 'Brace for impact!!!' in an otherwise polite British accent.

A stationary object might be avoided with fast reflexes on the control stick, but there aren't very many stationary objects in deep space. The more likely scenario is encountering something orbiting the sun in a path between Earth and Mars. If this object were coming at Bolo One head-on, or passing through the solar system at a right angle, there wouldn't be much time to dodge it. That's just one of the risks the crew knew they might have to face when signing on.

There has never been a robotic probe lost en route to Mars, due to an impact. Human error in planning, on the other hand, is another thing all together. This is what caused the failure of the 1999 NASA Mars Climate Orbiter. The Mars satellite was lost due to ground based computer software producing thruster output in English units of pound-seconds (lbfs), instead of the design specification requirements of metric units in Newton-seconds (N-s). As a result, the craft encountered the Martian atmosphere at too steep of an angle and disintegrated.

On Deck Three, Valerie began unpacking gear and setting up the Hydroponics Station. The heart of the Hydroponics Station is at the top of the ladder (just like the galley on the mid-deck). Directly ahead, at the highest part of the ladder, is a sign on the wall stating: *Weed 'em and reap.* Installed by the assembly team, it always put a smile on the faces of the crew.

To go beyond the work area, a crewman would have to pass through an airtight hatch and enter a small corridor surrounded by other airtight hatches, numbered One through Four, which lead into the four garden bays. To proceed yet further, the hatch you just passed through must be sealed and the corridor ventilated before opening another hatch. This is not as cumbersome as passing through an airlock, more of a high-speed intake/output fan, but it does cut down on the risk of cross-contamination, should there be a potato blight or crop failure of some type in one of the bays.

Bolo One's preloaded gardens are already growing well, with the seeds sprouting in the hydroponic troughs and almost ready to be set out. When Valerie was speaking to a group of reporters before liftoff and explaining the work she would be doing on the way to Mars, she told them, "To propagate future crops the entire crew will take turns assisting her and Brandon with seed germination, troughing, and feeding, before setting the taller plants in their nutrient-rich Rockwool packs. This natural fiber was developed to have all of the same properties as high-quality soil, but 90% lighter. For plants that would normally require ten pounds of potting soil, you only need one pound of Rockwool. If you have to transport dirt to Mars, make it the lightest dirt you can find.

"Typically, hydroponics means without soil, but by using the Rockwool as a medium for supporting the sprouts, less water flow will be required. Thus, less work for the pump, less power drained from the solar panels, etc. Initially, sprouts are started in the traditional hydroponic troughs, or trays."

"Are you taking any bees onboard to help with the pollination?" a reporter once asked. "At one time, there had been a discussion about bringing a hive of live bees for crop pollination," Valerie replied. "But, concerns about cross-contamination and a total crop failure (as well as a phobia about them getting loose) far outweighed the benefit of space travel with bees. Also, they didn't want to be swatting bees while dodging a stream of asteroids. That would be just a bit too hectic and hazardous to their health. A hive or two will be brought to Mars on a future mission, thereby helping to keep the greenhouses going strong."

*

Valerie and Jackie didn't plan a specific area on the ship as the designated 'Sick Bay'. There are first aid kits located throughout Bolo One, and it is small enough that anything can be retrieved in about two minutes, even if it's on another deck. Should the need arise; the main work area on Deck One is plenty large enough to set up a temporary surgical table or dental chair.

Also, one of the garden bays on the Hydroponics Deck could serve quite nicely as a medical quarantine area, as the rooms are specifically designed to segregate one crop from another.

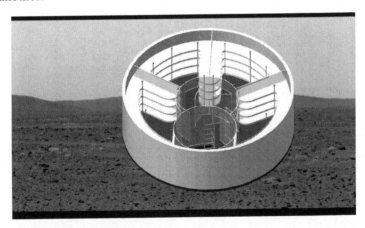

Everyone has received the necessary vaccinations to ward off just about every known ill. For the most part, their medical needs should only consist of treatment for scrapes and bruises while on board the Hab. God forbid they should need emergency treatment outside the Hab, once they are on the ground. A broken bone could be dealt with by splinting, using whatever tools are on hand, but a massively breached suit can only be handled by burial or storage of the body. Cremation on Mars would have to wait until proper facilities can be constructed.

The first deck has a pretty nice layout. The control area is not quite as large as the flight decks of the old Space Shuttles, but it doesn't need to be. In fact, above the foot pedals controlling pitch and yaw, there is a counter-top with surface-mounted digital displays, controls, and joysticks to operate the braking thrusters and roll. Arranged in a plus sign formation just above the thruster controls, is a pair of 17" monitors, sitting one above the other, and two more monitors, one on each side of the first two, for a total of four. When the crew is preparing to land, these monitors will display forward, below, left, and right, respectively. On the bottom monitor, they will be able to view the ground as seen from the area of the landing thrusters. Or, at least Tom can, as he will be piloting Bolo One down to the planet.

Carl will be sitting in the second seat, monitoring altitude and rate of descent, as well as viewing two other monitors - covering their butts, so to speak. While Tom is mostly peering forward and down, Carl will be checking rearward and down. The flatter the landing site, the better for everyone.

Two years prior to their arrival, the Fuel Processor 1 (FP1) spacecraft was landed by computer control in a predetermined location. A small, remote-controlled, light truck will have already scouted the surrounding area, dropping transponders for the Bolo One crew to zero in on.

Ideally, the crew will land Bolo One within sight of the FP1 lander. However, as planned for in the mission scenario, their craft carries with it a small, fully fueled, unpressurized rover having a one-way range of 500 km. Provided they only miss their mark by a distance within that range, they will be fine.

When the time comes, two crewmembers will drive the rover to the FP1 landing site, where a larger pressurized rover awaits. Even if the crew further misses the landing mark, there is another fuel processor (FP2) following them to Mars, two weeks behind them. The crew will guide it down to their landing site.

On the other hand, if all goes well with Bolo One landing near FP1, the crew will land FP2 further out, but still within the 500 km rover range. This will give the mission an even greater range of exploration. They will be able to explore everything within a 250 km radius of FP1, plus, after the 500 km trek over to FP2, everything within a 250 km radius of that site.

After the Bolo One landing, every two years henceforth, an exciting leapfrog event would occur on the planet. FP2 would then become the primary fuel processor for the following manned landing craft, basically the next mission's FP1. Thus setting up a chain of exploration and expanding the bases of operation.

Besides the control console, the first deck contains a full bath with laundry facilities, an Extravehicular Activity (EVA) prep room leading to two airlocks, and a specimen collection box. The box acts like a mini-airlock: a variety of samples (such as ore) are placed in the container from outside the ship. Then, the box is sealed to the outside and opened from inside the Habitat. As an added precaution, the box has a secondary seal so that any possible contamination is contained within the box. The person examining the specimens can easily see them through the clear lid of the box and conduct tests, after slipping their hands into gloves that are attached to the box from inside the Hab. A variety of tools and testing supplies compliment the box's laboratory features.

One of the more interesting attributes of the ship is the ladder-well. On each deck there is an airlock hatch. In the event of atmospheric depressurization, this enables any one deck to be sealed off from the other two until repairs can be made. In a manner of speaking, the entire ladder-well thus becomes an airlock.

The ladder-well also features a Jefferson Staircase, which runs from the first deck to the second, and another from the second deck to the third. Thomas Jefferson invented this type of stair for loft areas and places where a typical staircase wouldn't fit. It has a much steeper incline than a regular staircase, only requiring four feet of horizontal differential between the bottom tread and the top. It is quite easy to use because of the alternating half-stair design. The trick is to always start out on the right foot, or is it the left foot? After a few bruised shins, the crew will quickly figure that out.

Aboard Bolo One, Ty and Brandon wanted a place where the entire crew could gather in the event of a major solar flare eruption while en route to Mars. The ship itself will provide sufficient shielding for day-to-day background radiation, but a major solar flare (occurring about once per year, on average) can emit a very high dose in a short period of time. A shielded area was needed for protection. Running through all three decks, from top-to-bottom, the ladder-well seemed to be the best choice.

Another benefit of this ladder-well design is something that Ty helped Brandon work out. Claustrophobia can become a problem for people cooped-up in small spaces for long periods of time. It can affect many spacefarers, even if there was no sign of it in the psychological evaluations. So, the more open a space can be made to appear, the better for the crew's psyche. Mirrors were considered, which can double the visual size of a space, but they can also cause disorientation due to distortion and multiple images (as in a carnival house of mirrors).

To lessen the claustrophobic effect of this enclosed space, Ty and Brandon introduced the concept of constructing the interior walls from leaded, clear acrylic. While mostly transparent, the leaded acrylic still provides radiation shielding (much like the small windows used by X-Ray technicians). They jokingly referred to the moment they came up with this idea as a 'moment of clarity', but opted to build the staterooms out of opaque materials. Of course, they first wanted to make it even stronger and lighter by using a clear, leaded polycarbonate, reasoning that polycarbonate is 250 times stronger than glass and about five times stronger than acrylic. But, as leaded polycarbonate doesn't exist yet, and the leaded acrylic was already in common use and commercially available, it seemed prudent to go with that.

The two did, however, use clear polycarbonate in designing the interior walls on the Hydroponics Deck. The leaded version would have been nice to have, but would be sort of like 'Transparent Aluminum', the stuff of science fiction.

*

From: Carl Wilson
Subject: On our way
Date: Sagittarius 27, 0031 21:35
To: Mary Croft

_____(CLT): 5.09 sec

Hi Mary,

Here we are, on our way. I wish you could have made it to the launch but I know it's finals time. Senior year is always a bitch, making sure you have all the right classes and getting the right credits. So glad I don't have to go through all that again. I sure don't envy you, right now. But my heart goes out to you, in more ways than one.

Everything went as planned during the launch and we are on the trans-Mars trajectory and rotating at 1.06 rpm. That's the optimum for one g. with the tether length of 1.6 km. We could reel it out a little bit more for an exact one rpm, but once we hit one g. we decided the 1.06 was close enough.

It's going to be TORTURE, being away from you for the next 2 ½ years, but if you can wait for me to get back, I think we just might have a terrific future together. I know we agreed we aren't ready for marriage yet, and I'm not even going to attempt to propose via email. But, I wanted to let you know what I'm thinking. I didn't say anything about money before we left, but when we get home I could have over $7 million in the bank. That could be a really nice little nest egg for a young couple like us. What I'm trying to say is: I love you, and I know you feel the same way. I just hope that you will still feel that way by the time I get back home.

I realize we are both young and in the prime of our lives. If waiting becomes too hard, all I ask is that you let me know.

Be honest with me and I'll be honest with you. And as of right now, I honestly love you with all my heart.

Well, that's about all I can think to say, for now.

All my love,

Carl

< ≡ ♂ ≡ >

From: Mary Croft
Subject: Waiting
Date: May 13, 2018 11:32 p.m.
To: Carl Wilson

_____(CLT): 5.26 sec

My Dearest Carl,

Yes, I do feel the same way. You already know that, deep inside your heart. You are the most loving, kind, gentle, caring man I have ever known. I have been dreaming of us having a life together. I am waiting for your return with my heart wide open. Waiting for you to fill it with your love. I will always be waiting here for you to come home to me, but until you get back, I might go out to the clubs once in a while with the girls. Just something to do, not looking for hookups. So, you don't have to worry about that. I'm not going to be a nun, but I'm also seeking none other than you, sweetheart. LOL How's that for honesty?

Waiting for your return, with bated breath,

Mary

< ≡ ♂ ≡ >

From: Brandon Devlin
Subject: Update
Date: Sagittarius 27, 0031 23:52
To: Tyler R. Cody

_____(CLT): 5.28 sec

Hey Ty Rod,

How goes it? So, unless you've been sleeping for the past two days or hiding out under a rock, you know the launch went off without a hitch. We reeled out the tether, initiated spin, and acquired gee-force (or I should say 'Cee Force') right on schedule. The three-shift thing is working out, except for having to sleep when you're so psyched up. I just got off of my first work shift and dinner is heating in the microwave. The first half of the shift was monotonous, just sitting there and watching the monitors and instruments. During the second half, I went up to the HP and ran a pressure check on all of the hatches and checked the nutrient flow regulators. I know: BOR-ING!!! But I know you. You'd be in the medical supply closet making sure all of the labels were facing front. LOL Not that you're OCD or anything like that, you'd just be doing it for something to do. I remember that spring break when we stayed in Kalamazoo, instead of going home. You went around the apartment, gathering up all of the dishes and taking the rest out of the cupboard, washing them, and then working them back into the cupboard by size, color, and purpose. LOL

Well, enough with the boring stuff. I gotta tell ya, Jackie is gonna work out mighty fine. As I was coming on duty, I overheard talk about a poker game on deck 1, and the mental image of it turning into strip poker... well, let's just say I'd rather play with her than you, any day. ROFL

I'll keep you filled in as we go along. I hope that leg is healing OK. Be sure to follow the doctor's orders (both of them) and remember... I'm only a mouse-click away, if you need someone to talk to... for now. Naturally, about six months after we get to Mars, we'll be on the opposite side of the sun. Then, it'll be more like 24 ½ min. each way. So close and yet, so far away…

Stay in touch. I'll write more, later.

Go Broncos

BTW, Happy Birthday, dude. Party like no one's watching (come to think of it, I'm pretty sure no one is).

So here's an old revised toast:
To my old friend Tyler Cody
This birthday toast I give
May you live as long as you want to
And want to as long as you live. LOL
- Brandon

< ≡ ♂ ≡ >

Ty briskly closed the lid of the laptop resting on the wooden TV tray in front of him. He reached down, snatched up his four-footed cane and hurled it across the room, not really meaning for it to STICK in the drywall. 'Well, that was stupid,' he thought. Tears then began welling up in his eyes as he recalled a similar incident happening when he and Claire had been tiling a bathroom on the second floor of their new home, just a few short years ago.

Ty had been trying to cut a two-inch square ceramic tile on the diagonal, but it persisted in breaking each and every time. After the third or fourth unsuccessful attempt, he grabbed a piece of the broken tile and flung it across the room, impaling it like a throwing star in the far wall of the bedroom. "Shit!" he exclaimed.

Hearing this, Claire popped her head out of the bathroom, spotted the embedded tile, shook her head and calmly remarked, "Now you'll have to fix that, too." Then, without another word, she returned to her work in the bathroom, knowing that Ty's temper had just been extinguished by the momentarily violent outburst and nothing more needed to be said.

Whenever Ty remembered anything about Claire, his mind would then take him back to the night of the accident. How beautiful she looked standing there in the rain, with the bright headlights shining through the downpour. The lights reflecting off the ribs of the umbrella created a halo over his angel's head...

Ty was suddenly brought back to reality, rousted from his visit to the past by the trilling of the phone on the chair-side table. Startled, the .380 automatic dropped from his hand. He didn't recall picking up the Walter's PPH, but there it was. When the phone rang again, he quickly picked it up and answered. "Hello," he said, in a shaking voice.

'Dad, are you all right?' his son, Lonnie, anxiously questioned.

"Sure, never better. I was just checking my email and dozed off for a moment," he lied. 'How long had that gun been in his hand?' Ty's mind was reeling.

'Just called to wish you a happy birthday and see if there was anything you needed. You got any plans for the evening?' Lonnie asked.

"No," Ty replied. "Probably just watch some TV and go to bed early, as usual."

'How about I pick up a DVD along with some beer and your favorite pizza? We'll make an evening of it.' Lonnie was fishing for clues. He knew his dad well enough to tell something was amiss.

"That would be nice. Actually, I could use some company," said Ty. After speaking, Ty realized *that* wasn't a lie. Like a quiet cry for help, he really was feeling the need for the presence of another person tonight, not wanting to be alone with ghosts. "See ya soon. Oh, and make it Guinness. I'm in the mood for a stout, tonight," he said, before hanging up.

Ty picked up the PPH and returned it to the drawer of the small end table beside his chair. This was a .38 caliber replica of James Bond's Walther PPK, which was a .32 caliber. Ty had had the gun for many years, but only recently kept it within reach. And the more he missed Claire, the more he thought about joining her.

*

Unknown to Ty had been the cause of the blown tire eleven months earlier. For nearly an hour, a wiry, shadowy figure had been lying in wait for the approach of the bright yellow convertible. Even with the torrential downpour blurring his vision, the distinctive canary convertible was unmistakable. At the ready, he squeezed off a single shot, intending to bring the car to a stop and flush the driver out into the open. He did not expect Ty to so adeptly maneuver the crippled car nearly another half-mile. In his current position, this would still be a fairly easy hit, even in the dark of this rainy night. But, repositioning would guarantee a kill shot and with the time it takes to change a tire, there was plenty of time to relocate.

Stealthily scurrying through the woods, just off the road, the assassin found his next vantage point and dropped into position. Lifting the rifle's scope to his eye, he heard the skidding tires of Dave Weller's car and witnessed the violent collision. Since Dave had apparently done the deed, the shooter's task was completed. Seeing Claire flying through the air and striking the tree on the far side of the road, he assumed Ty was in just as bad of a condition. He had not intended to kill Claire. She was collateral damage and had not been a part of his contract.

Chapter 5

Monday, May 14, 2018 (Scottday, Sagittarius 28, 0031)

From: Tyler Cody
Subject: You did it!
Date: May 14, 2018 8:28 a.m.
To: Brandon Devlin

_____(CLT): 6.03 sec

Well space cowboy, how's it feel to finally be out there? I mean, I've known you were 'out there' for quite some time, but now *you're really out there*!! I'm proud of you, Bran. You knew going in that after the candle was lit, most of the ride would be boring.

As for me, I'm doing O.K... Check that, No, I'm Not. You can't know how badly I wish I could be right where you are. Sorry Bran, just feeling a bit jealous. Do me a favor, will you? Tell me what you see right now. Are the stars really brighter? I want to feel like I'm there. Could you do that for me?

Sounds like you and the crew are handling everything just fine. Hope I don't let it slip to Emma about the strip poker, next time I see her. Don't think she'd be too happy about that. (LOL)

Just remember, that same mouse click can find me too, if you need to talk about anything. Thanks for the birthday wish. This isn't how I pictured fifty, though. Gotta go, Bran. If you see Claire, tell her I miss her.

Ty

< ≡ ♂ ≡ >

(Note from Dr. Willis to Commander Lewis [he gets a report on almost every message Ty sends, as a matter of course], Commander Cody is still not dealing well with the death of his wife, recovery is slow, almost non-existent. I will monitor further emails and keep watch for signs of additional stress.)

From: Penny Castle
Subject: Knowing me and loving you
Date: May 14, 2018 11:47 a.m.
To: Thomas Castle

_____(CLT): 6.22 sec

Hey, Sweetheart:

You know me so well. That's what I love about you. You're always looking after me, even while you're far away. I went to the gym on Saturday and will go again after work. It does feel good when I go, and the stress melts away. Plus, I feel like I'm doing something good for myself.

Today it's back to reality. Monday has rolled around, way too soon. I could have used a few more hours of sleep after arriving home so late. I'm at work and thought I'd take a break to send you a note. Sometimes it seems like the week has more than one Monday. I've heard about that new Martian calendar of Brandon's. Put a bug in his ear, will ya? Maybe he can tweak the Earth calendar, too, and we can have several Saturdays, one right after another. Just a thought.

There's so much going on at work right now. End of year budget reports are due soon, department budget hearings coming up, expenditures still coming in, income not all received, same old, same old. I'll sure be glad when everything is closed out for the year. Oh well, that's why they pay me the big bucks. Ha, ha. Which reminds me, I heard a funny line the other day from my boss: 'I used to get paid weekly, but now I get paid very weakly.' Ain't that a hoot?

Right now I'm working on completing the class schedules for spring semester and beginning those for next summer. They seem to come earlier every year. We work about a year in advance of what is going to be happening during the next.

Oh, guess what, we filled the secretarial position. Yea! She starts next week. That will take some of the load off me. Then, I promise to take it a bit easier and not worry so much. You know I really do like my job and keeping busy. (The keeping busy serves a dual purpose; it also takes my mind off how much I miss you.)

But, it's not just the work. The people here make it a great place to work. Faculty members really care a lot about the students. You've heard me say how great the staff is, how we help each other problem-solve and sometimes become like family by sharing stories about our kids and lives. Spending that much time together, we see them more than our own relatives and they really do seem like family. You know my boss and that he's a great guy. We work together really well and complement each other in our strengths. We've become good friends and he 'has my back' when I need the support at work. And, he likes the ethical way I perform my job, questioning some of the things that come across my desk and whether they follow the proper standards, policies, and procedures. He runs ideas by me, asks and values my opinion - that's a rare thing in many office settings. I like the fact that he's a lot like you, same crazy sense of humor and so caring about others. This is why I sometimes kid him and say that he is my work husband while you're my home husband. He just laughs and tells his wife what we talk about. We always talk about our families, his kids, what we did on the weekend, and such. Don't worry your handsome head about it; he will never take your place in my heart (or anywhere else). Ok, that's enough about work. I would rather talk about you (and us).

You were right about Skype and that we're now out of range for two-way transmissions. I tried to call last night and it wouldn't even go through. I really would have liked to have seen your face and looked into your eyes. So, email is now our good friend, in addition to being a lifeline and/or love line (depending on who is talking and the mood of the day). We can attach pictures, though. Send me some of the crew and have them take a few of you to send to me, and be sure to enclose shots or videos of the stars scrolling by, too. Wait. Hmmm, this idea has possibilities. I'll get back to you on that.

1 4 3 always now and forever,

Your bright Penny

<   ≡   ♂   ≡   >

Penny works as the Office Coordinator in the Department of Teaching and Learning, within the College of Education, at Old Dominion University, Norfolk, Virginia. She works directly with the Department Chair, acting as his assistant, is involved with budget, payroll, personnel issues, class scheduling, is a problem-solver, a general go-to person, and really enjoys her job. At 40, she has been with the university since she graduated, about sixteen years.

Since most of her work is at a desk, a gym membership really helps her de-stress as well as fight the typical 'secretarial spread'. Of course, her self-image is much worse than reality. Tom loves the way she looks and couldn't ask for more.

Tom and Penny live in Hampton, Virginia, about six miles from Brandon & Emma, and within an hour or two of Jackie & Mike, Valerie & Steve, and Ty. Sally & Robert, on the other hand, call South Portland, Maine their primary home and Carl has lived in Boston since his sophomore year of college, where he met Mary.

From: Robert Hackard
Subject: Lonely
Date: May 14, 2018 4:14 p.m.

To: Sally Chung

_____(CLT): 6.62 sec

Dear Sally,

Glad to hear everything is going well for you. I wish you were still here instead of flying off through the stars. It's going to be pretty lonely around here without you, kind of like when you were on the ISS, but this will be a heck of a lot longer. Probably time to start a new project out in the shop, to give me something to do. Pick up a new company, maybe. Things might be better when you get home in a few years. Anyway, I sure hope so.

I'll write again, soon.

Bobby

< ≡ ♂ ≡ >

(From Dr. Willis to Commander Lewis. Chung's husband does not appear to be very supportive. This may affect Chung's mental and emotional state. Will watch for further signs of discord and advise.)

Bobby is far from being the happiest guy and is feeling abandoned, left here on Earth. In the romance department, he has known only Sally since they were in high school, some fifteen years past. He and Sally have been able to live in several places around the country. As an heir to the Pewlett-Hackard Corporation, Bobby has never had to work for a living and he's getting bored. The boredom is peaking now that the Canyon Copier Company has gone under and his family stock portfolio doubled in value, practically overnight. With any luck, the Z-Rocks Corporation will follow suit and make Bobby an overnight billionaire. Naturally, Sally is aware of his boredom with their life and marriage. She's not naive, just in denial, but

Bobby's latest email has shed a whole new light on the situation.

    From: Brandon Devlin
 Subject: Martian Calendar
    Date: Sagittarius 28, 0031 20:10
      To: Emma Devlin

_____(CLT): 6.96 sec

Good Morning M,

How ya doing this morning? I hope you slept well last night. Yeah, I just got up and it's really evening, but here it doesn't matter what you call it. It's always dark outside. So, no matter which shift you are on, when you wake up to start your day you can imagine it's morning. We are all on the first shift (to us).

Back in the '70s, there was a group at Stanford University that came up with a plan for building large space structures in orbit. One of the ideas called for putting three colonies in close proximity of a construction facility. By aligning the orbital habitats to produce a local sunrise at a particular time, it would have been a simple matter to set up different time zones. So, just as there are three 8-hour shifts in a 24-hour period on Earth, each of the three colonies (or settlements in orbital habitats) could be on different time zones, eight hours apart. Each colony would send a team of employees to the facility to work a morning shift, as it had been shown time and time again, that people are more productive when they are rested.

The psychological impact of that idea was really quite profound. Each team would be at their very best and most productive, because they are all on first shift (to them). No one is arriving at work in the middle of his or her day, on the second shift, and no one is coming to work when they feel it is really time to go to bed. This would be a win-win for everyone. Plus, visiting a different habitat would have had the feel of visiting a foreign country on Earth. You would experience that same eight-hour jetlag, albeit without having to travel 12 to 15 hours to get there. Travel from colony to colony would have been ¾ to 1½ hours, max. It would be like living in Denver and flying to Madrid for lunch.

You asked about the Martian calendar. So, here is your first lesson supplement from space. Ha, ha. If you Google 'Mars Calendar', you will come up with *The CMEX Mars Calendar*. This will give you some interesting data about the length of a Martian day and so on. For example: 1 Martian Day = 1.0275 Earth Days or 24 hours, 39 minutes, and 35 seconds, 1 Martian year = 686.98 Earth Days, but only 668.60 Mars days. *The CMAX* also has a 12-month calendar down the right side of the web page. But, if you add up the number of days in each month, the total is 672. Someone dropped the ball on that, I'm afraid. They also start the Martian calendar in1976, the first year of the Viking probes landing on Mars.

By comparison, Dr. Robert Zubrin, in his book, *The Case For Mars* based his Mars *Zubrinian* calendar on Mars' location within the constellations of the zodiac, as seen from the sun. There are 12 constellations and 12 months, with Gemini being the first. Martian months have a different number of days from Earth months, primarily due to the longer year. The breakdown of the 669 days, by month, is: Gemini 61, Cancer 65, Leo 66, Virgo 65, Libra 60, Scorpio 54, Sagittarius 50, Capricorn 47, Aquarius 46, Pisces 48, Aries 51, and Taurus 56. The reason for such diversity in the number of days per month is due to the elliptical orbit of Mars around the sun. The months are shorter when Mars is close to the sun, and longer when it is further away. Also, as viewed from the sun, not all constellations are created equally.

Dr. Zubrin also dated his calendar years earlier, beginning on January 1, 1961, for the first year of manned space flight. However, he chose to use Sunday through Saturday for the weekdays. If we were to adjust the clock to a Martian day or if a Mars day were 24 hours that would work just fine, but the extra 39 min, 35 sec each day throws a wrench into it. About every 52 days, there is a leap day. That is, you may start out with Sunday on Earth = Sunday on Mars, Monday = Monday, etc. But, after about 52 days, Monday on Earth is still only Sunday on Mars.

Now, the Devlinian Calendar (which was of course named after me, since it was my concept) uses Dr. Zubrin's calculations but with an eight-day week. Hey, let's keep the standard five-day workweek, but give us a three-day weekend...what everyone has always dreamed of (wink).

Since we now have eight-day weeks, I chose to name the days of the week for the first man in space, Yuri Gagarin, and the Mercury Seven astronauts, Alan Shepard, Gus Grissom, John Glenn, Scott Carpenter, Wally Schirra, Gordon (Gordo) Cooper, and Deke Slayton. Thus, we have Yuriday, Alanday, Gusday, Johnday, Scottday, Wallyday, Gordoday, and Dekeday.

So, that's the calendar we are using up here. Today is Scottday, the 28th of Sagittarius, 0031. It is the 31st Martian year, even though it has now been 57 Earth years since Gagarin flew in Vostok 1.

That should give your sixth graders something to ponder over. I left out the calculations for converting Earth days to Mars days, but that shouldn't be too technical for them. Let me know if you want them, though. Are your students doing algebra, yet? For the life of me, I can't remember what I was studying when I was a sixth grader, except of course, sixth-grade girls. Ha, ha. BTW, I'm looking forward to those questions from your students. That should be fun.

Well, it's a good thing I'm starting out on the HP deck today. I can get my breakfast anytime I feel like. Otherwise I might be late for work... LOL.

Lastly, Happy Anniversary, my love. I'm really missing you, too. The word fond doesn't come close to how I feel about you. I'm thinking about you every day and dreaming about you every night. We've been lucky to spend so many anniversaries together and I wish we could have today. Your anniversary poem was wonderful and here is my gift to you. I penned a tanka, just like yours.

Another Year

Now another year
Brings us closer together
Is it possible?
Can love grow any stronger?
Yes, it continues to grow

All my love today and always,

Brandon

HOLLAND

< ≡ ♂ ≡ >

From: Emma Devlin
Subject: Hi
Date: May 20, 2018 8:23 a.m.
To: Brandon Devlin

_____(CLT): 17.24 sec

Good Morning (and it really is morning, here),

It was so good to get your email. My students were very excited to learn about your Martian Calendar. They all agreed that using Zodiac signs as the months and astronaut names as the days of the week was really imaginative. They are having fun learning about the calendar and what you are doing on your mission. I have them studying the solar system and we're making drawings showing how Mars passes through the constellations as viewed from the sun. The hands-on work helps to reinforce the learning process.

Also, I dug your old copy of *The Case For Mars* out of the den and found the date calculations. Each of the students was able to figure out his- or her-own birth-date. I had them post their names and birthdays by Martian date, with the questions they sent. Oh, and thanks for sending the computer links. I added up the days in each month and I see what you mean. It's very odd. It still amazes me with what you can find on the web. Speaking of that, check out the attachment with questions from the class.

Stud — Questions…ents (1.2MB)

Changing the subject, yesterday, I talked to Mom and Dad. They're doing great and send their love. They may come and spend a few days this summer, around the 4th of July. This will help to fill the house with a little noise. It's very quiet with both you and Rich gone. He's planning to stay at Western and take summer courses. He says the quicker he graduates, the quicker he'll be working at engineering, like you. He's also expressed an interest in Nanotechnology. Rich's grades are all top-notch, and I'm so proud of him.

Speaking of our prodigal son, he called today. Rich was excited and thinks he will get into the same fraternity as you were in. He said one of his instructors was asking some questions about you, not knowing he is your son. I'm sure he'll be emailing you about it.

Whoops, I almost forgot to pass on some more good news. Laura and Nathan got to hear the baby's heartbeat, yesterday. She emailed the ultrasound images to me. It's incredible how much detail you can see. The baby appeared to be sucking its thumb - such a sweet sight. My younger sister is going to be having her second child, wow.

Well, it's getting late and I should get ready to head off to work. I hope you are sleeping ok. I've had some rough nights. Many times, I wake up and miss your warmth next to me. It's hard getting used to being alone at night. But, I'll survive. Sleep tight and don't let those bedbugs bite. I hear there's an epidemic. LOL

Always know that you are in my dreams and I can't wait until you are in my arms,

Emma

PS, HOLLAND forever

< ≡ ♂ ≡ >

From: Richard Devlin
Subject: blah, blah, blah
Date: May 21, 2018 11:47 a.m.
To: Brandon Devlin

_____(CLT): 19.03 sec

Hi Dad,

Well, I'm glad we got all that mushy stuff out of the way. Ha! Talked to mom the other day. Think I might be getting into your old fraternity. Acing most of my tests, having a good time blowing up stuff in the lab (just kidding) … along with not eating right and not getting enough sleep – typical college student stuff.

I was studying in the café @ Parkview campus this morning, looking @ the pix on the curved wall. I spotted one with you, the Sun Seeker car, and Jerry Bell. At least it sure looked like you. In fact it looks like me, since I look like you

did at my age. Jerry is my mechanical drawing instructor. I
haven't said anything to him, but he stares right at me like he's
trying to remember where or when we met. If he knew you're
my dad, he might ride me pretty rough and expect grades like
you had (even if you did sleep through a couple of classes – ha,
ha).

Anyway, on the wall next to the Sun Seeker was a
framed pair of black T-shirts (one front, the other back). On the
front was printed College of Engineering. The back has a
paragraph about life on campus and it starts out: 'I are an
engineer...' Funny stuff. I'll send you a picture of it later on,
after I charge my cell. Just hopped on the Bronco Transit bus for
the trip back to main campus. My next class is @ Sangren Hall
in 45 min. Need to send this off while I'm still in range of the
wireless. BTW, here's a little WMU trivia for you. Did you
know that WMU was one of the first totally wired (wireless)
campuses in the country?

TTYL,

Rich

< ≡ ♂ ≡ >

From: Brandon Devlin
Subject: Questions
Date: Sagittarius 37, 0031 20:08
To: Emma Devlin

_____(CLT): 24.55 sec

M, my love,

I hope your school day went well. I just read your email
and these are some great questions. That's a pretty bright class
you have. Hard to believe they're only sixth graders. Not sure I
was quite so bright at that age. Ha, ha. As I said before, the only

things I remember about the sixth grade were the girls. Ok, most grades. LOL

So, let me see if I can come up with some answers for these awesome questions.

* How does the whole crew work in the small space of the habitat without getting in each other's way? Aurora – Gemini 37, 0025 (02-07-2006)

Well, it's not too difficult. First of all, the Habitat is larger than it appears, with three decks each having about 530 square feet of floor space. So it's kind of like living in a house with almost 1600 square feet. In the image below, you can see how big Bolo One really is:

Secondly, we are working in shifts; two people at a time will be sleeping in the two usable beds. We have six staterooms onboard, but four of them are filled with items we will need when we get to Mars. Actually, we each use our own pillow and sleep sack on top of the mattress, so we're not really sleeping 'in the bed'. The good part is, once we are on the ground and those other staterooms are emptied, we'll each have our very own bedroom.

We work an eight-hour shift (though there really isn't much real work to do until we get to Mars) and then are off with eight hours of free time, before turning in. We get seven hours on the bed, and then have an hour to get ready for work and eat breakfast.

* What kinds of food do you have on the ship? Hannah – Cancer 23, 0025 (03-27-2006)

We have a pretty good selection of food to choose from. There are most of the usual things you might have in your cupboards at home, like pasta, crackers, canned soups, tuna, canned meats, peanut butter, salt & pepper, hot sauce, salsa, and many more pre-packaged things. From our hydroponic and traditional gardens we will be harvesting a lot of fresh vegetables and some fruit. We have strawberries, tomatoes, potatoes, sweet peppers, jalapenos, cucumbers, radishes, turnips, leaf lettuce, and spinach. To keep the food from getting boring, we brought along a variety of dried spices.

I like to have a bowl of cereal for breakfast, but we didn't bring a cow along with us to give us milk. So, we had to improvise. When planning for this trip we contacted a cereal company in Battle Creek, Michigan and asked them to make us a special kind of cereal – one that has powdered milk stuck right on the cereal. That way, all we need to do is add water and it becomes milky again. We have several varieties: plain and sugar-frosted flakes, cocoa flavored puffed cereal, something like granola or muesli, and an o-shaped oat cereal with freeze-dried bananas and blueberries mixed into it. We also have raisins to mix in with the flakes, my favorite!

• Are you floating around all the time? Jacob – Scorpio 38, 0025 (12-29-2006)

No, that's not necessary. On this trip, we are using centrifugal force to simulate Earth-normal gravity, so we don't feel the effects of zero gravity. Using a long tether, we have separated our habitat from our burnt-out primary booster rocket engine. By rotating these two parts around the center of gravity along the tether, at different speeds, we can make the artificial gravity as strong or as weak as we want it to be. When we come home from Mars we will start out at 38% of Earth's gravity (about the same as Mars's gravity) and gradually build back up to Earth-normal gravity. That way we won't be fighting the sudden change of Mars gravity versus Earth gravity.

In the early days of the Russian space station Mir, the cosmonauts would spend between six months and a year in zero gravity. Then, when they returned to Earth, their muscles were so badly weakened, the cosmonauts had to be carried. From this experience, we learned that without gravity, your muscles don't have as much to do, so they get weak. By exercising two or three hours each day, some of that effect can be overcome, but it's a lot easier on the body if we just take the gravity along with us.

* Do you get space sick? Amber – Libra 16, 0025 (10-06-2006)

From time to time, some astronauts do experience space sickness (basically, motion sickness). Others never seem to feel the effect, at all. A study was done once (I don't remember when or by whom) with a variety of people to see what type of person was most likely to get sick. It turns out that the more body fat one has, the less likely he or she is to get sick. There didn't appear to be any other signs to indicate how anyone might be affected. Age, height, male or female, none of it seemed to make any difference. The leading cause of space sickness is the effect of Zero Gee on the inner ear, and with the artificial gravity we have eliminated that problem. Check out my previous answer for some more information.

Do I ever get space sick? You bet! I did on my first mission, a lot. It kept happening until I became used to the feeling of flying through the air without wings. But now I think it's a lot of fun. The feeling is really liberating, and I hope all of you get to experience it someday. Not the sickness, just the feeling that you can fly. It is so wonderful!

* How do you go to the bathroom up there without gravity? Lee – Libra 43, 0025 (11-03-2006)

In the old space shuttles and on board the International Space Station, they had special toilet facilities, which use restraints to help hold a person in place, while using it. A system of air jets and vacuum pumps keeps things flowing in the right direction. We wouldn't want anything to back up.

Taking a shower is another challenge. The water just hangs in the air when there is no gravity. This can cause a severe breathing problem for someone taking a shower, as the water can float right up the nose and down into the lungs when you inhale. The shower stall has to be a very confined space, with air jets to keep the water away from the face. Surface tension causes the water to cling to pretty much anything it comes into contact with, so when the shower water is turned off, a squeegee is used on the inside of the shower. Then, a hand-held vacuum is used to remove the water from the skin surface, before tackling the walls, floor, and ceiling of the shower to get the rest of the water off.

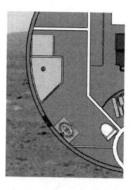

(Deck One Lavatory)

On board the Bolo One, we don't have any problems like that. The artificial gravity system makes it work just like an Earth toilet and shower. That way, we can use the bathroom the same way you do. Good thing, eh?

* Can you breathe on Mars without a space suit? Ricky – Virgo 59, 0025 (09-14-2006)

Not yet. The atmosphere of Mars is mostly carbon dioxide, about 96%. Then nitrogen follows that at 2.7%, argon at 1.6%, and oxygen at only 0.2%. From there, the quantities fall off even more for carbon monoxide, water vapor, nitric oxide, neon, krypton, formaldehyde, xenon, ozone, and finally methane at a mere 10 parts per billion. By comparison, Earth's atmosphere is 79% nitrogen, 20% oxygen, and 1% other gases. I say, 'Not yet' because there are a lot of very smart people working on the idea of terra-forming Mars. That is, to someday change the environment in such a way as to make the air thicker, warmer, and less toxic. Something like that will take a very long time, maybe several hundred to a thousand years to complete. Or perhaps someone who is in school right now might come up with a better way to make those changes in just a few decades. Who knows?

    * How cold is it on Mars? Grace – Virgo 02,0025 (07-17-2006)

    Very!! The minimum temperature as measured by the Viking lander was -107°C, and the maximum -17.2°C. And the Viking Orbiter Infrared Thermal Mapper has shown extremes from a low of -143°C (-225°F) to a high of 27°C (81°F). To find the difference between Celsius and Fahrenheit, you would take the Celsius temperature and divide it by 5. Then, multiply that number by 9, and then add 32. So, although -17.2°C sounds pretty cold, once you do the math, it's -1.04°F. When I was a kid, we would spend hours every day playing outside in temperatures like that. I liked to go sledding and ice-skating, then coming home to hot cocoa (Mom made the best).

    However, -107°C becomes -160.6°F. By comparison, the coldest temperature ever recorded on Earth was -89.2°C, on July 21, 1983 at Vostok Research Station, in Antarctic. There, you could toss a saucepan of boiling water into the air and it would drift back down as snow. I think that would be a fun trick for a party. Don't you?

    * How big is Mars? Brent – Gemini 57, 0025 (02-27-2006)

    The radius of Mars is half that of Earth, or about 3400 km. For a comparison, it's kind of like this: Set a small soccer ball on the table to represent Earth, put a baseball next to it, to represent Mars, and then a golf ball next to that to represent our moon. Try that. I think you'll be surprised to see just what that difference looks like.

Mars is not really as big as most people might think, but since there is no water, the actual 'land' area is about the same.

* Why does it take so long to get to Mars if it only took three days to get to the moon? Johanna – Leo 29, 0025 (06-08-2006)

This is an interesting question. The moon is only about 240,000 miles away from Earth, while Mars is (on average) 84 million miles from Earth. That is, Mars is 350 times further! So, if it took 3 days to go to the moon, will it take 350 x 3 days (about 2.9 years) to get to Mars? No, it won't, and here's why. The moon is traveling with the Earth around the sun, so to go from the Earth to the moon you don't have to go very fast. Also, you don't *want* to go too fast because the moon does not have any atmosphere to speak of, and very little gravity. That means when you get there, you have to use a lot of fuel to slow the spacecraft down, to fall into the lunar orbit. Otherwise, you'll shoot right on by, or worse, crash right into it.

But, going to Mars is different. Starting out at Earth, which is traveling around the sun at 33 kilometers per second, if you increase your speed by just 6 kilometers per second, you will be traveling 39 kilometers per second, which happens to be Mars' orbital velocity around the sun. So, if you leave at the right time, that speed will send you on a curving arc around the sun to catch up to Mars' orbit in just 6 months, instead of almost 3 years. And when you get to Mars, the atmosphere can be used to help slow you down, so you don't have to use a lot of fuel there either. The less fuel you need, the smaller the rocket needs to be to get you there.

So, for a given spacecraft and payload, we can get to Mars using less fuel than it would take to get that same spacecraft and payload to the moon. The politicians who thought we should build a way-station on the moon as a way of getting to Mars weren't thinking too clearly about that.

* How did the Bolo One get its name? Gary – Leo 65, 0025 (07-14-2006)

That's a great question! The South American Gauchos (or cowboys) used a device called a bola or bolo (from the Spanish word 'bola' meaning 'ball'), to capture animals. It was a set of either two or three balls, or weights attached to each other by cords. The Gaucho would swing the bolo over his head while holding one of the weights, or the cord where the weights came together. Once he had it spinning, he would throw it in an attempt to entangle the legs of the animal.

Referring back to the third question about artificial gravity, our habitat and burnt-out launch booster are spinning around the center of gravity of our tether, like two weights of a bolo. The difference is in our direction of flight. The thrown bolo flies flat, kind of like a Frisbee, but our flight path is at a right angle to that. So we are flying more like two objects out at the tips of an old plane's propeller. If you could see the tips of a propeller illuminated at night as it moved down a runway in slow motion, the two tips would appear to spiral around each other. That's the way our habitat and booster are rotating through space. And of course, the 'One' refers to this being the first mission to Mars using this artificial gravity technique. (Great question)

****

Well, that wasn't so bad. If you have any other questions from the class, let me know. For the next round, I'll talk to the rest of the other crewmembers and see if I can get them in on the fun. The more the merrier.

Signing off for now and enclosing all of my love,

Brandon

< ≡ ♂ ≡ >

From: Brandon Devlin
Subject: Starlight report
Date: Sagittarius 38, 0031 08:17
To: Tyler R. Cody

_____(CLT): 25.46 sec

Ty, my friend, you know they don't let angels fly in restricted space, but I'll keep an eye open for Claire, just in case.

Speaking of eyes, I wish yours *could* be here to see what I have seen and am seeing; it's amazing. We've both been to the ISS and experienced the view from the portholes. But, that doesn't hold a candle to the sight from this stateroom. As you are aware, the two staterooms we are using were chosen especially for the view they would get during the flight.

The problem with stargazing on Earth is the atmosphere. Only the brightest stars and galaxies are able to peek through. LEO is only slightly better, due to the light pollution from Earth. The best viewing possible in LEO is the short time span when you can get to the far side of the Earth from the sun, and then only when the moon is on the same side as the sun. But, that still doesn't beat this spectacular view.

So, to answer your question, 'yes', the stars truly are brighter out here beyond LEO. Not just brighter, the colors are super-vivid. Reds, oranges, yellows, greens, blues, purples, all of them twinkling, shimmering, like they're on fire (which they are, come to think of it)! I can see the entire Milky Way at this very moment (well, at least the parts of it we are NOT in) and the sheer quantity of stars and other visible galaxies is staggering. Being on the forward side of the ship, the ones passing this window are moving in a slow pinwheel counter-clockwise rotation. Fantastic! What a show!

Because of our rotation, the view from the side windows keeps moving past us, slowly scrolling upward on one side, downward on the other. It's a strange sight. Unfortunately, the side views are marred by the solar panels, which extend outward nearly 26m each way. On the backside of the Hab is the Sun, so we are keeping that window shuttered until we land. The spiraling dance of stars outside this stateroom window is so mesmerizing I have to force myself to draw the shade in order to get any sleep.

Sometimes, we all just need to draw the shade and get some rest. Go ahead and get some rest, ole pal. I'll keep a watch out for Claire.

-Brandon

< ≡ ♂ ≡ >

From: Brandon Devlin
Subject: Help
Date: Sagittarius 38, 0031 08:47
To: Emma Devlin

_____(CLT): 25.48 sec

Hi Babe,

I got an email from Ty, the other day. He's really sounding down. With Claire gone, all he's doing is sitting around moping about not being on the mission. His depression and injury are making him sit around a lot. And the more he sits, the more he obsesses on Claire's death. At least the mission would have given him a purpose. What a vicious circle. I don't know what to do or say to help him. If I were home, I'd take a few days off to visit Ty, take him out, get him drunk, and try to distract him from things for a while. But, I'm not there and it's so frustrating. The only thing I can do from here is to write and crack jokes, or something like that. As they say, 'laughter is the best medicine'. Maybe that's the answer I was looking for. Just keep telling him jokes and funny stories to provide a little diversion. What a great idea. Thanks, Hon. You always know the right things to say. Hah.

I'll write more, later on. I need to dust off the old mental joke-book and maybe research a few new ones.

TTFN, HOLLAND

Brandon

< ≡ ♂ ≡ >

Brandon spent a good part of the next two days attempting to come up with jokes and stories to lift Ty's spirits. While first testing them out on the rest of the crew, he found that the guys roared at the 'for men only' jokes, but Sally was the only one that laughed at all of the other jokes and rolled her eyes at the puns, and that was good enough for him. As engineers go, Brandon has a great sense of humor.

```
  From:  Brandon Devlin
Subject:  JotD (Joke of the Day)
   Date:  Sagittarius 40, 0031 20:15
    To:  Tyler Cody
```

_____(CLT): 29.08 sec

Ty,

Mornin', old man. Well, another day, another 78 cents after taxes, right? How's it feel to be fifty? The big 5-0! Yeah, I know I'm only a couple of years away from it myself. You know what they say, "When you stop getting older, they bury you." So this sure beats the alternative.

If it's way too early in the morning for a good joke, then put this away until later. OK, you had your morning coffee? Good. Here goes. A lady walked into a drugstore and asked a clerk if she could speak to the pharmacist, in private. The clerk fetched the man and he came out from behind the counter to greet the lady. Recognizing her as his next-door neighbor, the pharmacist said, "Hi, Mrs. Clark. What can I help you with?" "I want to buy some arsenic," she stated.

Wide-eyed, he glanced around to see if anyone else overheard what she had said. "Why on Earth would you want arsenic?" he queried in a whisper. Very calmly she replied, "I want to kill my husband."

Well now, the pharmacist was really taken aback by her statement and matter-of-fact attitude. He stammered, "I... I can't sell you arsenic! It's against the law! I... I'd lose my license! We'd both go to jail..." Well, before he could say another word she pulled a photo from her purse and handed it to him. It was a picture of her husband in bed with the pharmacist's wife. He studied it for a moment and then said, "Well, this is different. You didn't tell me you had a prescription." (That's the punch line where you should start laughing.) Bah DUM bum.

-Brandon

< ≡ ♂ ≡ >

Chapter 6

Wednesday, June 6, 2018 (Gusday, Sagittarius 50, 0031)

Boredom is a serious issue facing a crew while traveling through space for extended periods of time. Early one morning, Carl chirped at Tom, "Are we there, yet?" and Brandon thought Tom was going to smack him.

But, Tom was just playing around as he raised a backhand and quoted to Carl the old Stooges line, "Why, I oughta…"

Dating back to the Mercury, Gemini, and Apollo days, many of the astronauts have found space travel to be an almost spiritual experience. Maybe it was just the sight of earth form such a high altitude. Maybe it was the Zero Gee. Whatever it was, the experience has inspired some to compose poetry while traveling through space, and later after returning home. Others, such as Alan Bean, picked up a brush and began painting as a hobby and turned it into an extensive body of works shown in galleries worldwide.

Beginning in his senior year of high school and continuing in college, Brandon was quite a space advocate and wrote about it. During Brandon's sophomore year in 1992, one of the founders of the Space Studies Institute, Gerard K. O'Neill, passed away. That year Brandon penned:

Ode To Gerard K. O'Neill

Now we're strapped into our seats, prepared to launch at nine
Staring straight up towards the sky, your seat right next to mine

The Space Shuttle Atlantis, with passenger refitting
One hundred-sixty personnel ready, waiting, sitting

As soon as these clouds pass they're gonna light this candle
And then we're really gonna fly, so, find yourself a handle
In less than seven hours we'll eat our second meal
Then, over the horizon we'll see the great O'Neill

The flagship of our Starfleet, the Gerard K. O'Neill
The first of many starships built from lunar steel
The first ship ever built from ore mined from the moon
Although 'tis nearly obsolete and decommissioned soon

So, on its final voyage out, it's a fitting consolation
That the Jovian moon, Io, be its final destination
To haul up stores will take about a dozen flights or more
Plus ten passenger shuttles, brings our crew to eighty score

We'll rendezvous in geo-synch and board the mighty ship
Then stow our gear and settle in for the thirteen month long trip
Like lifeboats, smaller shuttlecraft are neatly stowed away
We'll set up runs down to the base and back, three times a day

Once in Io's orbit, the O'Neill will serve quite well
As construction shack, greenhouse, smelting plant, and hotel
Solar power satellites will spring from Io's sand
As corn and soybeans will rise up from the reclaimed land

Then after solar satellites our colonies, we'll build
In orbit around Io until the orbit's filled
Then, after all is said and done the O'Neill will have its place
As the one and only orbital museum that's in space

And on that far off day you and I may look with pride
Upon the Gerard K. O'Neill that once gave us a ride
To settle there, on Io and give birth to a new race
The Io-ens, our children, another life in space

While studying at the University of Michigan, Brandon became fascinated with the concept of Space Solar Power Satellites (SSPS). He read about a plan to build a base on the moon in order to strip-mine the surface for ore to be used in space. The plan called for a crew of 100 to 200 people residing on the moon, plus an undetermined number living in orbit at the ore processing construction shack.

Their job would be to process the raw ore and turn it into solar power satellites as well as a huge orbital habitat, a design variety known as a Stanford Torus. This latter item is a bicycle-inner-tube shaped habitat, one mile across, with a tube diameter of about 400 feet. The habitat was designed to house 10,000 people, living and working in space while building and maintaining solar power satellites and additional habitats.

The SSPS would generate electricity using photovoltaic cells or through concentrated sunlight heating helium to turn gas turbines. The electricity would then be transmitted by microwave beams to rectifying antennae on Earth and then patched into the national grid. This all sounded a bit far-fetched to Brandon, but the technology has been available since the mid-to-late 1980's. In fact, when working up the plan, in the 1970s, a cost estimate was in the range of $106 billion over a twenty-year time frame, very affordable in today's economy.

Also, the sale of such electricity could generate about $80 billion per year in revenue. And even if you factor in the inflation since the 1970s and double that figure, the payback would also be adjusted to $160 billion per year. But, since no one has seen fit to begin such a project, Brandon decided the least he could do is write about it:

The Alternative

Give us a place deep in space
Between the Earth and Mars
Where the sun shines bright both day and night
Like all the other stars

There we'll find the peace of mind
To unite the world as one
No threat of wars on distant shores
The fighting will be done
We all know the way to go
Is forward, never back
We must start soon to mine the moon
To save that which we lack
'Tis not so much the iron and such
But the cost of transportation
The gravity tax would break our backs
And wreak havoc on our nation
And why buy oil from foreign soil
Our future is burning away
Don't spend our cash on fossil trash
There is a better way
Solar power, every hour
Night or day, it doesn't matter
The sale of which will make us rich
Our wallets will grow fatter
There's just one way, as they say
To save our starving masses
And that's for us all to get on the ball
And off our lazy butts

     One evening, about ten years ago, Brandon arrived home
from work to find a phone message from an old high school
buddy, whom he hadn't seen in nearly fifteen years. Jeff had
also been quite a poet, back in the day. As they were getting
caught up on life events, Jeff told Brandon about a web site
called originalpoetry.com, where many poets share their work.
Once Brandon clicked onto the site, he was hooked and even
entered a contest, winning with the following:

The Starship Cynical

Sailing, sailing o'er the Milky Way
Far beyond our galaxy is where I long to play

Out among the distant stars, lies a destiny to explore
Give me a ship with solar sails and an ion-thruster oar
Don't burden me with anchors; they'll only add on weight
I'm off to visit Cassiopeia, with whom I have a date
Next, on to The Horse Head Nebula, to see where stars are born
'Second star to the right, then straight on till morn'
A crew of marauding pirates would truly serve my needs
Out among the natives, let them sow their seeds
We will take humanity and spread it to the stars
Scarring every planet, making each one ours
Conquer, pillage, rape, oh yes! After all, that is our nature
To spread among the cosmos, our bastard nomenclature
Then, go about our business, laughing with great mirth
We'll do unto others, in Heaven as it is on Earth

It had now been several years since he had composed a
space-themed poem. But, as it was a way to pass the time while
drifting through the cosmos, Brandon once again began to write:

Men Are From Mars

Men are from Mars
Now we're going back
But we'll be taking women with us
'Cause that's one thing which we lack
Of course, not completely
Or we would not exist
But, there is a definite shortage
And they are quite high on our list
We'll return to our mother-planet
From whence the Earth was seeded
We will then reseed Mars
As a backup home is needed
All our eggs are in one basket
And one never knows ones fate
We need to diversify
Before it gets too late
If the Earth is someday struck

By a comet the size of Maine
There will simply be nothing left
I think that's just insane
But with a colony living on Mars
Civilization will keep going
We will take with us our knowledge
And other things worth growing
Then someday if the Earth
Is once again worth improving
We'll return and re-germinate
To keep the cycle moving
Then outward to the universe
Other orbs we'll seek to seed
We will send forth our children
To build homes, which they will need
Onward, onward, evermore
Life will go on extending
Onward, outward, evermore
To the universe un-ending

  From: Emma Devlin
Subject: Summer break
   Date: June 12, 2018 9:16 a.m.
    To: Brandon Devlin

_____(CLT): 48.15 sec

My Dearest Husband (I really love the sound of that),

    Well, the summer break is finally upon us. School
hasn't been out for very long and I already miss those kids. I
always feel like I did the first time I put Rich on the school bus,
remembering how lost I was all day long without him. I have to
tell you about the end of the school year. We had a parent
visitation and student project day. My students displayed their
Martian calendars. You should have seen the parent responses to
the finished product. What great imaginations the children have.
The calendars are hard to describe because of the variety of

concepts and use of materials. I took snapshots and have enclosed them for you. If you can, add them to your video wall's photo gallery, kind of like we used to place Rich's drawings on the fridge.

To take my mind off how much I miss you, I've been trying to keep busy by cleaning and have now started to tackle the attic. What a job! Dirt, cobwebs, and spiders are all over everything. I was amazed at all the junk we have collected and all the things I haven't seen in years. How, why, and where did we ever get three fondue pots? Maybe they were wedding presents that we stuffed away (you never did like fondue). I kept out some items that I wanted you to take a look at before getting rid of them. There's room in the garage to store them until you get back.

I have been hitting a few yard sales, but the estate sales are even better. You and I have always found treasures at these on our weekend forays. I'm having fun and have picked up a few collectables. I even found some Star Trek Christmas ornaments – your other passion (besides me and your ship). I laugh and compare the different commanders, engineers, and crew of the series. Perhaps your voyage will get into the series. Having gone where no one has gone before... kind of catchy, don't you think? You'd make a cute ornament, too. I could put you in the curio cabinets with the other men of space. Ha, ha. Perhaps I'll write to Hallmark and make that suggestion. If they started with Alan Shepard, can you imagine the series they could build?

Next question. How are you doing today? From your letters, it sounds like everything is going as planned. E-mail was always a good way to keep in touch while you were away, but I think the writing of the emails is getting better. It's a lot like the old fashioned hand-written letters we used to stick in an envelope and send each other via *snail mail*. I wish we could Skype one more time before you get too far away. It would be wonderful to see your face, though touching it would be even better.

It's hot and sticky outside today. I've been working in the flowerbeds next to the pool. The flowers are simply gorgeous this year. I planted some of the wave petunias that Mom likes and created a stunning pattern. Most people wouldn't quite get the symbolism, but the layout and colors look like the Bolo One logo on your spacesuit. Pictures will be sent of these, too. You'll be impressed by my green thumb (and it's not fungus, ha, ha). I'm catching up to you in the gardening department.

I went shopping, picked out a new bathing suit, and have been sunbathing... a little. You know I don't normally spend much time in the sun due to the risk of skin cancer. I'll definitely send you photos of my tan lines. Those you might not want to put on your 'fridge'; keep them under your pillow. I will think about you kissing them before you go to sleep and when you wake. This is what I do with your picture each day. It is always carried next to my heart and you are constantly in my thoughts. I miss you so very much and it is hard to get through some days, especially during this summer when I am not at school. The children help to stave off some of the loneliness. They keep my mind and hands occupied during the day, but the nights are always for you. I miss having your body lying next to mine, and the passion in our bed. Remember to kiss my picture and it will get me through the night. Even though you are absent, I'll feel your lips on mine and imagine your hands in those special places. Brandon my love, please take care and come home to me. I wouldn't know how to go on without you. I'm sending all of my love and kisses until I hear from you again.

Love Always,

Your M

HOLLAND

< ≡ ♂ ≡ >

From: Brandon Devlin
Subject: Re: Summer break
Date: Capricorn 07, 0031 20:05
To: Emma Devlin

_____(CLT): 49.26 sec

Dear M,

I'm glad you're finding the Trek ornaments. I was chatting with Tom a few days ago and he told me that he and Penny have been collecting ornaments since they got married. How about that: just like us. Remember, the best values are the ones that still have the original packaging (in good condition). Back in the '90s, Hallmark printed a book every other year that listed values based on what collectors were willing to pay for the ornaments. Tom said one of the first pieces he bought was a $20 ornament from 1990 or '91, the Enterprise. However, since he didn't find it until three or four years after it was issued, he wound up paying $225 for it. At the time, the 'value' was nearly $400, according to the value guide. But then, people started buying and selling them on eBay and the value dropped to between $75 – 125. Tom & Penny now have three of them. Hopefully, the value will go back up with time - keep your fingers crossed.

So, if you find any at the yard sales, buy them for a few bucks if the boxes are in good shape. Look them up on eBay to get an idea of their current value, then just pack them safely away for the future. We'll need to make a list for the insurance company so we can cover them with a rider policy. You can catalog them if you like. Or, we can do this together. It would be a fun project for us.

My sweet Emma, I'm missing you very much and your picture is safe under my pillow. Know that kisses cover it every evening while my finger tips trace along your tan lines and my imagination runs wild.

I'll write more, later

Brandon
HOLLAND

< ≡ ♂ ≡ >

Chapter 7

Saturday, August 18, 2018 (Alanday, Aquarius 24, 0031)

From: Penny Castle
Subject: Crazy with loneliness
Date: August 18, 2018 10:04 a.m.
To: Thomas Castle

_____(CLT): 1 min 48.53 sec

My darling Thomas,

It's been a long week… very, very long. You know how days can be for someone working with budgets, funding issues, scads of deadlines, and so many more issues than I want to get into right now. We're just starting on the next fiscal year and my head is already hurting. Still trying to find rooms for some of the classes, don't have instructors for all of them, their letters of offer are waiting to be mailed, and so on. AARGH!!.. (OK, that's a smidgen better)

You always made me feel so much better when I came home all stressed out and tired. Actually, we made each other feel better after a bad day. But, my hubby is not here and I am lost and very lonely a lot of the time. You're always saying to me 'a penny for your thoughts.' Well, my thoughts are of you on this particular Saturday morning. It's now over three months since we've held each other. I miss you so much I could almost cry (or at least sniffle a little). The last time we spent any alone time together, was when we went to the cabin in Colorado for a three-day weekend.

Remember the delicate spring colors and the dusting of snow around the edges of the yard? How the hot tub steamed in the cold air? We took a long drive around the winding mountain roads and had our own private tour, taking in the budding trees and spring flowers. I've never forgotten and would like to relive some of that wonderfully romantic time we had together, and pretend you are near.

So, I've penciled in some vacation time, booked a flight to Denver for Friday afternoon, and am taking the laptop and camera along with me to the cabin. I'll be up there for a week or so and send you a video. I'm going to shoot the cabin, the trees, mountains, streams, and everything else that will remind me of you (and you of me) and our time together that wonderful weekend. I'll even take videos of the local wildlife (including me). Only, this nature film is for your private viewing, only. I just want to imagine you as close to me now, as we were then. It's so hard to cope with you being gone. Sometimes I am not sure how to get through the day.

Missing you so much it hurts,

SWAK

Your Bright Penny

< ≡ ♂ ≡ >

(From Dr. Willis to Commander Lewis: Penny Castle appears to be suffering some major separation anxiety due to being apart from Tom. Appears to show the beginnings of depression. She is scheduling a trip to their cabin in Colorado, which will help, but I am advising counseling. I recommend contacting her family doctor.)

Of course, Tom and Penny's idea of a cabin is only a little short of a luxury ski lodge. With one phone call before leaving for the airport, their good friends and neighbors, Ben and

Cassie, would head on up the road to the cabin, flip on the main breaker, set the thermostat to 70°, plow the drive, shovel and salt as needed, and switch on the front porch light. The hot tub on the back patio would be steaming, a bottle of wine set out to chill in the snow bank next to it, all so Tom and Penny could watch the stars twinkling over the mountain.

*

20:45 – Brandon was fixing himself a breakfast sandwich when Valerie strolled into the galley. There was a strange Cheshire-cat grin on her face and she had both hands hidden behind her back. "What are you up to?" he questioned, suspiciously. Just then, Carl, Jackie, Tom, and Sally all filed in behind her. Brandon and Valerie had just come on duty, Carl and Jackie were getting off, and Tom and Sally should have been on their way to the two staterooms. The five of them all began singing an off-key chorus of Happy Birthday. At the end of the song Valerie revealed what she had been concealing behind her back. It was a vacuum-sealed gift-wrapped box, about the size of a pack of dental floss. "What the heck is this?" Brandon queried. "And where did it come from?"

Valerie handed it over to him, saying, "I've been keeping this safe for you. It was slipped to me by Captain Clark and I can only guess where he got it." Everyone laughed. "Go ahead and open it." Brandon tore open the plastic pouch and suddenly had the strangest sensation that his wife, Emma, had just entered the room.

A bit disoriented by this, he glanced around, but naturally she was not there. How could she be? They were at least 20 million miles away from Earth. He tugged the end of the crushed ribbon to untie the package. It fell away easily. Then, Brandon folded back the wrapping paper; it wasn't even taped. Finally, the box top lifted off to reveal a sheet of rose-colored stationery, folded to nestle in the box. As he removed it, Emma was again beside him. He tentatively raised the paper to

his nose, inhaling the scent. 'Aha! Obsession... I think.'
Brandon continued to unfold the paper and the fragrance became
even stronger, as he read the note silently.

"Well?" prodded Carl. "What does it say?"

After first checking for intimate details, he read the
message aloud, "Happy birthday, darling. Surprise!! I smuggled
in this perfume to give you something to remember me by. I
hope it made the trip unscathed. Remember I love you and come
home safely, Emma." Everyone applauded as Brandon reached
into the box and pulled out the smallest perfume bottle he had
ever laid his eyes upon, a single dram in a tiny vial.

Valerie smiled broadly and added, "Captain Clark said
you would have to skip a dessert for this." Brandon knew
exactly what she meant. Clark was the team leader responsible
for weight distribution on the ship. Nothing goes onboard that
he doesn't know about. Everything had to be weighed so the
right amount of fuel could be planned for the flight.

"I'll need to have a little chat with the good captain
later," Brandon joked. They all took a few minutes to partake of
some toaster strudel, in lieu of birthday cake, before heading off
to continue with their daily routines.

      From: Brandon Devlin
   Subject: Missing you
      Date: Aquarius 25, 0031 00:24
        To: Emma Devlin

_____(CLT): 1 min 52.69 sec

My very dearest M,

Well, aren't you the thoughtful loving spouse? I doubt
anyone else would have ever thought to send a birthday present
along on a Mars mission, let alone have it smuggled on board. It
smells delicious, just like you. I know it's your favorite scent:

Obsession. I'll put a drop on my pillow tonight and dream of you all night long. As a special 'thank you' I wrote a little something to tell you how I am feeling. Why don't you go fill the tub, add a drop of perfume, and take a nice long soak in a warm bath. Then, put on something soft and sexy for me to imagine and climb into bed before reading about how much I love you:

Out of sight, out of mind, what a terrible thought to ponder
When you're out of sight, I'm out of my mind, but my heart still grows fonder
As the miles between us grow and years till again we meet
I'll hold fast to the memory of your lovely face, so sweet
I miss you dear, with all my heart, each fiber of my being
And when I close my eyes at night, 'tis you that I'll be seeing
I long to hold you in my arms, gently touch your skin, so bare
As you run your hand across my chest, your fingers through my hair
I'd kiss your palm, your wrist, your arm. I'd kiss your neck, then your breast
Working my way toward your knees and kissing all the rest
I want you wrapped around me, both feet up off the floor
Holding you gently, sweetly, till our legs will take no more
Then lower you softly to the bed, lying beside you, half atop
Holding you, holding me. My head's about to pop
Making love the whole night through, till the morning light comes in
A little bite of breakfast in bed, then start all over again
I'm missing you so much, my darling, but you have nothing to fear
I'll be sleeping alone tonight, and wishing you were here

Pleasant dreams, doll face.

Your loving and ever devoted husband,

Brandon

< ≡ ♂ ≡ >

From: Emma Devlin
Subject: Missing you more
Date: August 25, 2018 9:17 p.m.
To: Brandon Devlin

_____(CLT): 2 min 4.10 sec

Darling Brandon,

Reading your words of love made me realize how very much I miss you. I wept as I whispered them over and over. They touched my heart and filled my soul with longing. Late at night, I lie awake in our bed wanting to reach out and hold you in my arms, but you're not there, only a memory shares my bed. Lately, I've been doing the same thing with your Mesmerize cologne. A little mist on the pillow, I inhale your scent, and fall asleep dreaming of you spooning tightly against my back. I so miss the way you cuddled up to me.

But, dwelling on your absence doesn't do any good. It will be a very long time before I see and hold you again. What keeps me together is remembering how much we love each other, and your devotion to me. Bran, you have never given me a reason to doubt you. You've been a part of me for so long that I am only a shadow of a woman without the man I love. We complete one another. While you are gone, grasp my love in your hand and hold it near your heart. I am holding tightly to your love until you return to my arms.

I love and miss you so much.

Your wife and soul mate

Emma

HOLLAND

< ≡ ♂ ≡ >

From: Robert Hackard
Subject: Us
Date: September 08, 2018 11:30 a.m.
To: Sally Chung

_____(CLT): 2 min 37.02 sec

Dearest Sally,

You know I love you. I have loved you since the 10th grade, when we first met. I've never felt that way about anyone else... ever! But, I don't know if that's enough any more.

Since you've been away I've had time to think about us... a lot, and where we are headed in the future: whether it's together or apart. In the past several years, I know we have been just gliding along, living in a kind of static existence. No highs or lows, just drifting. I guess what I'm trying to say is that I love you, but I'm no longer in love with you. And I know it isn't just me. I've felt the way you have been pulling back, emotionally and physically.

We are still young and have long lives ahead of us. I'm just not seeing that life continuing on the same way for either of us. I think it is time for us both to move on and make some changes in our lives. It's fortunate that we never had any children to drag through this and hurt.

I'm starting up a new company and that is going to take up a lot of my time, physically and mentally. I've contacted my lawyers and had a divorce agreement drawn up, which I think you will find fair. You can keep the house in Maine and the condo on Majorca. For everything at home that you would call personal possessions, I'll have your friend Marie and my sister Bethany come in and box up for storage (all the clothes, jewelry, and the like). We've only kept photos on the computer, less the ones that are framed. I'll have Sissy run a copy of the computer albums and have duplicates of the framed pieces made for you, as well. That way, anything you don't want, you can delete.

I know that when you get back you won't be hurting for money, and it isn't about that. But I'm setting up a trust fund just in your name, with $20 million deposited in it. I want to be fair with you, so let me know your thoughts on that. Please don't argue. It will help to take away some of my guilt for making this decision while you are not here. With starting up a new company, the rest of our assets won't be very liquid for quite a while, but later adjustments will be possible.

There is also a provision in the agreement relinquishing any claim by me to your death benefits, if anything were to happen while you are on this mission. At your convenience, you will be able to assign those benefits to anyone else of your choosing.

I'm sorry to have to spring this on you in this way, but under the circumstances, there really isn't another way to do it. Please check over the attached copy of the divorce agreement. Make notes on it if changes are required and reply to me as soon as is comfortably possible.

I'm very sorry, and can't say it enough. I wish you the best of luck in your future endeavors. I hope all of your dreams come true.

Affectionately,

Bobby

Divo — Agreement...rce (1.6MB)

< ≡ ♂ ≡ >

(From Dr. Willis to Commander Lewis: Urgent! Please see attached message. I am recommending immediate counseling for Chung, with Dr. Thomas. Please contact me and advise course of action.)

From: Commander Morgan Lewis, Mars Support
Subject: Personal, URGENT
Date: September 11, 2018 6:45 p.m.
To: Dr. Valerie Thomas

_____(CLT): 2 min 45.81 sec

Dr. Valerie Thomas,

As the second in command and in light of your psychological training, I am asking you to assist with a tragedy that has developed. It is with deep regret that I have to pass along sad news that will affect one of the crew. Things like this are never easy to hear and even worse when one is so far away and unable to do anything.

Tom's wife, Penny, was found dead this morning. She was in her car, at the bottom of a ravine, about two miles from their mountain cabin in Colorado. It appears she may have been heading into town, possibly for supplies, and experienced a blowout just before a sharp curve in the road. She would have had little time to react and the car slid through the guardrail. Rest assured, she died on impact and did not suffer.

The duty to inform Tom thus falls to you, both as a psychologist, a friend, and the one on site capable of assessing his reaction and subsequent mental state. Please keep me advised if any action on our part is required, although there is really very little any of us can do at this point in the mission.

There are only a couple things that could be done, with none of them a good solution. An abort would involve continuing on to a Mars flyby, swing-around, and free-return trajectory, putting you back at Earth in about twenty-two months. Such action would need to be considered soon, as the primary mid-course adjustment is coming up within the next few days.

As the Hab was not built for Earth re-entry, we will also need to launch another Dragon capsule for you to dock with and transfer to, for splashdown. The safety of the crew is of the utmost importance. As you well know, such as in the case of Commander Cody, emotional distress can be a devastating and paralyzing event.

The families of Tom and Penny have both been apprised. Penny's mother, father, and sister are en route to tend to the funeral preparations. They have all been advised not to say anything to Tom until you have had a chance to speak with him. For everyone's sakes, please let me know when Tom has been briefed on this matter. Also as a personal favor, please pass along my condolences to Tom.

Thank you,

Cmdr. Morgan Lewis

< ≡ ♂ ≡ >

Valerie spent the next few hours emailing Cmdr. Lewis, Tom's mom & dad, Penny's mom & dad, and getting all of the details she could. A bit shaken, Valerie glanced at the clock, 04:35. She and Brandon were now getting off work, Carl and Jackie were about to hit the rack, and Tom and Sally would be climbing out of bed. Valerie stabbed the intercom to the control deck, "Brandon, is Carl down there?

"Yes," he replied. "Do you need him up there?"

"No, I'll be right down. I need to talk with both of you, right away."

Minutes later Valerie stepped out of the ladder-well on the first deck. "What's up, Doc?" Carl mugged.

"No laughing matter, I'm sorry to say. I need your help. Could both of you pull a twelve hour shift for the next few days or so? I just received a confidential email from Mission Support notifying me that Tom's wife, Penny, has died. I have to break it to him and I believe he will need to take a few days off. He'll need time to grieve and deal with matters as best he can. He shouldn't have to worry about the daily duties."

"Wow!" Carl exclaimed. "First Sally, now Tom."

"What about Sally?" Valerie asked, sharply.

"She didn't tell you?" Carl asked in return. "She got an email from her husband, two or three days ago. He's filing papers for a divorce. I would have thought she had told you about it." Valerie was silent for a few moments wondering why she was just finding out about this. Dr. Willis would have seen the email from Bobby to Sally. Valerie was surprised that Pam hadn't given her a heads-up, since the two have been personally acquainted since college. But, Pam must report directly to Commander Lewis, so she isn't permitted to contact Dr. Thomas directly regarding any email correspondence.

"It seems we have a couple of issues to deal with," she said, finally.

"Well, I doubt you'll have to worry about Sally," Brandon said. "I was talking to her yesterday and the subject of relationships came up. She confided in me that she was looking forward to moving on. I got the impression things had been a little rocky for some time, now. I'll keep tabs on her, if you like."

"Great!" Valerie threw up her hands. "And which one of us is the ship's counselor? Anyway, I'll need the two of you to assist with Tom's duties for a few days." They both assured her all would be taken care of. Brandon would work over for the next four hours, while Carl got a little sleep. Carl had taken a short nap earlier and felt that four hours would do him just fine. Valerie sighed, "Now for the hard part, I have to go and tell Tom."

"Tell me what?" Tom asked, stepping out of the ladder-well. "What's up?"

"Let's go back up to the mid-deck, Tom," Valerie replied with a solemn look on her face. She gently took hold of his arm, as they walked back into the ladder-well.

When they were both at the top of the ladder and out of earshot, Carl slowly shook his head saying, "I sure wouldn't want to be him, right now."

Brandon thought for a moment and quietly added, "Nor her. Can you imagine trying to tell someone his wife has died? They've been together since high school, if not longer. Emma and I have been together just over twenty years... well, I guess they have too, come to think of it. Still, I can't imagine living without her."

Carl was quiet for a while, just sitting there, thinking about Mary and how much he would miss her, if something like this was to happen to her. After a few moments Carl added, "I'd better get a nap. I'll be back down at oh-900."

"OK," Brandon said. "Get some sleep. See you at nine."

Meanwhile, on the mid-deck Jackie was sipping a cup of herbal tea before bed, while Sally was lingering over her morning cup-o-joe. The creases on one side of her face and her disheveled hair indicated that she had been sleeping hard. "May we use the commons?" Valerie asked, referring to the mid-deck common area, as she stepped off the ladder and through the hatch, followed closely by Tom. "We have something private to discuss."

"Sure," Jackie said, picking up her cup and heading for the stateroom.

"I'll go on down to the control center," Sally agreed, as she grabbed her cup and juggled the hot toaster pastry that had just popped up.

"That's fine, thanks," said Valerie. "Oh, and Sally, I'd like to have a chat with you also, later on today."

Sally shot Tom a worried look over her shoulder, then started down the ladder, but stopped to let Carl complete his climb, as he was on his way up. The puzzled glance Tom returned her way as he shrugged told Sally he didn't have a clue as to why the doctor wanted to speak to him in private. His thoughts immediately focused on his medical exam from three days ago. "So level with me doc. How long have I got?" He tried to smile and play it off, but knew by the look on Valerie's face this was something very serious.

"Pardon me, just passing through," Carl announced as he headed off toward the other stateroom, barely glancing at Tom.

"I wish it were that simple," Valerie told Tom. "I'm recommending you take the next few days off. You're not even going to want to be here when I tell you what has happened. Sit down, Tom." Valerie pulled out one of the stools to sit on. Tom followed suit. "Tom, I'm so sorry, but there's no easy way to say this…" tears began to well up in her eyes and trickle down her cheeks, as she choked out the words. "It's Penny. She's gone."

It took a moment for the statement to sink in. "What do you mean: gone?" he asked, in a whisper. Valerie reached across the table and tightly grasped his hand.

"Penny was at your cabin in Colorado. It looks like she may have been heading into town when there was a blowout. The car smashed through a cliff side guardrail. She is dead, Tom."

"No!" Tom shouted, bolting to his feet and then slowly sinking back onto the seat. "She can't be. It must have been someone else!" He was shaking, his eyes darting from side to side, trying to find a plausible explanation, and failing. "How can… Are they sure? How do they know, for sure?"

"Tom, they wouldn't have notified me if they weren't. Penny's folks got the call from the sheriff yesterday afternoon and contacted Mission Support. Her mom, dad and sister are en route to tend to things on your behalf. You can get in touch with them when you are able and let your wishes be known. Other than that, we're stuck out here with at least twenty-two months to go. Twenty-six if we land."

Tom blinked a few times, wide-eyed and bewildered. "If we land?" he repeated, while swallowing as if to keep from being sick.

"Well, if it came right down to it, Morgan said a fly-by, swinging around Mars with a free-return trajectory could put us back home in about twenty-two months. They would have to launch a splashdown capsule for us, but it's an option... Just in case we need it," Valerie patted his clenched hands, trying to comfort him or trying to lend support.

"Tom, I know this is totally out of the blue. No one could ever have imagined a freak accident like this happening to one of our loved ones. Hell, I didn't even have a clue about Sally getting divorced until just a few moments ago. But, turn this around and look at it from the other side." She gave him a moment to comprehend, but it just wasn't sinking in.

"Go on," he said.

"OK, look. When we signed up for this mission, we did so with the full knowledge that one or more of us might not make it home alive. Agreed?"

"It's not the same thing!" Tom jumped to his feet again, this time knocking the stool over, and started pacing across the small space. "Not the same thing at all. I didn't sign on for my wife to be the one killed! That get-together we had with all of our families and spouses was to get them used to the idea that one of us on the ship might not make it back... to assure them they would be taken care of, for life... but that was for them... to get them ready, just in case! Not us! I'm not prepared to accept the fact that Penny might be dead!" Tom added, as he righted the stool and collapsed back down onto it, dropping his head down onto his crossed arms.

"I understand, Tom. There are terrifying and evil things in our lives that we just don't ever expect to happen and would never even think to prepare for. If I had to pick one of the crew, predicting he or she wouldn't be able to cope with a tough situation, between you and me, the top of my list would have been Sally. But, she seems to be coping quite well with a pending divorce. It will be tough and overwhelming, Tom. But, mourning, grief, and sadness are all natural reactions to a loss of this magnitude. Even anger, rage at the world and yourself. Always remember: What defines who we are, is how we deal with the challenges.

"Now, we can turn tail and run, if you can call it running. We can return to Earth in twenty-two months, or we can do what we came out here to do… explore Mars, because going home early won't bring Penny back. I know that sounds terribly harsh right now, but give it a few days," Valerie could hear the soft sounds of Tom's muffled sniffling. "You've got to let it out, Tom. Go ahead." Reluctantly raising his head to look at her, tears were pooling in his eyes. Valerie stood up slowly, walked around the table, wrapped her arms around his shoulders, and lowered her cheek to his head. "Go ahead, let it out. It's ok to cry." Tom cried as Valerie's tears dampened his hair.

At a point about half way down the ladder, just out of sight, Sally had heard everything. She stood there, sobbing into her hands, mourning both for Tom's loss and her own.

Chapter 8

Over the next four weeks, Tom managed to work most of his own shifts, but spent the majority of his off time working with the computer. When he wasn't reading or responding to emails from friends, family, or the public, he was surfing the web for articles about grief management and some of the strategies and methods used for dealing with the loss of a loved one, especially a spouse. Tom quickly realized Valerie was right about the mission and that aborting for a slow return to Earth was out of the question. Bolo One had been approaching the mid-course adjustment point: to land on Mars or return to Earth. A Mars fly-by with the gravity assist to send them on the free-return trajectory would not allow for a landing had they changed their minds later on. On the other hand, with the mid-course adjustment made in favor of landing, a mission abort from orbit could still be accomplished, though with more difficulty.

As it turned out, the one person that became Tom's biggest confidant and source of support during this time was not anyone on the ship, but Ty. Tom would reminisce about the times spent together with Penny, and Ty would tell tales about what he and Claire had done together throughout the years. At first, the monologues were more like eulogies, followed by long sessions of overwhelming grief and wounded cries. But after a long while, their talks slowly turned into something more closely resembling home movie narrations, being more of an event telling than an experience.

One night, as Ty sat in his living room typing his latest reply to Tom over a few beers, a pre-Claire memory came to him of the 'good old days' when he and Brandon were roommates, at the Western Michigan University. In the note to Tom, he wrote, 'Ask Brandon about the beer-crisper.' As college roommates, Ty and Brandon were in agreement that vegetables left in the bottom drawer of the refrigerator would never get eaten (out of sight, out of mind). Therefore, any and all fruit and veggies (when they remembered to buy any) were kept on an upper shelf, in plain sight, and the bottom drawer served another, more noble purpose.

With the two young men being more than fond of craft beers, the large single bottom drawer of the refrigerator was just the right size for beer bottles, alternated cap to the back, cap to the front. A case of beer would fit easily, but the weight caused the drawer to pop off the track, until Brandon acquired drumsticks from their marching band neighbor. Laying the sticks in the bottom of the refrigerator, under the drawer, they rolled the beer in and out, smoothly.

Once the bottle fit and optimal storage arrangement was confirmed, the drawer became known as the beer-crisper. Ty and Brandon stocked it with many varieties from their favorite local brewpub, Bell's Brewery: Double Cream Stout, Oberon, Two Hearted Ale and Consecrator Doppelbock. They also believed in the motto: 'Friends don't let friends drink Bud', a running joke among their cronies. If you're gonna drink beer, drink BEER.

Plus, whenever their parents stopped by, the fruit and veggies on the upper shelf always made a great impression. Their friends were impressed by the novel and creative way Ty and Brandon kept their beer a few degrees cooler than what one might find on an upper shelf.

Then, one day while Brandon's mom was visiting, she decided to do some cleaning for the boys, wiping down shelves and putting away dishes. She thought the veggies should be in the crisper, but when she opened it, she found the beer and had some stern words for Brandon, only twenty at the time. But Brandon and Ty didn't consider themselves to be future alcoholics or even lushes. They were budding connoisseurs.

And besides, Ty was of the legal drinking age, with every right to purchase the beverages.

*

Whenever she could, Sally would stay nearby, to keep Tom company and offer a compassionate ear, while he waited for the replies from Ty. With communication lag-times of nearly ten minutes by this point in the journey, their 'talk sessions' could sometimes run into eight to ten hours at a stretch. On more than one occasion, Valerie found it necessary to sternly remind Tom and Sally to log off and get some sleep. "The email will still be there in the morning," she would admonish.

But on the day Tom replied, "Yes, mom." Valerie knew he would be OK and she could stop hovering. Having Sally around seemed to do him some good and he treated her more as a friend, than a subordinate. And right now, Sally also needed a friend. With her own sadness, spending time together was good for them both.

*

04:45 - Brandon was working at the germination station on the Hydroponic Deck, about to set out a new batch of strawberry plants when there was a sudden dull thump. It felt as if he was sitting in a parked car and someone bumped it with a car door, but their vehicle is half way to Mars. Curious, he stepped over to the nearest window and gazed out, but couldn't see anything unusual. Rather than risk contaminating a fresh planting by entering one of the other garden bays, he turned toward the ladder-well and climbed down two decks to where the others had gathered in response to this jarring sensation.

Tom and Sally had just gotten up from their bunks and everyone was awake and crammed around one of the half-meter wide portholes. "What was that?" Brandon inquired, in a low tone. As Tom turned, Brandon could see concern reflected in Tom's face and that it was not good news.

"Take a look," he said. The crew parted to allow Brandon access and he moved to press his face to the window.

Peering out, at first all appeared normal. The stars were passing by the window in a slow upward movement, as if the ship and crew were falling through space in slow motion. As he shifted position to look more aft-ward, his view was blocked by the solar panel as usual. Tilting his head to view further out the length of the panel, however, he realized something was amiss, or more accurately, missing. Brandon did a double take and looked again, amazed that the far end of the panel was no longer there.

The solar panel, formerly measuring 26 meters in length, was now more like 10 meters and appeared jagged at the tip. An asteroid about the size of a small bus had narrowly missed the Hab by 10 meters.

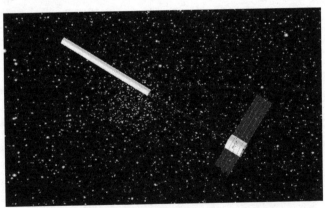

"No warning on the monitors?" Brandon asked.

"No," Valerie replied. "There was nothing on the monitors and then a second or two before impact, there was a single beep from the radar. This thing must have gotten knocked out of the asteroid main belt and was headed in towards the sun, rather than orbiting."

"And moving like a bat out of hell, to sheer that panel off like that without putting us into a spin," Carl added as he sat down at the control console, just below the porthole.

"How bad do you think it is? Looks like we only lost about a two-thirds of the panel, right?" Sally asked, obviously worried but trying to sound optimistic. By that time Carl was checking the power meters.

"I wish it were that simple," he responded, with a sigh. "The way these things are wired, it looks like we may have lost use of the whole panel. See there?" he said, pointing. "The normal readout from the top half of each panel is on one gauge, with the bottom on another. These four gauges represent both panels and their operating capacity. Right now, there are no readings on gauges one and two."

Tom then added an observation, "Carl, pull up the Power Loss Protocols in the computer and, while you're at it, send the Alert call to Mission Support, coded 'Stable, but guarded'. They will be reading the voltage drop on their consoles soon enough. Let's let them know we are still alive."

Carl acknowledged the order and sent the message. Next, he typed in the phrase *Power Loss Protocol* and the monitor displayed the instructions outlining what to do in the event of a total loss of power, as well as various degrees of power loss. Most of the instructions were the same:

Step 1.) Turn off all un-necessary equipment and lights.

Step 2.) Locate the source of the power drain.

Step 3.) Affect repairs as quickly as is SAFELY possible.

Step 4.) Gradually turn lights on while monitoring power gauges.

```
Watch for spikes to the load.
```

Etc.

"Well, I'd say we can check off number two, right off the bat," Brandon pointed out. "So, for now we're on… what, half power, right? Let's go with that, ration our usage and check our options. One thing that comes to mind is to pull out the surface RTG we have stowed away in Stateroom Five. What other ideas do we have?"

Jackie stared off into the distance thinking out-loud, "Riding the exercise bike more; it's already configured to generate some level of electricity."

Valerie retorted, "Yeah, but not enough to compensate for all the extra showers we'll need to take. That thing generates more sweat than it does electricity."

"I certainly hope we can come up with something else before firing up the nuke," Tom quickly replied. "We are still a month out from Mars. And that thing puts out a lot of radiation for such a confined are like inside the ship."

"I agree completely," Brandon added, "As for step three: we don't have a back up solar panel to deploy. I seem to recall Skylab having a one-panel configuration, but I can't remember if that was by design or some sort of failure."

Carl was just finishing the message to Mission Support, clicking on 'Send'. "I remember reading about that a few years ago," he volunteered. "One panel was lost when a micro-meteoroid shield broke away during launch, taking the panel with it. Plus, there was a problem deploying the other panel. The first crew was able to install a replacement shield and got the remaining panel to deploy, but that was in Earth orbit. If this had happened while we were in orbit, we might have waited for FP2 to launch and borrowed one of its panels. But it's not like we can stop here and wait for FP2 to catch up. That won't happen until we get to Mars orbit."

Brandon continued, "I think the best we could do with the damaged one, would be to re-attach some of the wires so as to complete a circuit and get partial use out of what's left. However, that would mean a lengthy spacewalk and whoever pulls that duty is going to be pulling some big rems by the time he gets back in here. But, you're absolutely right. We should be able to come up with some kind of a workaround."

Valerie observed, "And, it may be a cold thing to say, but logic dictates that if it comes down to an extended spacewalk as our only option, one crewmember with a fatal dose is better than six."

"Rewiring that panel could take days of attaching and testing. Perhaps two people for as much as a week. I'll contact Mission Support and see what they have to offer," Tom said. "They may have some useful ideas as well." He turned to the communications system as Sally and Jackie went back to peering intently out the window. Valerie looked on as Carl began running some wiring schematics on the main monitor, and Brandon headed in the direction of the HP deck. As the end of his shift was approaching, he still needed to wrap up the work he had been involved in. Upstairs, while shutting down the shop, he wanted to make sure all unnecessary lights were flipped off, as well.

There was a small water pump with a variable flow regulator, propelling water from a reservoir into an irrigation line. The water flowed through the line, branching off to six trays, which would be seeded the following afternoon. Brandon decided to shut off the flow, reasoning again, to save power during this emergency. As he turned the knob, the pressure increased and water sprayed everywhere. He quickly turned the knob the other way. At that moment an idea flared brightly in his mind and he froze for a moment while considering it. 'Sufficient water pressure could drive a paddle wheel to turn a generator', he reasoned. "A millwheel in space! But, it takes electricity to run the pump," he thought out loud, talking to himself. "But, I think you're on the right track."

After checking the computer inventory of plumbing supplies on board, he sat down, pulled his iPad over and started drawing what he hoped would be a solution to their thorny problem. Their drinking water is stored in a series of one-inch tubular pipes running through the corrugated fiberglass outer walls of the Hab. The pipes are positioned in two courses around the ship, staggered like the thin side-walls of a compressed accordion, and wrap almost all the way around the spacecraft, except where there is a hatch or window. In those cases, there are elbow pipe joints to bend the water around the hatches and windows. Six inches of foam insulation fill the corrugated fiberglass walls encasing the tubes. Enveloping everything is the traditional thin metal skin on the outside, coated with several thin layers of a sprayed-on foam insulation.

After water is used for drinking, cooking, plant irrigation, showers, and waste disposal, any waste liquid (including urine) is passed through the scrubber/recycler where it is purified to the same standards used by water bottling companies on Earth. This water is then pumped back into the wall storage tubes for reuse. In addition, a dehumidifier collects evaporation from the Hydroponics Deck and even that from perspiration. Not all water is recovered. The human body requires a portion of the water consumed. So all things considered, they are able to recycle nearly 92% of their water.

An hour later, Carl and Jackie had still not yet gone to bed. Tom was occupied by the same task as Brandon had been, attempting to come up with a workaround, with Carl lending a hand. Meanwhile, Sally was closely monitoring the computer screens at the control console, as if something were about to attack the ship at any moment. Jackie was assisting Valerie in the galley, both endeavoring to come up with ideas for nutritious meals that did not require cooking. On all of their minds was the sobering fact that the less electrical power they needed to use, the better. There were plenty of fresh vegetables ready to eat such as carrots, potatoes, turnips, and radishes, as well as strawberries and cherry tomatoes. Cold cereal will be readily available, and Pop-Tarts don't *have* to be toasted to taste good. The electrical issue wouldn't make the crew go hungry.

At 06:30, Brandon toted his iPad down from the HP deck to join Tom and Carl in the general lab area on Deck One. "We may still need to do a space walk," he said. "But it should only take an hour or two. I have an idea," he proceeded to explain his plan.

Thirty minutes later, Carl and Jackie were off to the staterooms to get back on track with their sleep. They reasoned that a case of sleep deprivation wouldn't help the situation.

As Mission Support had assessed the situation and determined that rewiring the panel was the best option, there was natural reluctance to Brandon's idea, at first. But, once it was thoroughly explained that the necessary spacewalk would be only one to two hours instead of ten to twelve hours per day, over several days, the go ahead was given. If this plan ended up failing, the fall back plan would be to have the crew rewire the panel.

Valerie volunteered to relieve Sally on the monitors after her four-hour stint. Spying Sally's glazed eyes, she was afraid that Sally might not have blinked at all during that whole time. A near miss with an asteroid could have that effect on just about anyone.

Tom and Brandon set to work gathering various types of pipe and fittings, collecting tools, finding sheet metal, snatching up more tools and basically grabbing anything else they thought might be needed. One of the largest pieces of the puzzle was a water pump that had been brought along, in hopes of finding an underground reservoir to tap. They then carried the vast collection of parts and equipment up to the HP deck. For the size and complexity of the task they were planning to undertake, Deck Three was the only place on board where this project could be done, without interfering with vital ship operations.

The water purification system had to be shut down to prevent unintended consequences. If they had accidently cut into one of the tubular pipes while it was running, the ship's entire water supply would have been pumped out within a matter of several minutes, flooding the compartment. What was needed for this process was a double bypass. First, they cut into the tubes near the top of the wall, attaching elbows and short pipe segments as they went about their construction. As the pipes ran continuously top to bottom in columns, zigzagging their way around the ship, Tom and Brandon only needed to cut into the pipes near their top end. By doing so, they isolated a section of pipes that became self-contained, now separate from the rest and thus created a by-pass. The two men determined an area of six or eight pipes should hold a sufficient amount of water for their purposes in this location and they would repeat the procedure on the opposite side of the Hab.

In the central corridor on Deck Three, Brandon and Tom would then construct a jury-rigged steam-powered electric generator. Once the unit is assembled, a spacewalk is needed so someone can gently peel back one or two thin layers of the sprayed-on insulation from the area directly outside of the critical pipes in question. The spacewalk involves some risk as one side of the Hab is constantly bombarded by sunlight while the other is in the shade, with a 500° temperature difference between the two sides.

If it all works as planned, one set of pipes will transmit steam to the generator. The other set then cools the generator and condenses the steam back into water, to re-circulate it. The real trick will be in not removing too much of the insulation, or the ship will either get too hot or too cold, causing the plants on the HP Deck to die. The water on the shaded side must be replaced with a non-freezing liquid (such as glycerin) to prevent the pipes from freezing solid and bursting into space.

The next fundamental questions are: Will the spacewalker be able to rappel down the side, while wearing a suit and hauling a full pack of gear, as the ship is rotating at a full One Gee? Or, will they need to slow the craft's rotation? The spacewalker would have a difficult time first having to suit up, climb the ladder to the hatch carrying all his gear, and then rappel slowly over the side down to the area needing to be worked on. "A slower rotation is definitely the way to go," Tom determined. "We'll keep it moving just enough to prevent things from becoming airborne on the inside, maybe zero-point-three gee."

"Good idea," Brandon agreed. "Then, the one doing the work will only weigh... oh, about 40 kilos or so, including spacesuit and gear. Now, which one of us is going outside?"

Tom grinned, "I'll flip you for it."

Chapter 9

Thursday, October 11, 2018 (Gordoday, Pisces 31, 0031)

From: Brandon Devlin
Subject: No worries
Date: Pisces 31, 0031 06:47
To: Emma Devlin

_____(CLT): 4 min 30.44 sec

My darling M,

Just a quick note, with news about the mission. I don't want you to get worried or be afraid for me when you turn on the news. One of Bolo One's solar panels was slightly damaged by a small asteroid, a couple of hours ago. It hit near the far end, on the port side of the ship. We are currently operating on half power and working to get things back to normal as soon as humanly possible. This should only take us a few hours to fix. No one was injured and we are not, I repeat NOT in any great danger. Tom had to report it to Mission Support and, of course, they will be alerting the media by holding a press conference. So, I wanted you to read the real story here, first. You know as well as I do, how the media is going to blow this whole thing way out of proportion. Coverage of the Apollo 13 mission had almost become a back page note until their mishap. Then there was a non-stop media circus, 24-7.

I'm not comparing this to the Apollo 13 disaster, by any means. I want to stress that this is only a minor setback. We're going to have it fixed in a jiffy, and you know that is right up there with three shakes of a lamb's tail. (Smile, that's a funny!)

Please let Rich and the rest of the family know what's what for me, ok?

I love you so much and will come back to you safely,

Brandon

< ≡ ♂ ≡ >

*

Later that night CNN broke into their segment on dangerous beauty fads with: "This just in: the first manned mission to Mars may be in dire straits if the crew members are unable to repair a damaged solar panel on their ship, Bolo One. The two solar wings extending outward from the side of the spacecraft generate electrical power for the crew's journey. This morning, one of the two panels was completely destroyed by a huge asteroid, estimated to be the size of an ocean liner. Had it come a mere forty-five feet nearer, the entire ship would have been destroyed and the full crew of six would be lost.

"A disaster of this magnitude would surely spell the end of manned operations beyond low Earth orbit for the foreseeable future. It is now a waiting game to see if the Mars undertaking will continue or the order to abort will be conveyed. Just what actions will either event demand? How long will the crew of Bolo One be able to survive with only half of the power supply necessary to operate life support, perform ship functions, and carry out the many other crucial tasks affecting their very lives? CNN will keep you updated as further details unfold.

*

It was nearly three days before the rigged-up steam plant was ready for testing. During that time, Carl had come up with an extensive inventory of reasons why he should be the one to venture outside. He had always kept himself in pretty good shape and over the course of the trip so far, had even lost ten to fifteen pounds. "I'm the youngest, most agile, quickest, and if something happens, the most expendable," Carl rationalized.

"Can't argue with that," Brandon laughed. "But when it comes down to experience with space walking, Tom has you beat by thirty hours and me by twenty, for that matter." During the AGAS tests, Tom had set a new record for a single EVA, while he was examining the connecting tethers as his ship orbited the moon. The previous record of 8 hrs, 56 min was set on March 11, 2001 by Susan J. Helms and James S. Voss on STS-102. Tom beat that record by 1 hr, 12 min with his 10 hrs, 6 min walk on June 26, 2014. "But, since this was my idea..." Brandon smiled and raised an eyebrow.

"Look," Tom said. "I know you are both qualified, in fact every member of the crew has been through the necessary training to perform a space walk. As the Mission Commander, I could pull rank and just do it myself, but as you all know, that's not my thing. I think of us as more of a family, so I'm willing to put this to a vote. But, like the Mercury Seven, we need to make the rule: you can't vote for yourself," he laughed.

"Commander, may I remind you that Starfleet Code section 12, paragraph 4 states that commanding officers are prohibited from going on away missions," Carl added in a flat emotionless tone." Everyone started laughing.

Valerie chimed in at that point, "Boys, why don't you stop flexing your testosterone and simply draw straws? Shortest straw wins. I'll even draw one with you."

"Count me in, too," added Jackie. "Let's get this thing up and running." To the crew, drawing straws did appear to be the only fair way to choose. Sally was more than willing to hold the straws for the rest of them to pluck out the winner, while refraining from drawing one of her own.

Though short on real straws, matchsticks and the like, they determined zip-strips served the purpose quite well. Sally found that she could hold the strips upright, with the length concealed up her sleeve, without difficulty. Jackie reached out first, pulling out a twelve-inch nylon strip and laid it on the table. Valerie drew an identical strip. "Well, either we're both going or neither one of us is," she hooted and they all laughed. Next, Carl slowly stretched out a hand, then he quickly jerked a zip-strip out of Sally's grip, almost causing a friction burn to her fingers, as he kept the zip-strip hidden from the rest of the crew. "Sorry," he told her, seeing the flash of pain on her face.

"OK," said Tom, with a bit of an eye roll at Carl. "I'm up next." Tom's zip-strip was an eight-inch, which he laid next to Jackie's.

"Is there any point in me picking?" Brandon inquired.

Smiling broadly, Sally came back with, "Sure, there is always a chance yours will be shorter. No pun intended."

They all laughed again, but Brandon stopped short and growled out with mock ferociousness at Sally, "You've been peeking." He pulled the last zip-strip. It too, was eight inches. Then, Carl held out his arm and closed hand, opening his fist slowly, before widely grinning like a Cheshire cat. There in his palm was the only six-inch zip-strip on the ship. Ready or not, Carl was elected to be the one heading outside.

From: Emma Devlin
Subject: Not Worrying
Date: October 12, 2018 10:23 a.m.
To: Brandon Devlin

_____(CLT): 4 min 37.65 sec

My Love,

I received your e-mail. Thanks for letting me know so quickly that you are ok and what had really happened. I'm glad I heard it from you before I saw the news. It has been a zoo with reporters calling and asking me for a quote, about how I was doing, had I heard from you, was I frantic, wanting to get the woman's view, and so on ad nausium. They have sure had a field day with speculation and predictions of doom. But, I know you and am confident in your ability and your assurance that all will be well. Darn media, anyway. Why can't they stick to predicting the weather and the election outcomes? Come to think of it, they're not so great at either of those, either. Smile.

As soon as I heard from you, I called and spoke with Rich, let him know you were ok, and warned him about the press. I know he likes his anonymity and doesn't want everyone to know about his parentage and attending WMU. Then, Mom and Dad called and I explained to them both what was going on. They were worried, but accepted my guarantee that you would be ok.

By the way, how is Ty doing, really? Better, I hope. He seems OK whenever I've talked to him on the phone, but still, I can tell he's hurting and depressed. I haven't seen him in several weeks with everything that's been going on. Are you seeing the same things when you hear from him? I think about Ty from time to time and wonder how he is coping without Claire, especially around the holidays. It's impossible to think about losing you. Those words are not in my vocabulary.

Oh, I almost forgot to tell you the news, according to the latest ultrasound, Laura is having a boy! Isn't that exciting? She and Nathan are dancing on the ceiling. He really wanted a boy and has finally gotten his wish. Mom has already started making a baby quilt. It's a block quilt, done in shades of green, and has the ABCs stenciled on the blocks. You'll be impressed when you see the finished product. I'll send you a couple of pictures of the quilt and the stuffed animals I bought for the baby (couldn't resist them). You know, I still have the one Mom made for Rich when he was a baby. That seems like so long ago, but only yesterday. Maybe a little bit of both. Does that make any sense? I guess it really doesn't have to. A mom can feel both.

I've composed another little ditty for your reading pleasure, since you enjoyed the tanka I sent you on our anniversary. I know it doesn't compare with your clever lines. I think as long as it tells you my story, all is well...

Now I lay me down to sleep,
Wishing my husband was here to keep,
While I lie here wide awake,
For him my body does softly ache.

I really do miss you so very much. It is hard to sleep in that big bed and not have you next to me, breathing softly - or snoring. I don't even mind the snoring, because it means you are there. I know I've said that before and can't help but say it again. We have never been apart this long. And, especially, never gone so long without joining in the oldest of dances. It doesn't matter whether we're caught up in a gentle waltz and floating along, or fused together in a fiery tango with clothes all asunder. Even hard rock would feel good, you rocking me in your arms, you rocking inside me until we explode. After, we'll drift off to sleep to a lullaby, wake the next morning at first light, the music will play, and we'll dance. I'm giving you fair warning: be sure to get plenty of rest. When you come home to me, I plan to dance with you until dawn.

I'll let you go now. Since you're not here, in the morning it's off to school and having the pleasure of enlightening young minds. They're a lot of fun and I'll keep you informed about our projects. This is a whole new class and who knows what they'll come up with this year. Write soon. I'll be waiting to hear from you.

All of my love

Your M

HOLLAND

< ≡ ♂ ≡ >

*

Reducing their rotation speed by 80% required a couple of hours of the small station-keeping rockets being fired in reverse. The whole crew was having a great time bouncing madly around the Hab. This activity looked much like the space-suited astronauts on the grainy TV images of the Moon landings, occurring nearly fifty years earlier. The big difference was the lack of space suits on five of the six crewmembers. Carl was in the process of suiting up and, like two mother hens, both Tom and Brandon were hovering over him lending assistance physically and imparting advice verbally.

Getting into a spacesuit is a rather complicated procedure from start to finish. Not knowing how long the EVA would take, Carl began with a lengthy stay in the lavatory, prior to donning a customized diaper. Next in line is what is fondly referred to as the 'octopus'. This contraption is a collection of wires and electrodes, which will help Valerie monitor Carl's vital signs while he is outside the vessel. This is followed by a full body undergarment of thermal long johns, which is much more heavy-duty than anything one might wear when snowboarding or slogging through snowdrifts in the Arctic.

Finally, all is topped-off by the canvas helmet. This specialized head covering contains the communication earpiece and throat-mic, as well as the water mouthpiece. Once the mouthpiece is attached to the body-mounted canteen by a flexible tube, the user need only bite down gently on the end to initiate the flow of water. This soft canteen, like a Bota wine bag, is strapped to the waist and positioned at the user's lower back, out of the way. This location allows body heat to keep the water from freezing solid and the tightened straps of the backpack provide the necessary pressure to generate the flow needed to push the water up to the mouthpiece.

Now Carl is ready for the outer suit. Like the undergarments, the outer suit is tailor made for each user. For this first Mars mission, a little personalization was permitted in the design phase of the individual suits. Two two-inch wide bands around the bicep area of each arm are highlighted in a color chosen by each user. There is a matching three-inch band around the right thigh and another one over the top of the helmet, front to back like a racing stripe. Carl's preference was Hunter Orange and when the others asked why, he grinned and replied, "I don't want anyone shooting at me, mistaking me for an alien."

Sally laughed at that and pointed out, "When we get to Mars, any life we may encounter will be the natives. *We* will be the aliens, and besides, no one should be doing any shooting in the first place." She chose a color called 'Georgia Clay', saying that if they did meet any Martians, she wanted them to think she was one of them as her chosen color most closely matched the red, iron oxide rich Martian soil.

Valerie chose fire-truck red, against the otherwise white suit, so she would be readily spotted as the chief medic. Tom picked a rich blue, a color that perfectly matched Penny's sparkling eyes. Brandon went with the traditional Kelly green of his ancestry and also to go with his green thumb. Jackie, on the other hand, requested the opportunity to use two colors: brown and yellow to emphasize her African/American – Chinese heritage. As Bolo One is the *first crew*, she was obliged by the design team and given the two stripes, but each at half the width.

The spacesuit is, for all intents and purposes, an unpowered spacecraft. It is an airtight vehicle, which provides the occupant protection from the vacuum, heat, and cold of space. It also supplies crucial air and water, and contains a receptacle to get rid of waste. As to the last item, keep in mind that whatever you do in the suit stays with you until you take it off. As with small children in snowsuits, a trip to the head before getting dressed is a prudent.

Before donning the spacesuit, it is pressure tested by attaching the myriad components together, just as if the person was inside. The suit is pressurized above the ambient pressure of the room. Then, as the arms, legs, and torso are bent and twisted around; the pressure gauge on the left sleeve is examined for abnormalities. Any drop in pressure will be a 'NO GO' on that particular suit until repairs can be made. Submersion testing while being pressurized, was performed on all suits prior to launch, but leaks have a way of developing when you least expect them. Each member of the crew has a set of five identical suits. These are all constructed with interchangeable components so that a faulty helmet from one may be switched with the helmet of another, or pants for pants, and so on.

To begin the process of entering the suit, Carl slipped on the boot liners. These are sort of a felt-like material, designed not so much for cushioning the feet, but to wick perspiration away from the body. Due to the rigorous activities involved, Gemini and Apollo astronauts had been known to lose several pounds of water-weight during a single EVA. That is why the boot liners provide a way to trap perspiration and the suit has a canteen to prevent dehydration.

After that, come the pants with attached boots, which eliminate two connection points where air might leak. This is followed by the top, which locks to the pants by means of an airtight fitting, which twists and snaps into place like changing the lens on a camera.

Then, the gloves are pulled on. These too have a similar fitting that locks to the sleeves at the wrists. The last piece of the outer suit is the helmet. On the surface of Mars, the racing stripe model will be used. But for deep space, a slightly larger model is better suited to the task. It features a clear faceplate behind an adjustable gold visor to aid in blocking out the much more intense sunlight, unfiltered by an atmosphere.

Prior to the helmet being placed on the head and secured, the suit is hooked up to the umbilical line. This line is a flexible air-hose having electrical lines running through and is connected to a compact backpack built into the top of the suit. The backpack is stuffed with the medical monitoring unit, communications device, and power links for the onboard air conditioning and heating systems. There are two EVA umbilical lines onboard, both being in the ladder-well, near each of the hatches. One is on the lowest level near the floor-mounted hatch and the other near the hatch above the third deck ladder.

After testing is completed, everything is connected, the helmet goes on, and the suit is pressurized. At only 20% of the weight the crew normally hauls around, Carl is now able to move about easily, as he feels like he is only 25 kg including spacesuit. Looking every bit like a five-year-old in a snowsuit, it is now time for Carl to go outside to play.

Chapter 10

Saturday, October 13, 2018 (Yuriday, Pisces 33, 0031)

6:00 p.m. "Good evening and welcome to CNN News. At this very moment in deep space, a hazardous undertaking is under way. We have learned that the veteran astronauts aboard Bolo One are sending the youngest member of the crew, Dr. Carl Wilson, outside the spacecraft to perform a harrowing space walk.

"Mission Support has not, as yet, shared all of the details. We only know that Dr. Wilson will be removing some of the insulation from the outer hull. The reason for removing the insulation is unclear. There are many electrical components and life support systems, as well as the ship's water supply, housed in the outer hull. Depending on what part of the hull is exposed to the extreme temperature fluctuations between the sunny side of the ship and the shady side, experts warn that the water supply will either flash freeze, or vaporize into steam. And of course, as the craft is spinning through space, this freezing and boiling could oscillate back and forth from one extreme to the other, every minute.

"This reporter is wondering just what are they thinking. More after this short word from First Galactic Savings & Loan: Making your savings astronomical..."

*

Of course, as the ship is traveling in its unique configuration, it is deliberately keeping one side to the sun and one side to the shade at all times, by design. The reporter was obviously unaware, or at least poorly informed, of this fact.

Before depressurizing the ladder-well, Tom and Carl climbed the two Jefferson ladders up to the Hydroponic deck. Tom made a final visual check of the suit and attached the umbilical line. Then he helped secure the helmet in place. "If I had known this was going to happen, I'd have suggested we put the EVA Prep room on the third deck," Carl wisecracked. "Fewer stairs to climb."

Tom laughed and replied, "If we had known this was going to happen, we would have outfitted the HP with a steam-powered generator before we left. OK, you're all set. I'll give you a 'Go' once I'm back on Deck One, indicating the hatch is sealed and the ladder-well is depressurized."

"Roger that," Carl replied. He began climbing the rung-ladder to the roof hatch, as Tom descended the two Jefferson ladders. Before opening the roof hatch, Carl paused, listening to the first deck hatch being sealed, the hiss of the air being pumped out of the ladder well, and then the headset, "OK, we're just about ready," Tom said.

"Good. How's my Comm?" Carl asked.

"Reading you wall to wall," Tom said over the earpiece. Then, turning to Valerie, "Medical and Environments?" he queried.

"Go," she responded.

Then to Brandon, "Transport?"

"Transport is a Go," Brandon replied.

Tom then announced over the Com, "Carl, you are Go for EVA."

"Roger that," Carl answered back. "I'm opening the hatch, now."

Carl released the clamps and pushed upward. The hatch opened easily. At 20% Earth Normal Gravity, the hatch felt as if it only weighed about 4.5 kg. He closed the sun-blocking gold shield-plate before proceeding further up the ladder and then drew himself up one rung, followed by another until the rim of the hatch was at chest level. Carl unfastened a small, compact electrical winch from his utility belt and attached the power-spool end to the top rung of the ladder. The other end, he attached to the handle-like ring built into the chest-plate of the suit (the design inspired by the Star Trek movie, *The Wrath of Khan*). He was now secured to the spacecraft by something more substantial than just the umbilical line. Placing a portable magnetic video camera atop the Hab near the hatch for Brandon to scrutinize the operation, Carl reported, "Ready to deploy."

"Roger, I have you on camera," Brandon acknowledged and began operating the winch remotely from the first deck. "Proceed." As the small motor on the winch began turning, it reeled out the cable, allowing Carl to move further up the ladder.

Carl clambered up and out onto the top of the Hab, remaining perched on his hands and knees to maintain a low center of gravity. For a moment, he felt slightly disoriented, as the Hab was still rotating, albeit much slower than it had been. From his prospective, everything was moving around him as if he were the center of the universe. His better judgment whispered not to try standing up, if he didn't need to.

As Brandon reeled him out little by little, Carl slowly inched towards the sunny side of the Hab. Lacking any handholds on the side of the craft, Carl would have to rely on Brandon to lower him into place, just out of sight of the camera.

As he began turning around to lower himself over the edge, feet first, Tom shot up a hand to get Brandon's attention and called out, "Hold up there a moment, Carl." Brandon stopped the winch and Carl came to an abrupt halt, nearly bringing him down onto the side of his faceplate. "Sorry about that," Brandon apologized. Tom continued, "Carl, I would like you to set out over the edge, headfirst. The location to work on is high on the side, so you really shouldn't need to go past your waist."

Sally was standing-by on the Hydroponic Deck to assist. At this point, it was sealed off from the ladder-well, along with all of the other decks. Tom then ordered, "Sally, in bay 3, using the headset and infrared scanner, let Carl know when he is in position. Where the bulkhead is exposed on the inside, we want Carl to peel back the insulation on the outside."

"Roger," Sally acknowledged.

Tom continued, "Carl, you've got that old Android Tablet on you, right?" Now that Carl had re-adjusted his orientation, Tom and Brandon were once again viewing the soles of Carl's boots, as Brandon resumed reeling him out, in the direction of the sunny side of the ship.

"Affirmative," Carl replied. He began to extract the small, somewhat antiquated multi-media device from the left thigh pocket of his suit. It had been a graduation gift from his mother, when he acquired his Engineering degree.

"You won't need it until you are in position," Tom told him. "But when we are ready, I'll have you manipulate it to cast a shadow on the outer bulkhead."

Carl smiled in understanding. "Gotcha," he said. He could visualize the plan as Tom had explained it. As Carl shades an area on the sunny side of the ship, Sally will be able to view the cooler reading on the inner bulkhead using the IR scanner and thus be able to guide him to the exact point on the outside.

A moment later, Sally was in position and they were ready to go. With Brandon operating the winch, Carl dangled headfirst over the edge, stopping as he was suspended at waist level. Sally could distinguish Carl's silhouette on the inside of the bulkhead, moving slowly and shape-shifting, as re-exposed areas regained heat while other regions became shaded. "Carl, can you hear me?" Sally inquired.

"Loud and clear," he responded, already holding the five-inch by seven-and-a-half-inch Tablet at arm's length, with his right hand. Sally could easily make out the rectangular shape well enough to ascertain where it was.

"OK, switch it to the other hand," she directed, then waited for the image to stop moving again. "Good. Now, move it ten centimeters to the left."

Being upside-down, Carl's instinct was: 'as seen by an observer on the outside, right side-up'. So he moved his hand to the right.

"No, my left..." Sally began to say, then added with a smile in her voice, "and yours too, for that matter."

Carl paused a moment, then mugged, "D'oh!" Everyone on the circuit laughed, including Carl, as he shifted his Tablet the other way.

Sally waited for the image to stop once more. "OK. Now reach up about ten centimeters. That's toward your belt," she said, with just the right amount of sarcasm to show it was all in fun and not meant to offend.

"Yes, Mom," Carl groaned, mockingly.

Trying not to laugh, Sally went into a mock orgasmic romp gasping, "Um, that's it. That's the spot. Yeah, right there,

Ooh."

Tom broke in at that point, "OK Carl. Mark that spot and commence removing the insulation, as we discussed. At a meter or less from the bulkhead, the outline of your Tablet should be just about the right size section needed. Just peel off one layer at a time, leave it un-shaded till I tell you if more is needed or not, and we will go on from there. Copy?"

"Roger that, Commander. Can I go back to listening to Sally, now?" Carl chuckled.

Tom replied, "We need to finish this side, get you turned 180 to the dark side (although I see you are already there, mentally), repeat the process, and then send you back inside immediately after. Ok, boys and girls, fun time's over for now, I'm afraid."

In unison, Carl, Sally, and even Brandon, expressed a long drawn out, "Aaawww."

*

From: Brandon Devlin
Subject: JotD
  Date: Pisces 34, 0031 20:13
   To: Tyler Cody

_____(CLT): 4 min 47.30 sec

Hey Ty,

How's life treatin' you these days? Better, I hope. Better than up here, anyway. I'm sure you saw the news flash the other day.

But hey, don't believe everything you see and hear on the tube. That asteroid wasn't much bigger than a semi. I saw a video of the broadcast and if I hadn't been here in the flesh, I'd think we were goners, too. It did take us a smidgen longer to repair than I thought it might (most of three days), but we came up with a workaround that'll knock your socks off. And, we got Carl's first spacewalk out of the way in the process. The kid aced his mission and is now a veteran and certified space cadet. How about that?

Tom and I talked him through a procedure of stripping insulation from the outer hull. This will allow us to super heat a little water on one side of the ship to produce steam and chill it on the other, so it condenses back. We built a damn good steam-powered electric generator on the hydroponics deck. It's really a combination system drawing on solar and geothermal energy. It's cranking out almost as much power as both of the solar panels, before the accident. Sometimes, the old ways are just as good as the new. Only, let's not go back to the paddle-wheel boats or steam-engine cars. Ha, ha (We are leaving the panels attached, JIC).

I'd like to keep this gadget operating once we're on the surface of Mars, but we'll be experiencing day-night cycles, along with possessing a planetary atmosphere, so it won't work properly. Well, that's why we brought along the RTG.

Hey, and specking of electricity, you heard about Ben Franklin and his kite, didn't you? Well the way I heard it, Ben was out in the back yard one day with a kite and he couldn't get it off the ground. His wife hollered out the kitchen window, "Ben, what the heck are you doin' out there?" He said, "I'm tryin' to get this here kite up in the air, but it won't go." She said, "Well, you idiot, what you need is some tail." Ben shouted back, "I told you that this morning and you told me to go fly a kite." Ba DUM bum

Catch you later,

Brandon

< ≡ ♂ ≡ >

From: Brandon Devlin
Subject: Resting Up
Date: Pisces 34, 0031 20:40
To: Emma Devlin

_____(CLT): 4 min 47.34 sec

My Darling M,

It's startling how much alike some of us are on the ship. Ty and Claire were so deeply in love with one another. Just like Tom and Penny, and you and I. I don't know if I could ever cope with losing you in such a violent way, or in any way come to think of it. Just the thought of being without my wife and soul mate makes me feel short of breath, as if the air has been knocked out of my lungs. But, Ty is starting to come around and crawl out of that black hole called grief. It's been a long, slow process for him.

After Penny's death, I think Tom would have lost it too, if it hadn't been for Ty. The two of them have been going through a sort of one-on-one 'group counseling' via their email exchanges. He and Ty have both started opening up to each other, at least. So that shows they are trying to accept what has happened and move forward.

You know it's really hard being someone's closest friend when you are literally millions of miles away. It's so frustrating! We've always been close, our line of work and the possibility of death from so many ways creates a bond. Words can't always describe just what it is we want to say. Well, I guess I'd better change the subject now or I'm the one that's gonna be needing counseling.

So, Laura is having a boy. That's super. I can just see Nathan bouncing around with excitement. I hope they don't name him something like Nathan Montgomery II, though I suppose there are worse names. Wouldn't it be hilarious if they named him after me? Brandon Montgomery, that has a nice ring to it. LOL

Is Sarah looking forward to having a little brother or have they not told her, yet? What is she now, 3 or 4? I never can remember. She's always been a little sweetheart, like her mother and aunt (meaning you). I wonder if the baby will take after his mom or dad? I remember Nathan telling me about the jokes he used to play on people. He was quite a little terror when he was younger. This ought to be interesting.

Now let's focus on the next part of your letter. You say you want to dance all night. That's ok by me. Let's start with that waltz, then set our selves on fire with a tango, and finish up pulsating to that hard rock by rocking hard. Thrusting together, rocking and a rolling to our own beat is exactly what I dream of every night. But, instead of a lullaby, I want us to drift off in exhaustion after the fireworks (John Phillip Sousa, eat your heart out). You see, I was thinking more like staying in bed for a week. I can't wait to get you home alone, and then I'm gonna turn you every way but loose. You might not want to be wearing an expensive negligee, because it'll be in the way and I may shred it with my teeth. With these calluses I'm building up on my hands after reading your letters, my hands might be a little rough. I'm afraid I might cause bruises, though you know I'd never intentionally hurt you. It's just that it's been so long and I may hold on a bit too hard. ROFL

Loving and missing you more than I can say (in print at least). When I come home, I'll let my hands and lips do the talking.

I'll write more, later. Something just came up I need to deal with. Hee hee

Brandon

< ≡ ♂ ≡ >

From: Emma Devlin
Subject: Fireworks
Date: October 19, 2018 6:45 p.m.
To: Brandon Devlin

_____(CLT): 5 min 10.37 sec

My Love,

I must say that you really know how to be subtle (ha, ha). When I know you're coming home I'll put in for two weeks of annual leave. One week to spend in bed with you and another week to recover. You might want to do the same. You know I tend to nibble a bit when excited, and teeth marks take a while to fade. And, you like it when I use my imagination… my imagination has been working overtime, dreaming of our (next) first night together.

I may wear that negligee anyway as the thought of you removing it makes me shiver with anticipation. I know just the one. There's a surprise for you. I've always wanted to have photos taken, for you, by one of those places that do glamour shots, with women in beautiful outfits and suggestive poses. Take a look at the attached calendar page. I'll be sending you one each month until you are home. I love the romantic outfits and there's not much on beneath, in some nothing at all.

Imagine where your hands and lips could be exploring (sometimes that's all I can think about). Now, for the December photo, visualize what we could be doing together on a rug in front of a roaring fire, and it won't be roasting marshmallows. That one will come to you soon and you'll see what I mean.

There's something I've been meaning to ask you. Do people at Mission Support read our letters and see the pictures I've sent? I hope not. They would think I am a sex addict when it comes to you. On second thought, what if they do. They'll see how much in love we are and how much we miss each other (and, it might give someone a hard on, tee hee).

All my love,

Your M

HOLLAND

< ≡ ♂ ≡ >

(Dr. Willis laughed quietly to herself and blushed slightly at their passionate exchanges. The love shared between these two always touched a chord in her heart, and left her a little envious. This is one exchange where Commander Lewis would have no reason to be copied.)

*

In the big corner office, Commander Lewis was situated behind his desk, tipped back in his chair, and perusing the daily reports. He brought his chair back into position with a thump when the familiar 'DING' sounded, indicating a new message had just hit his inbox. Glancing over at the screen and seeing the message was from JPL, he decided it was worth interrupting his labors.

From: Rick Battles, JPL Mars Tracking
Subject: Mars Quake
Date: October 30, 2018 10:23 a.m.
To: Commander Morgan Lewis, Mission Support

_____(CLT): no delay

Commander Lewis,

Good morning, Morgan. I just received an alert from one of our team members monitoring the FP1. Last night, they recorded what appeared to be 6-7 minor tremors at the Avernus

Colles landing site. The vibrations were minute, just 0.1 to 0.3 or so intensity, but the duration was a minute or more for each. None of the other rovers, still transmitting anywhere on the planet, recorded anything at all, so it was a rather odd occurrence. The operations tech that reported it said it was almost like a 600-pound woodpecker had been pecking at the outside of the vehicle. Very strange.

All of the other displays are reading 'Systems: A-OK'. The fuel processor is functioning within normal parameters. I just thought you should be aware of a possible malfunction. We'll keep an eye on it and let you know if it occurs again.

R. Battles, JPL

$< \equiv \male \equiv >$

As he finished reading, Commander Lewis frowned. The communication from Rick was rather casual and not really what one might call a proper report, written within the prescribed format. Checking to see that his office door was closed, he reached down into his bottom drawer, fished out the hidden bottle, and poured two fingers of scotch into his water glass. As he downed the scotch with one hand, he stabbed the delete button with the other, transporting the message to the netherworld. Then, he poured another drink as he resumed analyzing his mountain of reports, as if the message had never arrived.

Chapter 11

Wednesday, November 7, 2018 (Alanday, Aries 10, 0031)

From: Carl Wilson
Subject: The view from here
Date: Aries 10, 0031 22:00
To: Mary Croft

_____(CLT):   6 min 50.81 sec

Hello Sweetheart,

Sure wish you were here to see this view. We're preparing to go into Mars orbit in two days, and I haven't slept in nearly three. I can't get over this spectacular sight of Mars. If I stand with my back to the door of the EVA Prep room and peer out the half meter sized porthole above the control console on the other side of the lab, there is the thinnest of margins of space surrounding the planet. It's like back on Earth, during moonrise of a full moon: hold your hand out at arms length and make a ring with your thumb and index finger to view the moon through. It looks HUGE!! Have you ever done that? Try it if you haven't.

We'll be arriving with about 40 days left in the dust storm season, but if we get a break in the weather, so to speak, we'll land at the first opportunity. These past six months have been terribly confining for everyone. When it comes to the claustrophobia of a closed space with no exits, this is about like being in the brig, on a submarine, under the polar ice cap. If that asteroid hadn't hit the solar panel last month and stirred up so much excitement, I think I might have gone space happy. Although I don't know why they call it 'happy'. I kind of feel sorry for all of my crewmates that didn't get to go out on the EVA. But, fair was fair and I won the draw. I got to experience the vastness of space, first hand.

Oh, and speaking of that excitement and the EVA, our new 'steam-powered' electrical generator is putting out nearly as much power as both of the old solar panels did. While going over the numbers with Tom, a few days ago, he said it reminded him of a story he heard about the early days of the Apollo Program. He said there was an 'urban legend' that goes like this:

When NASA was getting ready to send the first astronauts to the moon, they thought, 'How are the crew going to take notes in zero gee if there isn't any gravity to pull the ink out of the pen (you know how, if you write upside-down for a few seconds, the pen stops working)?' So the Fisher Pen Company designed a pen that was pressurized to about 50 PSI that would write in zero gee (at a design and development cost of $50k, mind you).

Well, that particular expenditure was during the 'Space Race' days when big spending was the norm. But, then once the U. S. was co-operating and collaborating with the Soviets, someone asked them how they solved the problem. Tom said, "The Soviet cosmonauts said they used one of these." I glanced over and Tom was pulling a short pencil out of his shoulder pocket. (LMAO) He said he's carried a pencil on every flight since he heard that. And, I found out yesterday that Brandon carries one, too.

After doing a little digging I found out that the Fisher Pen Co. developed the pen on its own dime and then approached NASA. But, the result is the same: it makes for a cute story. The point is: sometimes the old ways are the best. Who would ever have imagined we would be using a steam-powered generator on our way to Mars.

Unbelievable, everyone might say. The technology is very old, but that's exactly the kind of (out-of-the-box) thinking that the Mars Direct Plan was built on: make some of the fuel on Mars, instead of taking it all with you. Have it waiting for you when you get there. That's why we need people on the mission. Rovers can't think and problem-solve the same way we can. Of course, on a robotic mission, it could just be flown without life support, so no big shakes.

Well, let's see... by ye olde Earth calendar I see today is November 7. With any luck we'll be sharing our Thanksgiving dinner with the locals. (Har har). That should be just about two weeks away. Sure wish I was sharing it with you. I really miss you, Mary. You'll never know how much. Say hi to your folks for me.

All my love, Carl

< ≡ ♂ ≡ >

During the next two weeks, the dust storms appeared to increase in intensity, instead of tapering down. From the beginning, it had been planned that the crew could ride out the storms, in orbit, for up to two months, if necessary. But, that was before the asteroid incident. It had taken a considerable amount of fuel to slow the ship's rotation and then speed it back up again. This emergency procedure reduced the amount of fuel available to dwell in orbit for any long period.

Staying in orbit requires occasional thruster bursts to maintain the proper orientation and altitude, due to the gravitational pull of both Mars and its two moons: Phobos and Deimos. With current fuel reserves, the end of November will be the cut-off point for making the go /no-go decision to land or head back to Earth. Unfortunately, that would still leave 19 days remaining in the dust storm season. The scientists at Mission Support are minutely scrutinizing every detail of the weather reports from the Mars Express Satellite, which has been in orbit since late 2003.

Since the crew can't land yet, the sleeping arrangements have remained the same, with only two usable staterooms. But, after the asteroid hit and some of the supplies and spare parts had been used, as well as there being a smaller stockpile of food now, Sally started a new project in her spare time: redistributing the remainder of the other items in one of the storage staterooms which contained a lower bunk. Working steadily, she excavated a path to the bed and cleared it off. Now, if someone wanted to have some solitude or lie down during his or her off duty time, they would have a place to do so.

While Tom scanned the latest message from Ty, Sally wandered into the unused stateroom to inspect her handiwork. Having plopped down on the bed and stretched out on her back, she began daydreaming of meandering through a meadow of tall grasses and wildflowers. Sally envisioned a beautiful summer day with just a hint of a breeze lifting her hair from the nape of her neck. With not another soul for miles, she peeled off her clothes, letting the sun and breeze wash over her bare skin, and laid down in the grass for a little sun bathing. It was so warm and peaceful in her fantasy world, and Sally's mind continued to drift... after a while her right hand migrated to her furry mound. It had been so long since she had shared herself with Bobby. With trembling fingers, her imagined self began stroking her moist crotch, softly and slowly at first, then ever faster.

Moaning softly in the quiet stateroom aboard Bolo One, Sally's right hand slid down inside the front of her shorts as her left hand began gently massaging first one breast and then the other, squeezing the nipples lightly. It didn't take long for Sally to find the pleasure she had been seeking in her fantasy. In a matter of minutes the release left her gasping.

Sally opened her eyes to find Tom, standing at the door, his gaze riveted on her. As their eyes met, he blurted out, "I'm sorry. I wanted to show you the note I got from Ty. I didn't realize..." as he turned to walk away.

"That's OK," Sally whispered as she jumped up and moved quickly toward him, her hand outstretched asking for understanding. "It's my fault. I should have shut the door." She was embarrassed but also searching his face for any sign he liked that which wasn't meant to be seen. All she could make out was a shade of crimson staining his cheeks.

Not knowing how long he had been watching, Sally hesitantly placed her arms around Tom's waist and pulled him close. She could feel the bulge in the front of his pants straining firmly against her pubic mound, which told her he had been at the entryway long enough. Tom's hands immediately found their way to Sally's lower back. It was an automatic reaction beyond his control.

She moved one hand to the back of his neck to draw his lips down to hers. As Tom began to lean in closer, he abruptly stopped himself. "I'm sorry. I'm not ready to let someone else into my life yet. It's still too soon," Tom said as he pulled her arm down. "I can't..." his voice trailed off as he reluctantly stepped away from her grasp and hurried back down the stairs to the control deck. Sally slowly went back over to the bunk and lowered herself to the mattress, placing her elbows on her knees and hiding her face in the comforting shelter of her palms, allowing the stillness to envelope her.

From: Emma Devlin
Subject: Excitement!
Date: November 23, 2018 4:55 p.m.
To: Brandon Devlin

_____(CLT): 7 min 53.59 sec

Sweetheart,

Great news! We have a new family member: Brandon Richard Montgomery; 9 lbs. 2 ozs; 21 inches; born at 9:02 am, a very sensible baby. Laura gave birth yesterday. (Thanksgiving Day if you haven't been keeping track by your calendar. How'd you like Miss November?). She's doing fine, but is tired. I'm going to stay with them while she's recovering and help take care of the baby. Nathan is awfully funny. You know he doesn't smoke, so he's passing out bubble gum cigars. He looks like Groucho Marx (or Churchill?) with that pink cigar clenched between his teeth. You know, I don't think his feet have touched the floor yet. He's been so sweet and thoughtful to Laura and won't let her do a thing, making sure she rests. I like that in a man. The baby reminds me of Rich, with that mop of dark hair. Babies born with hair are always adorable. Some people might argue that those having baldpates are cuter, but I like curls.

Cradling him and nuzzling that tiny neck brings back so many memories. And, I've always loved the smell of baby powder. A few days ago, before I drove up to Boston, I lugged the photo albums out of the closet and started flipping through photos, reminiscing about our lad. I wish you were here with me to share these memories. It's hard to imagine that we were that young, though I don't feel much older now than I did then. Memory is a funny thing. I'll scan and send you a few of the best shots. Wait till you see them. We were quite the good-looking couple, if I do say so. Let me know what you think.

Also, while Laura was taking a nap earlier, I went to meet Mary for lunch in downtown Boston. She is really missing Carl and is so proud of him for his part in the mission and his first spacewalk. I had only met her the one time, at the press conference, but she is a really sweet girl. I guess she and Carl will be getting married when you all get home.

Oh, and getting back to YOUR son (LOL), I received a piece of news from Rich. He's planning on traveling to India during the university's winter closure period in December. There is a conference on Nano-Technology that one of his professors has invited him to attend, along with a couple of dozen other students. He said they are getting a discounted group rate through Western's Travel Services, so the cost per person won't be a killer. And, they'll be arranging flights, making hotel reservations and the like. The students will be in conference for a week, then spend a week playing tourist. He was being funny and said they would be visiting a cemetery for one person (meaning the Taj Mahal). One of his friends suggested everyone ride the bus to their tourist destinations, so they learn more about the country and its people. I hope it's safer than it used to be. Yes, I know he's twenty now, but it's going to be like sending him off to summer-camp. I may be worried the whole time he's gone. (That's a mom's prerogative, ya know)

But, I know he's been working hard and deserves to relax. Don't know when he might get another chance to have an adventure like this. I do know that his engineering program is pretty intense, but Rich seems to thrive on the challenge. He is SO much your son. Think I'll stick to teaching. It's also a challenge and I like working with the youngsters.

I'm relieved things have improved and you're all now safe. I tried not to worry too much, but that's part of a wife's job description (kind of like being a mom). That contraption really works well, from what I heard from Mary. What a terrific idea. You've always been a very resourceful person and the six of you make a great team. They ought to have a parade down Broadway when you all return. Wouldn't that be something to see? I can even see the president presenting you with a medal or at least... what was in that old Star Trek movie.. *'a commendation for original thinking'* when Kirk reprogrammed the computer so he could beat the Kobayashi Maru no-win scenario? LOL

I will be incredibly glad when you are home. I just can't get used to sleeping by myself, and wake up because you're not here next to me. When I do drift off, I dream of your body next to mine, snuggled around my back, your warm breath on the nape of my neck, and your hardness pressed against my rear. That always feels so very good. And, I feel safe, and oh so loved, when I am in your arms. Better stop now, so I don't start crying. I love you and miss you more than I can say. Think I'll go hug that baby again. That'll cheer me up to no end.

Soon, December's calendar page will be on its merry way. On Christmas day, I will dream of you and picture us together in front of that fire, with you removing my nightie in that special way you mentioned. Sweet dreams.

Enclosing all of my love,

Your M

HOLLAND

< ≡ ♂ ≡ >

From: Richard Devlin
Subject: Christmas break
Date: November 25, 2018 8:15 p.m.
To: Brandon Devlin

_____(CLT): 8 min 1.54 sec

Hey Dad,

Happy Turkey Day! How goes it on the Starship Enterprise? Me, I just got to main campus from Parkview. I'm sure glad they have these Bronco Transit buses. Parking places are at a premium on campus; same as when you were here. Don't think that will ever change. The car has been parked in the Valley II lot for quite a while and has only been used to go to Bilbo's for pizza and Bell's Brewpub for... soft drinks, yeah, that's it, soft drinks (same old haunts as you frequented. How's that for heredity or perhaps programming?).

And speaking of the Bronco Transit, a friend of mine was chatting with one of the drivers, yesterday. The driver owns an apartment house in the Stuart Historical District and will have an available unit, after the first of the year. My buddy and I are going to rent the apartment. It's about a two-mile bike ride to campus (in nice weather) and after splitting the cost, rent will run me $425 per month, including utilities. The driver said his wife also works at Western and they get to see each other on their breaks and eat lunch together. It's nice to see couples that like each other so much. Kinda like you and Mom.

I guess Mom told you I will be spending winter closure at a conference on Nano-Tech, in India. My NT Prof. says we are going to learn how to put an elephant on the head of a pin:

AN ELEPHANT

I suggested they should have held the conference in Micronesia, but he said it wasn't going to be that big of a deal. (Get it... Micro... Nano?) ROFLMAO We'll be going in a large group, with lots of "grown-ups", so not to worry. You know how Mom gets.

She emailed me about Aunt Laura's new baby. That's really awesome.

Dad, I really love these engineering classes. I think it is in my genes (or at least in my shorts). Woot! I had one Prof. tell me two weeks ago that I was a "chip off the old block". He's really old, so I think he may have been one of your instructors and has figured out I'm your son. His name is Edward Michelson. It really made me proud to be compared to you.

I think the word might be getting around, tho. There have been a few odd people on campus that really seem to be keeping on eye on me. It's kind of creepy. For the past week or so, it feels like I'm being watched. I don't like that very much. Probably tabloid reporters or something.

Well Pops, I guess I will head to class and pretend I'm paying attention. LOL

Catch ya later,

Rich

< ≡ ♂ ≡ >

(From Dr. Willis to Commander Lewis, could Devlin's son, Richard, be in danger on the WMU campus or possibly be experiencing a little paranoia? I recommend contacting his mother and/or their family doctor for evaluation and possible counseling if paranoia.)

After receiving the report and a copy of this e-mail from Rich to his father, Commander Lewis suggested Dr. Willis might be experiencing paranoia and should go to submitting monthly reports rather than weekly. In his opinion, the psychologist's time could be better spent on other projects, rather than frittering it away on these re-occurring threads. He was getting tired of reading all of these mundane reports, as she appeared to be trying to make herself appear useful to the mission. Being taken aback by the rebuke, the psychologist applied for and was granted an immediate two-week vacation.

*

From: Rick Battles, JPL Mars Tracking
Subject: More Mars Quakes
Date: November 25, 2018 10:38 p.m.
To: Commander Morgan Lewis, Mission Support

_____(CLT): No delay

Morgan,

It's happened again. Same as before, but worse. Intensity 0.6 – 0.9 for 2 ½ minute duration, a three-minute pause, then the same thing all over again. Then it stopped. I'm at a loss to explain it. Can your people fire up the truck and get the camera on this? Let me know what you find out.

Rick

< ≡ ♂ ≡ >

From: Commander Morgan Lewis, Mission Support
Subject: RE: More Mars Quakes
Date: November 25, 2018 10:45 p.m.
To: Rick Battles, JPL Mars Tracking

_____(CLT): No delay

Rick,

Thanks, I'll look into it and get back to you in a few days. I doubt it's anything to worry about.

Morgan

< ≡ ♂ ≡ >

After clicking the send button, Morgan shut down his computer, flipped off the light, and left for the night. It was nearly 11:00 pm when the gate guard saw Morgan on his cell phone, as he sped off the base.

*

05:15 - Just before bed, Jackie was lounging in the stateroom, casually perusing her email, when up popped a new message from Chen Kaiying, an old teammate and good friend from the '08 Olympics. This was odd, as Jackie had not heard a peep from Kaiying in more than five years. That was about two years after she moved back to the U.S. from China.

While in their late teens, Jackie and Kaiying were an inseparable and mischievous pair. Their gymnastics trainer would often scold them for acting up, especially when there were young men about. In school, Jackie and Kaiying would pass notes back and forth chatting about the boys in their classes. The two weren't worried about the messages being intercepted and examined by their teachers. No one would know what was really being communicated as the notes were in a secret code devised by the two of them.

It was a pretty simple cipher in which a number at the bottom of the page would be the 'key'. For example, if there was a number 4, one would read the first word of the first sentence, the second word of the second sentence, and so on, through the fourth sentence, then start once more with the first word of the fifth sentence.

Jackie wistfully recalled how the two of them had been devoted friends, while training together during the years between the '04 and '08 Olympics. Throughout these years, Jackie had lived with the Chen family in Shunyi, located northeast of the Capital International Airport, about 20 km outside of Beijing. Jackie and Kaiying had spent many a night together in each other's rooms, doing whatever young girls do at that age.

Although Jackie had made several attempts to contact her over the years, she had not received a response from Kaiying, so this communication was very unexpected and somewhat startling. She swiftly glanced toward the bottom of the email and her eyes widened when she saw what, at first, appeared to be a jagged line, but was actually a row of number eights, inscribed in flowing Chinese characters. Jackie didn't bother reading the entire email message, but instead started counting words and silently translating the message.

From: Chen Kaiying

Subject: Greetings to my friend
  Date: November 26, 2018 5:15 a.m.
    To: Jackie Miller

_____(CLT): 8 min 6.36 sec

Hi Jackie,

We have not heard from you in a very long time and all miss you here at the gymnastics school. And need to hear from you, soon. How are you doing? I really hope to get a letter from you about your experiences. What will we ever do while you are away on this adventure? Maybe we will think of something fun. I think it will be hard for us. I am wondering if you are missing us also. If you have time, write to me and tell me how you are and how you like living in space. Can you email a picture of you? If you don't have one, that's ok. I haven't met Mike yet. When I'm in America, will I get to meet him? I hope no one will die or become injured on your mission. That would be sad.

Your good friend,

Chen Kaiying

⁊\

< ≡ ♂ ≡ >

Jackie went pale, the blood draining from her face. Her mind began racing as she struggled to understand the impact of the message.

Chapter 12

Monday, November 26, 2018 (Johnday, Aries 28, 0031)

From: Jackie Miller
Subject: What are you talking about?
Date: Aries 28, 0031 05:30
To: Chen Kaiying

_____(CLT): 8 min 6.39 sec

Where is Michael and what are you planning to do to him? What the hell is going on and why the hell are you doing this to us? Screw the damn code.

$$< \ \equiv \ ♂ \ \equiv \ >$$

After striking the send key, Jackie began pacing unevenly around the tiny stateroom, waiting in agony for the reply. At this distance from Earth, it would take just over sixteen minutes before the reply is received, at the earliest. After what seemed like hours, the reply came in and she began reading. The significance of the message slammed her in the chest like a boulder, and she slumped to the deck.

From: Chen Kaiying
Subject: Michael
Date: November 26, 2018 5:55 a.m.
To: Jackie Miller

_____(CLT): 8 min 6.45 sec

165

Michael is safe for the time being. We are holding him hostage in your home and he is secured to prevent escape. Your husband will be killed though, if you fail to help us complete our assignment. It is no coincidence that you are on this particular mission. This undertaking has been in the planning for over two years. It was arranged for you to replace Commander Cody. That particular car accident worked out to our advantage, as no one discovered what had been planned.

It is essential that your spacecraft does not land on Mars. How you prevent that is of no concern to us. No one needs to die on the ship. It will be sufficient to abort the landing and force a return to Earth. You will be compensated ten times what you would otherwise receive, plus Michael will live. Think very carefully about your decision and the penalty if you do not comply. Whether Michael lives or dies is in your hands.

Chen Kaiying

< ≡ ♂ ≡ >

Jackie was dumbfounded. She quickly fired off a message to Mike.

From: Jackie Miller
Subject: Your status
Date: Aries 28, 0031 06:15
To: Michael Miller

_____(CLT): 8 min 6.47 sec

Michael,

My darling, please let me know if you are all right. What is happening there? I just got a very strange and disturbing email from an old gymnastics teammate from China. I am very worried about you and your safety. I need to hear from you immediately.

Love,
Jackie

< ≡ ♂ ≡ >

    Jackie's mind was in a dither as she dispatched the email. Bolo One had been in Mars orbit for nearly two and a half weeks, waiting for the dust storm to subside. They were all becoming impatient, itching to get down to the planet's surface and begin their work. How could she justify any compelling reason for turning back to Earth now that they were so close to landing? But, without a good rationale, how could she 'cause' the mission to abort. 'That's called sabotage,' she deliberated. What would that process involve? Was there a way she could actually 'cause an accident', so that it would appear genuine and not look like sabotage? On the other hand, Kaiying said they would pay her ten times the wealth she would otherwise receive for completing the mission. Jackie shook her head from side to side, in denial. This was all senseless. How could she believe a word Kaiying had written? Plus, even if she did co-operate, there were thugs at her house and what would prevent them from murdering Mike if and when they no longer needed him?

    Jackie took a quick look at the clock. Now, after sending the message, it would be another sixteen plus minutes before she could expect a reply. She had been in her quarters on scheduled slumber time for nearly an hour and a half. She should be asleep, but with this latest crisis, how could she even think of closing her eyes? Still fully dressed, Jackie stumbled across the common area and into the galley for a cup of herbal tea, longing instead for a good stiff drink. Valerie was there, sipping a cup of tea and inquired, "Are you still up and about? Anything wrong?"

    "Oh, just a little antsy, I guess," Jackie replied. "Bad news from home." Instantly, she wished she hadn't said that. Now she might have to explain.

167

"What's happening at home? Is everything OK?" Valerie asked, with concern in her voice.

"Well, I can't say, just yet. I'm waiting for an email in about twenty minutes, before I'll know anything for sure." Jackie was being as evasive as she could while trying not to appear rude. If it became necessary to sabotage the ship, she was afraid she might have already said too much.

But Valerie was sharp and very intuitive. With her educational background and clinical training, she recognized her friend was carrying a very heavy burden on her soul. Not much ever got past Valerie.

"So, is there anything you need help with or want to talk about? I have plenty of time," Valerie shrugged with a grin. The waiting to land was almost becoming a joke.

"Not just yet," Jackie replied. "I'll let you know." After preparing her tea, she picked up the cup, and headed back to the stateroom. Once there, Jackie sat on the edge of the little round stool and mentally started sifting through different possible replies from Mike, in her head. One might be: 'what sort of message did you get from your friend in China? What has gotten you so worried?' In which case, Jackie would know that he was OK and Kaiying was just blowing smoke up her ass. Any variation of this response would be acceptable. A few more, less pleasant thoughts flitted through her head before 'DING'. The email message indicator displayed the receipt of one new message. She looked at the clock. It had been thirty-seven minutes. Holding her breath, Jackie opened it quickly.

From: Michael Miller
Subject: Don't Worry
Date: November 26, 2018 6:52 a.m.
To: Jackie Miller

_____(CLT): 8 min 6.56 sec

Don't worry about me. Just try to enjoy yourself on the
flight and have a good time. And if anything comes up, I'll be
sure to let you know. You are so funny, sometimes. We are so
good together, you and I. You won't find another one like me.
So don't take any un-necessary chances out there. There could
be no one to take your place. For as long as I live, you're the
only one for me and vice versa. In an hour, I'll have to leave for
work. Does this answer your questions?

All for you,

Mike

< ≡ ♂ ≡ >

In shock, Jackie's numb fingers parted and dropped the
melamine teacup to the deck. As it bounced across the floor, she
tried to scoop it up and instead toppled her stool, with a clang.
Valerie happened to be descending the ladder from the HP deck
to pour another cup of coffee for herself, when she heard the
clatter. She tapped on the door, "Jackie, are you OK in there?"
she called out.

"Fine!" Jackie snapped back. "Please go away and leave
me alone!" Valerie slid the door open.

"If you are having a problem, you know I can't do that.
Besides, you're my friend and I'm worried about you." Valerie
could see Jackie had not yet changed into her sleeping togs. The
cup was lying on the floor, trailing liquid across the
compartment. Jackie righted the stool and as she straightened,
tears filled her eyes. "What is it? Valerie pleaded. Let me help
you."

For a moment, Jackie stood there mutely and didn't
know what to say or do. Then, she suddenly stepped forward,
hugged Valerie tightly, and with ragged breath choked out,

"That." and nodded toward the monitor. The screen was close enough for Valerie to read without shifting position.

"I don't understand why you're so upset. Mike sounds OK to me."

Jackie released Valerie and moved away. "Mike is being held hostage. In the sign off, 'All for you'… the number four, it's a code. If you read the first word of the first sentence, second of the second, third of the third, fourth of the fourth, then start over, it translates 'Don't try anything funny. We won't take no for an answer." Valerie stared intently at the screen for a moment, as she counted off the words.

"Are you getting space-happy? You're looking for hidden messages that aren't really there."

Jackie sobbed uncontrollably, the tears streaming down her face. "No, it's true," she went over to the computer and used the mouse to scroll up to Chen Kaiying's first message. She explained, "When I was growing up in China, Kaiying was a close friend and teammate in the Olympics. When we were young, we used to pass notes back and forth to each other in class. To keep anyone from reading our messages and getting us in trouble, we came up with this code. See the strange looking marks at the bottom of her first message? Those marks are the Chinese symbol for the number eight. So take a look at the first word of the first sentence, and so on through the eighth, then start again." Jackie sat slumped on the bed as Valerie sat on the little stool and deciphered the first message and then went through the rest of the emails.

"I'm so glad you showed me this." Valerie pronounced firmly.

Puzzled, Jackie stared at her, her red eyes widening, and blurted out, "Why? Are you going to help me sabotage the mission?"

Chapter 13

Monday, November 26, 2018 (Johnday, Aries 28, 0031)

08:40 - When Tom knocked on the door to the stateroom, Carl had been asleep for a mere three and a half hours. Groggily he yawned, "Are we there yet?"

Tom smiled wryly and replied seriously, "Yeah, but we may be leaving soon. Get dressed and meet us in the control center. We have a sticky situation we need to discuss. Come on down and we'll fill you in."

Four minutes later, Carl popped out of the ladder-well on the first deck, his left cheek still red and wrinkled from resting on his pillow. "What do you mean, we're leaving? What's up, Doc?" he punned, lightly punching Jackie on the shoulder. She turned her head and gave him a weak, trembling smile. He could see by the redness in her eyes and trail of tears on her cheeks, that she had been crying. "No, seriously, what is it?" Alarmed, he pulled up the empty stool next to Jackie and sank down to the seat.

Everyone was now here. Valerie stood up and, addressing the group, relayed the contents of the emails Jackie had received and explained everything that had occurred during the past few hours. "Has Mission Support been notified?" Carl queried.

Tom replied, "I'm not so sure we can do that... not just yet, anyway. In the message there was something mentioned about plans being made as far back as two years ago." He turned

171

and asked Jackie, "Do you know who it was that brought you into the program, maybe a sponsor?"

Jackie thought intently for a moment, her brow furrowing, "I'm not sure, but my dad said a friend of his was one of the mission developers, and he had suggested I apply for admission to the program. He said if anyone found out he had said anything, it might look like he was playing favorites. So my dad never even told me who it was. But, that was several months before the mission was even announced to the public."

Tom continued his train of thought, "Val showed me all of the messages, and it appears there is someone of high rank in the program who is in on this and controlling our moves. We're not sure how far up in the command chain this goes. I suppose the traitor could be a mission developer. But, it appears a big name has apparently recruited Jackie and arranged for her to be on this ship, to replace Commander Cody…" Tom's voice trailed off. Then he turned to face Jackie straight on, "Wait, you said you were contacted prior to the mission being announced? None of us had backups prior to the announcement, not until about three months into the preparations. I mean, it could be just a coincidence that you had the same chemistry and medical background as him, but…"

Tom's mental deliberations abruptly headed in another direction: Ty and Claire's accident may not have been an accident, after all, and what about Penny? Was there a previous plot meant to take her hostage that went awry? Could someone have accidently killed her while trying to take her hostage, thus forcing him to abort the mission? Could they have now taken Mike hostage after their failure to capture Penny?

"Penny," he whispered. A cold sweat broke out over Tom's body as bile rose into his throat. His eyes stared around the room, seeing nothing, as his mind whirled in horror, and he exclaimed, "Do you think someone attempted to kill Ty to replace him with Jackie?" After a moment, Jackie's face went ashen and then turned green as she realized the implications of Tom's statement. She suddenly lurched forward and sprinted toward the lavatory, not quite making it before vomiting noisily on the floor, spattering the toilet.

"I'd take that as a yes," Carl stated. Sally jumped up and moved quickly, following Jackie, to assist.

After taking a deep breath to calm himself Tom began, "So no, I don't think we can let on that we are aware of their plan, just yet. But, I know it is up to us as a team to find a solution to this situation. At this moment, I just don't have a clue as to what it may be that we can do out here, on our way to Mars, to stop kidnappers back on Earth."

Brandon considered this a moment, "You're right, what the hell can we do way out here? We're at their mercy." Then, a notion flashed through his mind, "Wow! If Ty had any idea his wife may have been murdered in an attempt on his life... he'd be on the next flight to... well, anywhere after those bastards, even if it led him straight into Hell."

Valerie had an inspiration. "I've got an idea for us to consider. We may just have a couple of aces up our sleeve they aren't counting on. Perhaps Ty should be informed," she started to say.

"Are you space happy?" Brandon broke in, almost shouting as he jumped up to his feet. "That would really shove him over the edge."

Valerie raised her hand. "Hear me out..." she paused. "Ty lives in Richmond, Jackie and Mike, in Charlottesville. So he's only about an hour away by car. I think assisting us could do him a lot of good. Maybe even make him feel better by knowing he is taking part in resolving our problem and striking back at those who snatched Claire from him. It'll make him feel like his life has purpose again, and that his loss was not in vain.

"Of course, I'm only speculating about Claire, so we need to be careful in what we say to him. His accident might really just be a big coincidence, after all..." Valerie paused, weighing how much she should say next. "Remember on the day we launched, there was a second big news story involving a terrorist cell being taken down in Chicago? Well, that was my husband Steve and his team."

Brandon smiled sarcastically, "The military or the terrorists?"

Valerie snorted, "Cute. The military, or more accurately, extra-military. They are an ATAC team, which stands for Armored Tactical Assault Command," and she pronounced it 'EH tack', putting the accent on the first part of the word. "I'm going to contact Steve, and see if he and his team can lend a hand. I know I mentioned that he is a federal civilian employee, but it's a bit more than that. The ATAC is a covert ops division," she made air quotation marks with her fingers to emphasize the term covert ops. "I'm not allowed to talk about what he does, but if he can help, I'm sure he will.

"We can have him co-ordinate with Ty on site and strategize. But, it may take a few days until Steve and company can gather their gear and get over to Jackie and Mike's place. Ty could go in and stake out the neighborhood, keep an eye on the house, and report back to Steve if they try to move Mike."

Jackie and Sally were just starting on their way back over to the group, and overheard the conversation. "I think that's a great idea," Sally said. "It's like we have our own 'A-Team' riding to the rescue." She was speaking mainly to bolster Jackie's spirits, as she referred to the old TV show. Little did Sally know just how right she was. The Armored Tactical Assault Command team, led by Steve, basically IS the A-Team: highly skilled in the three I's: infiltration, interrogation, and intimidation, as well as possessing the usual marksmanship and combat expertise. Each team member was handpicked from the best of the best: all former Special Forces (Green Berets, Airborne Rangers, Seals).

Standing near the pressure hatch to the ladder-well, Tom suddenly dropped down onto one of the stools, looking distraught, face twisted with inner anguish. "What is it, Tom?"

Brandon asked, concern mirrored on his face.

"I'm wondering if Penny might also have been slain by someone attempting to force me to abort the mission, through sabotage or by other means. Mission Support was pretty damn quick to identify an abort maneuver, and not offer alternative tactics. What if that was part of their grand design? First Ty and Claire, then Penny, now they're working on Jackie and Mike. There could be a person right in Mission Support that's trying to stop us from landing."

"What about Emma and Mary?" Brandon asked. "They could be in danger, too."

Valerie considered that for a moment. "I doubt that we will have to worry about them, just yet. Typically, subversive groups usually target a single objective at a time. Hypothetically speaking, if they fail in one objective, *then* they move on to the next.

"So, with Mike being held captive, Emma and Mary are very likely safe for the time being. Let's work on getting Mike rescued. Then we can see to the safety of Emma and Mary."

Positioned at the control console, Carl nodded slowly as his concern for Mary eased slightly. He was closely scrutinizing the monitors and gauges. "You'd think that if it's someone with any clout, they could just come up with a good excuse and order us to abort. But anyway, the latest readings from the satellite feed indicate dwindling dust storm activity and that the atmosphere will be almost completely cleared over the next forty-eight hours," he reported. "We may actually have an opportunity to land, at that point."

"But if we touch down, they'll kill Mike!" Jackie interrupted Carl with a loud wail and began weeping, once again.

Valerie leapt into the conversation, "Ok, we need to get busy, quick. Brandon, send an urgent note to Ty. Fill him in on everything that has occurred up to this point and give him Jackie's address, if he doesn't already have it. Make sure he knows damn well that this is reconnaissance only, until Steve can arrive with his team and relieve him. We don't want him getting himself killed. Don't mention our speculations about Claire or that this may be connected to his accident. I'll contact Steve and have him get there as quickly as he can. I'm simply afraid that if we land they will murder Mike, but if we abort the mission they might take his life anyway, no longer needing him for insurance. So for now, we have to hold orbit and stay where we are. I'm going to e-mail Dr. Willis too, and suggest she put a hold on any email reports about these messages for a few days. I've known Pam since grad school and she is the one person I am sure we can trust." Valerie was unaware of the psychologist's revised reporting schedule to Commander Lewis, and that Pam wouldn't see any messages until after her vacation.

"Good plan," Brandon observed. "Except for one little problem. Our fuel situation is becoming critical. In about four or five days, we will have to land or fire the thrusters for the trans-Earth trajectory anyway. Spending so much time in orbit was anticipated, due to the dust storm season when we arrived. But, the asteroid impact and having to slow our rotation for the repairs and speed it back up again, used a lot of fuel. So, it's forcing us to make a decision, one way or the other. We can't hold in orbit for very much longer than… perhaps five more days, six at the very most."

"Then, let's get busy," Valerie declared, moving from her place near the control console.

"I'll run the numbers and try to pin down a more accurate time-line for fuel consumption and landing," Carl volunteered, turning back toward the computer screen. Sally went over and pulled up a stool next to Tom, sat down and draped her arm around his shoulders, then squeezed him slightly.

"We'll get this thing figured out," she promised him.

"I know that. It's just going to take so much time." He sighed quietly, leaning over and momentarily resting his head on her shoulder. Carl was busy at the console, Valerie and Brandon were heading off to start sending their emails, and Jackie was proceeding back up the ladder to fix another cup of tea and try to get some much-needed rest. Sally reached across, gently placing her hand on Tom's opposite forearm, and lightly kissing the top of his head.

"I'm here if you need me," she quietly whispered. Tom glanced up at Sally and gave her a tired smile; gratitude clearly etched on his features as he placed his hand atop hers and affectionately squeezed it.

*

A few hours later, Carl was number crunching with a program written in "R" that he had quickly hacked up, when Brandon stepped out of the ladder-well.

"Well, I've drafted the note to Ty and made sure he had all of the facts he needs and none that he doesn't. It's on its way, now. What's the verdict on your end?" he questioned.

Carl replied, "I've given the situation a lot of thought and gone over these numbers several times. If, whoever it is in Mission Support, *believes* Jackie has sabotaged the ship, then that might buy us a little extra time. So here's what I came up with: If we can pump the fuel from one of the almost empty fuel tanks into one or two of the other remaining tanks and then jettison and blow the empty one, it will create quite a good sized response on the sensors. Of course, we can pump some of the liquid waste into that tank to dampen the explosion, but this will give the impression of a lot more damage and loss of fuel than there actually will be.

"When Mission Support contacts us about the explosion, we tell them that we may not have sufficient fuel to execute an atmospheric entry and barely enough to operate the escape thrusters. We report that we will have to head back to Earth, but it will be another twenty-four hours until we line up for the maneuver. I think whoever is involved in engineering this plot will back off and put a hold on killing Mike, waiting to see if we really do perform the maneuver. Do you think they'll buy it?"

Brandon thought about it for a moment before replying, "That's a fairly risky plan, but I like it. However, if you don't mind, I'd like to go over those numbers of yours with Tom. What may initially appear to be a lot of damage could actually wind up *being* a lot of damage, if you know what I mean."

Carl smiled and replied, " I'd have said the same thing if one of you had come up with this crazy proposal. I understand completely. Just so we're clear on what will happen. If and when we blow the tank, some time in the next forty-eight hours, Mission Support will be expecting us to fire the trans-Earth thrusters, right around twenty-four hours after that. This is all based on my calculations concerning the amount of fuel we will have supposedly lost. There's no ifs, ands, or buts about that. In reality, we'll still have only about seventy-two hours to make the decision about whether to land or not."

"Then we'd better marshal the troops and produce a consensus," Brandon resolved. Carl turned back to the console. Considering Carl's plan, Brandon smiled and thought, 'Carl's really come a long way, and not just in astronomical mileage. This kid's gonna do all right.'

Chapter 14

Tuesday, November 27, 2018 (Scottday, Aries 29, 0031)

Claire's brother, Billy, had an old six-person camper mounted on the back of an even older pickup truck, that he used to use in the fall and winter for deer hunting. Ty figured that if he was going to go on a stakeout, it might be easier to keep an eye on the house from the window of the camper, than from the front seat of his car. In the camper, at least he had a bathroom, refrigerator, and microwave. Also, the camper had sign-art windows with hunting scenes printed on them. This allows someone on the inside to see out quite well, but seeing in was nearly impossible, unless it was dark and the lights were on inside. Since Billy had already shot his limit, a quick phone call secured the use of the camper, no questions asked.

On his way to Charlottesville, Ty picked up a grocery bag full of essential stakeout supplies, such as candy bars, chips, frozen burritos, energy drinks, and the like. Once he arrived in town, Ty stopped at the Burger King on Riverbend Drive and grabbed a couple of Whoppers, before turning down Jackie and Mike's street. As Ty exited the drive-thru, Claire's voice whispered in his mind, commenting on his poor dietary choices. She would not have approved, but somehow Ty thought she would forgive him, this one time.

Once Ty reached Jackie and Mike's neighborhood, he circled the block twice before finding a good parking lot about a block and a half away. There, he could easily view the driveway and garage, not appear too conspicuous to the neighbors, and most definitely not be seen from the front window of the house. Billy had left a pair of binoculars in the camper that would work out perfectly for this job.

Brandon's email suggested Ty set his cell phone to vibrate. When the commandos arrived, Steve would then be able to contact him, while he remained concealed. But, at this distance from the house, that would not be necessary. Ty would be able to listen to a ball game on the radio without the kidnappers being made aware of his presence.

*

Steve and his team are based at the U.S. Naval Air Station, in Virginia Beach. When Steve found time to read the message, Valerie had sent it nearly thirty hours earlier. The good news was that the team had just completed an assignment, so they were, indeed, available to assist. The bad news being that the assignment had been in Seattle, Washington. In responding, his email was guarded, as standard operating procedures dictated.

From: Steven Thomas
Subject: Work
Date: November 27, 2018 11:25 a.m.
To: Dr. Valerie Thomas

_____(CLT): 8 min 8.22 sec

Dearest Val,

Hi babe. I only now got a chance to catch up on my email. Just closed a big deal out here in Seattle. Will be back at Virginia in about eight or nine hours and I'll round up some buds to help clean the garage when I get home. I know how you hate having chaos reign out there. It will be ready for Mike and Jackie's party, though. I promise. We'll be leaving here in an hour and I can get about a six-hour nap on the plane. That way, I'll be all bright-tailed and bushy-eyed when I arrive. LOL I'll write more as soon as the mess is all cleaned up and fill you in on where the bodies are buried, so to speak. (Ha, ha)

All my love always,

Steve

< ≡ ♂ ≡ >

When this message arrived, it was very welcome news to the crew. They had hoped that Steve and his team could have arrived in Virginia sooner, as the deadline to land or fire trans-Earth thrusters was drawing near. Midnight would be the twenty-fourth hour after the communications to Mission Support regarding the explosion set off by the crew, simulating a disaster. Eleven hours, thirty-five minutes remained from the time Steve sent his reply.

Steve had secured the willing aid of all seven of his squad members, before they boarded the plane. After a quick computer check of the satellite view of Charlottesville and debate of tactics, the crew created their preliminary action plan. "OK, ladies, get your beauty sleep while you can. You're not likely to get any prettier, later on," Steve advised his men, in his standard wrap-up spiel at the end of a planning session. They were all so used to it most just grunted in agreement and proceeded to hit their airborne racks.

Unable to fall asleep, Steve continued going over the details in his head, scrutinizing them for flaws. It's about a two-hour drive from their base in Virginia Beach to Charlottesville. With flight time cutting it so close, at most they would have only an hour to complete their tasks: rescue Mike and email the results of their mission.

This particular type of operation is what Special Op organizations call a 'quick and dirty' mission. The team usually spent a week or more in preparation for a similar exercise, but this mission necessitated execution within eleven-and-a-half hours, from start to finish. The waning moon was just over half full, and if the sky was clear over Virginia, they will have to keep to the shadows. Unlike the Chicago al Qaida takedown,

181

this plan called for surrounding the house late at night and sneaking in. During the late night/early morning hours, most of the targets should be asleep or at least groggy and less vigilant.

The biggest difference here, would be not having an inside man. To compensate, the team decided to utilize infrared headgear to locate the occupants within the house. They would move in with the stealth of ninjas, quietly negate the threat using silenced weapons and lethal hands, and liberate Mike. After that, a quick email to the Mars crew would bestow the green light for landing.

Having worked with this same team for so long, Steve had the utmost confidence in each and every one of them. He trusted every man in his group as well he did his own reflexes. Steve had been in the army since he was eighteen, first in the Airborne Rangers, then advancing to the Green Berets. After twelve years in the military, he had been tapped to head up the first, newly formed ATAC team.

These days, Steve wondered just how many missions he had left in him. He was beginning to feel 'old' at 40 and he knew, deep down, the numbers were against him. He had never been wounded or even came close to it. And the longer he continued deploying on missions, the greater his chances were of catching a bullet. It was just a matter of time. 'Someday,' he thought, 'I'm gonna have to find another line of work.' After having finally settled the details in his mind, Steve drifted off to sleep for a good six-and-a-half hours, before the plane began its descent.

*

22:57 - Steve quietly rapped his knuckles on the camper's rear door. Alarmed, Ty dropped his half-eaten sandwich and nearly choked on the large bite in his mouth. Glancing out through the curtain, Ty expected to find a police officer, or at least a security guard, questioning him about being parked in this shopping center lot. Spotting Steve, dressed in all black and sporting a futuristic headset, Ty opened the door and whispered, "How did you find me, here?"

"Sorry if I startled you, but it wasn't very hard," Steve replied, his fingers tapping the infrared headgear perched above his brow. "Yours being the only heat signature sitting in a cold camper, I approached from the rear to see if it was you or one of our targets standing guard. If I were going to set up a stakeout, this is a spot I would have picked. My infrared set showed someone sitting in a position to view the house, so I figured it must be you. I'm Captain Steve Thomas (referring to his prior military rank was a hard habit to break since all of his team called him Captain). We met at the press conference the evening the mission was announced. I assume you were informed I would be arriving." Steve held out his hand to greet Ty. "Has there been any movement?"

"No," Ty answered, shaking Steve's hand. "That is, one suspect left earlier in the day, around 15:00, but came back about an hour and fifteen minutes later with what looked like two small bags of groceries. Nothing since then."

With his other hand, Steve reached in and patted Ty's shoulder, "I really appreciate the assist. Now, we'll take it from here. You should head home and catch up on your sleep." Glancing around Ty and spotting the crumpled up assortment of fast food, candy bar and gum wrappers, Steve observed, "Looks like you've been on stakeout for quite a while."

"Yeah, I guess you're right," Ty squinted tiredly at his watch. "Almost thirteen hours, but I'm going to wait until you go in, so this old engine starting up won't rattle the neighborhood. You probably don't want the kidnapers looking out the windows while you're trying to sneak up on 'em."

"Good thinkin', man. Thanks, again," Steve told him, then turned quickly and faded into the darkness under the trees lining the road.

Steve's team had worked closely together for nearly eight years, with all of the same men remaining on the job. One or two had been nominally wounded on more than one occasion, but so far they had not lost a single man as a result of being killed in the line of duty. When Steve recruited his team, he and his trainers at the Federal Law Enforcement Training Center (FLETC), near Brunswick, Georgia, had really done their homework. Two years worth of homework in fact, training Steve as a Federal civilian, finding the men for his team and convincing them that civilian government work was more rewarding than their current military life.

Aware of each other's strengths and weaknesses, these fraternity brothers are able to perform seamlessly and communicate in several ways. Line of sight communications could be exploited by a system of precise hand signals, adapted from American Sign Language, with the team relaying messages down the line from one man to the next. Messages to all were conducted via a series of specific clicks on their two-way radios, similar to Morse code, and heard only through their earpieces. They communicated silently, safe from the eavesdropping enemy.

It didn't take long for the team to take up their designated positions. By means of four vantage points, with each commando having a different view of the house through their infrared headgear, they obtained four head counts for comparison. Conferring, they concluded there were four people in the house: Mike slumped in a straight back chair in the middle of the living room, with one figure continuously pacing around him, and two people reclining in the two main floor bedrooms. No one was on the second floor, making a stealthy attack much easier. Gliding through shadows and sidling up next to the outside of the house, the commandos utilized miniature cameras to examine doors and windows for booby-traps and as possible entry points. From a window, the kitchen door could be seen clearly with no signs of danger from entering that way. Following a stealthy check of doorknobs, no open portals were found and it appeared the kitchen door would be their best bet.

Though an unlocked door may appear inviting, it would also be too easy an entry and might well be wired to alert the perpetrators, or booby-trapped. The team always erred on the side of caution, especially in situations involving human life. As another precaution, suction-cup microphones were affixed to windows to pick up any conversations from the kidnappers inside, or other sounds that might affect their plans. No unusual sounds were detected and the team decided to proceed. A specific series of clicks on the radios signaled 'go'.

The strategy was to take out each perpetrator, one-by-one. Gonzales, who had been the Chicago inside man, shifted from his position behind a small shrub near the garage door, to the kitchen door. He silently pulled open the storm door, propping it open with the slide catch on the closer mechanism, before picking the lock of the main door, eliciting a subdued 'snick'. He slipped inside the dimly lit room and pushed the door closed, stopping for a count of several heartbeats to check if anyone had heard the slight noise.

Moving through the kitchen to the dark dining room and on towards the first of the bedrooms, the infrared goggles helped Gonzales to avoid bumping into the scattered furnishings. Once inside the bedroom, he quickly located the man sprawled on the bed, lying with one arm flung over his eyes and the other stretched out to the side, near the nightstand. As Gonzales came within reach of the bedside, a squeaky floorboard spoiled the surprise. The suspect started up and went for the handgun on the nightstand, bellowing out a warning. A well-placed kick from Gonzales broke the suspects arm, while a karate chop to the throat silenced his shouting, albeit too late. A second chop fractured his neck, eliminating this threat.

Through his open throat-mic, Gonzales alerted the rest of the team to the conflict inside. Two other team-members followed Gonzalez's lead, raced toward the kitchen door and kicked it open, then rushed through the house. Upon hearing the commotion from the bedroom and resounding crash in the kitchen, the pacing guard in the living room darted behind his captive. He jerked a large knife from its belt sheath, placing the blade tight against Mike's throat. He then faced the front door, anticipating a frontal attack from that direction.

Suddenly, a small, blurry, red dot flashed on his temple, lingering there less than two seconds before being replaced by a slightly larger round hole, as the driveway side window crashed inward reacting to the bullet's trajectory. Once again, Hawkeye had hit his mark perfectly. From his vantage point, he first had used the infrared goggles to find his target. He was then able to gain a line-of-sight through the side window, albeit dimly through the sheers.

As the kidnapper's body fell away, his knife skidded across Mike's throat, but lightly, leaving the equivalent of an oozing paper cut. A couple of minutes of pressure would stem the bleeding without the need for so much as a bandage, much less stitches. Calamity averted, the partially sedated Mike was a very lucky man, indeed.

Approaching cautiously and entering the second bedroom with weapons drawn, the pair of team members following Gonzales, Charlie Cook and Ralph Jacobson found the third suspect on his knees with ankles crossed and his fingers tightly braided together on top of his head. "I'm not resisting," he called out. Shoving him down flat on the floor, the team members frisked his person for weapons and securely bound his wrists behind his back with a nylon zip-strip. By the time he was hoisted to his feet and frog-marched into the living room, Mike had been freed from his restraints and the bleeding staunched. Suspect number three was shoved down onto the chair, which had previously been occupied by Mike for the greater part of the past four days.

Turning to Mike, Steve began, "Mr. Miller, you might not remember me, but my name is Steve Thomas and you and I have something in common. Our wives are both orbiting Mars in the Bolo One. Now, while we interrogate this guy to find out who he is, who he's working for, and determine what the hell is going on, you'll need to relay a message to your wife. There isn't much time left to do so, but you have to convince her that you are safe and they can go ahead with the landing. In a few minutes, I'll send the same to mine. Can you do that?"

"Gladly!" Mike replied, rubbing his reddened wrists, massaging where the quarter inch nylon ropes had dug in deeply from his attempts to struggle free.

"You won't get any useful information from me," the suspect snapped, heatedly. "I am a Chinese citizen, attached to the Chinese Consulate in Richmond. I possess Diplomatic Immunity, so it is illegal for you to hold me captive like this. Release me immediately and my government will not file a grievance against your government."

As he was speaking, Ty entered from the dining room, wanting to get a better look at the bound Chinese agent. Steve spotted him across the room as he entered, but figured the situation was contained now, so there was no harm in him being there. Glancing over at Ty with a malevolent grin, the suspects eyes brightened as he declared, "Oh, I see you appear to have recovered nicely from your little mishap with the car; my fault for not following through. That is one mistake I shall not make, again. Sorry I can't say the same for your lovely wife. Such a shame that her life ended in such a brutal fashion." Ty's face first went ghostly pale, then turned crimson as the meaning of these words sank in. Brandon had not provided Ty with all of the details of the suspected conspiracy, but what this man was saying now, filled in a lot of the remaining blanks, bringing total clarity to the situation.

Steve cuffed the agent on the back of his head, "I don't think you realize the situation you are in. You're in no position to demand anything, and we are the ones with a grievance, asshole. You'll be lucky if you make it all the way to Guantanamo. And what do you know about this man's accident?"

Suddenly, a cell phone in the suspect's shirt pocket trilled loudly. Quickly removing the phone from its hiding place, Steve pressed the barrel of his automatic tight against the man's temple. In a deceptively calm and quiet voice Steve told the agent, "I'm going to put this call on speaker. You will reply as if nothing is wrong. Do you understand me?" With eyes narrowed and glancing sideways up at the gun, the fanatic slowly nodded his head up and down. The phone trilled for the third time, Steve thumbed it open and pressed the button to answer the call. There was a pause before the kidnapper began speaking, as if debating whether he should cooperate or not. Steve jammed the gun harder against the man's skull, with the tip of the barrel grinding into flesh.

"Hello." The man in the chair barked into the phone. A disjointed voice on the tiny speakerphone said, "Yeah, it's me. In just about ten minutes, I will be transmitting a command to the spacecraft, ordering them to fire the thrusters for the trans-Earth injection. It will take about eight minutes for the message to reach them, but once the thrusters are fired, they will be on a return trip to Earth. Well done! Our efforts have at last succeeded in aborting the landing. Feel free to dispose of our friend, Mr. Miller, and get the hell out of there as soon as you can."

CRACK! A shot echoed in the enclosed space. It did not originate from the man in the chair following the orders he had just received, nor had Steve or any of his crew fire it. Six weapons swiveled and locked on the figure across the room. Ty, still standing near the dining room entrance with arm extended, had discharged his own .380 automatic. Steve pressed the cell phone's button, hanging up on the caller, before dropping the phone on the nearby end table. There was nothing more to say to the person on the other end. The shot said it all. The man in the chair was now slumped forward with a major portion of the back of his head messily decorating the floor. His sharp tongue and diplomatic immunity proved no match for Ty's PPH, though he had been right about one thing: he wouldn't be making that mistake again.

Steve glanced from Ty to the corpse, then back to Ty. He lowered his gun, then pulled a black handled folding knife from its belt pouch and sliced through the zip strip, releasing the deceased's hands. Picking up the cut pieces, Steve handed them to one of his men. He gingerly stepped over to Ty and cautiously eased the gun from Ty's grip. Steve glanced around the room, looking at each of his men, having clearly caught the implications of the kidnapper's greeting to Ty. Steve simply said, "Looks to me like he was trying escape." Glancing back at Ty, "Unfortunately, we didn't find out who was giving the orders. Ralph, search the phone's call history to figure out who the caller was." Steve's men followed his lead and lowered their weapons, also.

Staring, with a far away look in his eyes, Ty volunteered, "That won't be necessary. I recognized the voice on the phone." Eyes suddenly focusing with crystal clarity and alertness, he looked directly at Steve and snapped out, "How quickly can you get me to Houston?"

Steve shot Ty a worried look, saying, "Not too sure we can do that. This little… uh, 'rescue' is not what you might call 'sanctioned'. We're not even supposed to be here. As far as anyone else is aware, we're assumed to be in Virginia Beach for some much needed R & R."

Ty looked thoughtful for a moment, and with his back now ramrod straight, he faced Steve squarely. "Captain, as you may recall, I am a US Naval Commander. I've been on somewhat of an extended medical leave, but, if you'll follow my orders, I'll personally sanction this mission and take full responsibility for the consequences. Would you like to see my I.D. card?" Ty asked, reaching for his wallet.

Steve's worried look morphed into a grin as he saluted and barked out, "Sir, no sir. That won't be necessary." He popped the clip out of Ty's gun and jacked the cartridge out of the chamber before handing it back to Ty, recognizing the sudden change in the man before him as nothing less than an epiphany.

Transformed, Ty now appeared to be the dynamic and self-confident leader he had been a year-and-a-half ago, before

Claire's death. "I know who called and as far as he knows, this asshole just killed Mike. We have to get to Houston, ASAP. I also need to convey a message to the Mars crew, if I may use your computer when you're through?" he addressed Mike.

"Sure thing, anything!" Mike quickly replied, very thankful to all of these men that had just saved his life and returned his freedom.

"While you're doing that," Steve began, as he turned to his men and ordered, "Gonzalez, you and Jacobson will stay here and take care of Mike. Make sure that bleeding stops, then get him to a safe location. There may be others on their way to take the next shift. We don't want them finding Mike or these bodies, so contain this scene and give me a status update later. Charlie, I'll need you to track us down a jet... Air Base, Airport... I don't care which, just something big enough to get six or seven of us to Houston, like right now. Beep me with coordinates when you have it set up."

"Roger that," Charlie replied as he exited the room on a run and headed out the door.

From: Michael Miller
Subject: Safe at home
Date: November 27, 2018 11:25 p.m.
To: Jackie Miller

_____(CLT): 8 min 9.56 sec

Stick the landing, Babe!

I love you,

Mike

< ≡ ♂ ≡ >

Knowing that Jackie would have just read the message from Mike, Ty sent his message directly to her.

From: Tyler Cody
Subject: Message to Tom
Date: November 27, 2018 11:28 p.m.
To: Jackie Miller

_____(CLT): 8 min 9.56 sec

Dr. Miller,

Please give the following message to Tom: A lot is happening here. Momentarily, you will be receiving a communication from Mission Support, with orders to fire thrusters for trans-Earth injection. Acknowledge the command and then cut or block your comm. and telemetry, so they can no longer track you. Continue on to the landing site, if you are still able to do so. I am here with Captain Thomas at Mike and Jackie's place. We will soon be en route to Houston to place Commander Lewis into custody. He is a murderer and a traitor. I will send you an email when we are finished, but for now, it is imperative that he be convinced the Hab is either returning to Earth, or better yet, destroyed. You can expect to hear from us within a few short hours.

Cmdr Tyler Cody

< ≡ ♂ ≡ >

(Another message that would not get passed on by Dr. Willis)

Chapter 15

Tuesday, November 27, 2018 (Scottday, Aries 29, 0031)

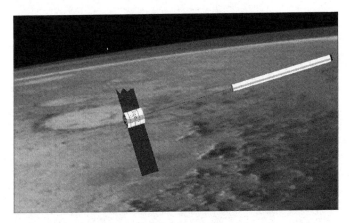

    The crew was wandering about the control deck in their flight-suits, waiting for word from home that Mike is safe and they can proceed with the landing site. Or, if that message doesn't arrive before they hear from Mission Support, the crew will need to come up with an excuse for not firing the thrusters to place them on a trajectory back to Earth. Only seventy-two hours is left before they have to decide to either land or head for home. All that is left to do is don their helmets and gloves and strap into the landing seats, now re-attached to the deck, while Tom and Carl will be strapped in at the control console.

    Feelings are mixed among the crew. Tom is sorely missing his dear, sweet Penny. Though longing to be home, he understands that being there won't bring her back to life. He glances over at Sally. She looks back at him and smiles, dimples appearing at the corners of her mouth. He is finding it easier now to answer her smile with one of his own. Sally has been a wonderful friend and crewmate.

Gazing again at Sally, Tom now truly sees the beauty that she holds, both inside and out. A new thought flickers through his consciousness; they are going to be spending the next two years together. This is a very pleasant idea, especially now that she is single. Since the two of them share a background in geology, Tom sees them spending a lot of time together, exploring Mars and making new discoveries together. Perhaps discovering a deeper relationship with each other... someday.

Sally is contemplating the landing to come, not wanting to return to Earth without first setting foot on the surface. The fact that she will be one of the first geologists to set foot on another planet has her feeling like she is striding about a foot off the deck. There will be times when she will assist Carl in his geochemistry tests on the planet, but like Tom, she sees the two of them working side by side at every opportunity.

She is also relieved to be free of her marriage. Sure, she will miss Bobby. After all, they were together for seventeen years and comfortable with one another. Apparently, that wasn't enough for Bobby anymore.

Even before the split, Sally had come to the realization that it was not enough for her, either. Instead of being crushed by the divorce, she was feeling emancipated by the possibilities that it would bring. Sharing a glance with Tom, she notices the look on his face and wonders what he is thinking and smiling about. Is he feeling what she is? His eyes again touch her lightly and a warm feeling fills her breast. Could he...

Carl is eager to descend to the surface and start scratching around in the dirt. His mind was going over the exciting work to come. The geochemistry of a planet will tell you about the chemical processes and reactions that govern the composition of the soil and rocks. This is in addition to the interactions of the hydrosphere (hopefully, they will find one) and atmosphere, and how the cycles of energy and matter transport the chemical components through time and space.

There was only one big down side to the Mars landing, as far as Carl was concerned. It would be another three-and-a half months longer before he and Mary could be wed, than if they were to head home now. He loves Mary with all his heart and the wait will be agonizing. But, the additional paycheck will come in handy while they are starting out. Then, a short while later it will be time to sit back and pen a book or two about the trip and their findings. Heck, he can start writing that first book, right now. Why wait? Maybe Mary could join him on the lecture circuit and he could introduce the world to her, through his eyes. Huh, all of this before the age of 30. Not, bad. Not, bad at all.

To spare Mary any undue worry, Carl has intentionally kept her in the dark about Mike and the possibility of them not being able to land. If they can't land and have to head back to Earth, that will be the time to fill her in. Why should she be made to worry, un-necessarily?

There are two things back on Earth that Brandon is yearning for: to hold the love of his life, Emma, in his arms, and to see Rich, their son. It has been almost unbearable being away from Emma. And, he is so incredibly proud that his son would want to follow in his footsteps. What more could a father ask for.

But, he's also looking forward to the prospect of walking in the slightly dimmer sunlight on the surface of Mars. What an adventure this will be! He is visualizing setting up their new state-of-the-art greenhouse on a wide flat expanse of terrain, as well as a different type, just beneath the Martian surface. In just the right locale a few meters underground, such as a lava tube, there could be acres of crops growing by the time the crew gets ready to head home in a year-and-a-half. In his mind, he is already going over the logistics of greenhouses vs. lava tubes, grow lights, CO_2 levels, nutrients, water, and a thousand other details to be worked out.

One big question to be answered: What is the possibility of finding liquid water on the planet, or at least a large supply of water-ice? Of course, they can always make their own water by distilling carbon dioxide down to carbon monoxide and oxygen, then combining that oxygen with some of the hydrogen, brought with them from Earth.

But, if liquid water were to be found, that would take care of one of their greatest concerns. With water in an underground reservoir lying far enough down to maintain a liquid state, they would then only need to pump it up to their temperature-controlled greenhouses. This is the type of challenge Brandon is eagerly looking forward to undertaking. Bring it on.

Like Carl, Brandon had not mentioned their current situation to Emma. No need to cause her any undue worry. The disappointment of not being able to land, will give them many hours of email discourse during the long twenty-month trip, should that become the case.

Valerie would willingly remain on Mars for the rest of her life, growing her own food and living off the land, if only Steve could join her. She had often fantasized about settling down on Mars with Steve, hanging out her shingle, and waiting for the first immigrants to arrive from Earth (the proverbial small-town country doctor in the bad-ass frontier town).

With the *'Mars Direct Plan'* moving to its ultimate advantage of a manned flight every two years, it isn't hard to imagine scores of settlers arriving in less than twenty years. A decent little boomtown, along with a thriving community, could spring up by then. This time frame would only put Valerie in her late-fifties to early-sixties, very doable. She would have a busy and productive life for many years, especially considering the reduced gravity and how liberating that could be on aging bones and muscles.

Of course, Steve would eventually need to retire from his paramilitary career before linking up with her on Mars. But, a boomtown could use a good sheriff, if only to keep the immigrating colonists on the straight and narrow. Besides, knowing human nature, it wouldn't be long before someone set up a still and started manufacturing Two-Moonshine, began running games of chance, or launched other types of commerce; setting in motion a myriad of problems requiring law enforcement. His background in subterfuge and policing bad guys would make Steve a natural for the sheriff position. Or, just as there are U.S. Marshals, Mars could have a U.M. (United Mars) Marshal. 'I'll have to bring that up in my next email,' Valerie thought.

Jackie is also excited about the prospect of landing on Mars, but in her heart of hearts, she is ready to have the combined genius of Tom, Carl, and Brandon design and build her a transporter, propelling her straight home to Mike's loving arms. This anxiety is almost more than she can endure. Jackie might topple over and curl up into the fetal position at any moment, if she could only let herself stop pacing long enough to do so. If she knew for sure Mike is all right, it would make everything else a little more tolerable. Then, she would be able to get back to the task at hand: planning her next year-and-a-half stint on Mars.

With her diverse training, Jackie will have a full schedule to fill her time. As a chemist, she will assist both Sally and Carl with the chemical analysis of the planet. In addition, as a physician, she will assist Valerie with medical situations, as well as tend to Valerie herself if the need arises.

"Fifteen minutes everyone," Tom announced. "Whatever the decision, up or down, we need to be strapped in and ready to fire thrusters in fifteen minutes. That's One Five minutes, people! Make certain all of the hatches on each deck are secured, police your immediate area and nail down anything on this deck that even *thinks* it's loose."

"Up or down?" Carl asked. "We still have that seventy-two hour fuel buffer. I'm not ready to give up, yet."

Tom replied, "Me neither, but what if we get the word from M.S. that it's time to fire Trans-Earth thrusters? How long are we going to be able to stall?"

Brandon offered, "I've been thinking about that. We could say 'we will try to dock with the ERV in a couple of days for a safer, more comfortable ride home. That might give us the added time we need."

"Yeah!" Carl exclaimed. "I'll start running a plot for the rendezvous."

"OK," Tom agreed. "I doubt they'll go for that, but it's worth a shot."

"Tom, I'm gonna need to keep my laptop with me when I strap in," Jackie insisted.

Tom was against that idea at first, as it could slip out of her grasp and become a projectile, bouncing wildly around the cabin. But, knowing Jackie's fragile state of mind, he obliged, "As long as you hold onto it real tight. If we wind up having to fire thrusters before the message comes in, you won't be able to read it until we're back in zero-gee and coasting again. And, if that thing gets out of your hands during the momentum, someone could get badly injured."

"OK," Jackie agreed. "I'll hang on with a death-grip. I want to have it in hand, just…" DING!

Jackie almost dropped her laptop on the floor when the message indicator sounded. She sheepishly grimaced at Tom, quickly recovered her composure and her grasp on the computer, then clicked onto the waiting message:

    From: Michael Miller
 Subject: Safe at home
    Date: November 27, 2018 11:25 p.m.
      To: Jackie Miller

_____(CLT): 8 min 9.56 sec

Stick the landing, Babe!

I love you,

Mike

< ≡ ♂ ≡ >

"They did it! He's safe! We're free to land!" Jackie was literally jumping up and down in her exhilaration and excitement. Standing nearby, Carl looked over her shoulder and glanced at the message.

"Wait, it says to stick the landing. As in: 'where the sun don't shine'?" Carl queried. Jackie laughed as she set the laptop on the table.

"Oh, no. When a gymnast 'sticks the landing'," she explained using air quotes, "that means she lands standing up straight with no loss of balance, no half step to catch herself. In other words: a perfect routine with no faults. Sticking to the floor."

To demonstrate, Jackie made a short hop in the air, came down lightly with her feet together and knees slightly bent. She paused for a second, then stood up straight with her arms up and out in the traditional victory stance, her body appearing like a block letter Y, and finally bowed to the rousing applause from the group on the control deck.

"Alright, let's get serious. Everyone strap in and make ready for the landing sequence," ordered Tom. He displayed a confident smile and radiated a sense of leadership that had only been at half power for the past two-and-a-half months. "You can stow that laptop now, Jackie. We won't be needing it again until we're on the ground."

"Aye-Aye, Sir," Jackie snapped him a smile followed by a smartly executed salute. But just as she reached for the laptop, it emitted another DING! The screen for the email was still open. Jackie looked at the subject line and sender. "Tom, there is another message here, addressed to me, but it is a message to you. It says: 'A lot is happening here.....'," Jackie read the message aloud and then interjected, "Commander Lewis? I wouldn't have thought him to be a traitor. He must have been the one my dad was talking about that suggested I apply to the program. But, it was strange: Dad said he didn't want me to know who he was, supposedly because he didn't want it to look like he was playing favorites. So Dad never told me who had recommended me. It could have been any of a dozen big-wigs that Dad knew."

Tom's mind began to swim, as this new revelation sank in and he thought, 'So, that's why Morgan was so gung ho about us aborting the mission and returning to Earth. He must have been behind this plot from the start, or at the least, approached very early on. Ty's message referred to murder. Had Morgan been party to a plot to kill Ty and Claire, and possibly Penny?' Tom considered the notion, horrified. And the more he thought about it, the worse he felt. He could sense his face reddening and his heart thudding harder.

"How's our time?" he asked of Carl, in a raspy voice.

"We have twelve minutes until we can fire the retros for atmospheric entry," Carl replied, calmly.

"Ok, let's get ready to land. Brandon, as soon as we take delivery of that message and I send an acknowledgement, I'll give you a cut-off signal. Then, I want you to kill the microphone and telemetry. We'll keep the comm. open so we can receive, but activate those firewall rules you wrote to block all outgoing traffic. Carl, start reeling in the tether now. That way, when we fire the explosive bolts on it, it might appear as a malfunction. To repeat, when I give you the signal, then you'll cut mic and telemetry, blow the tether and the solar panels, all at once. We're gonna make it look like Bolo One blew up and hopefully, we'll be down into the atmosphere before they can get a satellite view of us."

"That should work," Brandon remarked as he checked the radar screen for any satellites in their area. "And the good news is, we'll be on the ground a couple of hours before they realize we even left orbit. No blips on the screen," he added for good measure.

Less than four minutes passed before the communications system chirped; a slightly nasal voice intoned, "Bolo One, this is Commander Morgan Lewis at Mission Support. We have analyzed the condition of your fuel reserves. Due to the loss of that tank yesterday, I am sorry to say, it does not appear you will have sufficient fuel for the thrusters to perform the necessary maneuvers once you have entered the planet's atmosphere. Therefore, it is with deep regret we must order you to abort any attempt to land the Habitat. You will, instead, make preparations to fire the trans-Earth thrusters at precisely 23:42 and 12 seconds. This movement will take you back out of orbit and put you on the free return trajectory toward Earth.

"We realize what a great disappointment this is, especially after having come so far, and getting so close to your objective. However, the safety of the crew vastly outweighs the importance of any benefits derived from the mission. We are all thankful that the failure of the fuel tank didn't cause more damage than had occurred or result in loss of life. Preparations will now begin to launch a Dragon capsule for you to dock with, upon your return. Godspeed Bolo One and our prayers go with you on your return to our home planet. Please acknowledge this message and its directive."

Tom swallowed and fought down the burning urge to convey to Morgan his true feelings. He wanted, desperately, to reach through the radio link and wrench the commander through the connection and into the Hab. Were that a possibility, Tom would have destroyed the commander with his bare hands. Instead, taking a deep breath, Tom keyed the microphone and calmly answered, "Mission Support, we acknowledge the command to abort. Repeat, we acknowledge abort. We are now preparing to fire the Trans-Earth Thrus…" As he spoke, Tom made a quick slashing motion across his throat, signaling Brandon to cut communications. Brandon flipped the switches, turning off the communications link and the telemetry, as he nodded his assent. "Now, firing the bolts on the tether and solar panels," he reported.

The Hab shuttered slightly as the mild shock of the exploding bolts propelled the one-and a-half solar panels and the spent Falcon 9 booster away, each slowly tumbling end-over-end to eventually burn up in the planet's atmosphere. There was no turning back at this point. If they changed their minds now and really did want to head home, without the tethered counterweight of the booster, the crew would remain in zero gravity for the next twenty months.

But the crew were firmly committed to the next step in the landing sequence: firing the retro rockets that would slow the Hab's orbit, allowing it to fall into the atmosphere of Mars and toward the small, un-named crater on the Avernus Colles. Lying on their backs and strapped into seats on the floor and at the console, they could feel the push against their backs, the result of a twenty-seven second burst from the retros. At the end of the burn, Tom directed Carl to jettison the retro pack. Carl punched the button to fire the next set of exploding bolts, releasing the clamps. The retro pack was fired away and a large Kevlar bag instantly inflated. This action created a flexible bowl beneath them; a bowl that was two meters thick and four times the diameter of the Hab, engulfing it and doubling as a heat shield.

Referred to as the aero-brake, this bag/bowl would begin slowing the Hab's descent, as soon as the atmosphere became thick enough to start providing some resistance. When that resistance becomes so great that the heat begins burning the bag away, it, too, will be jettisoned. At that time, parachutes will pop out of the Hab's top and landing thrusters will begin firing to further slow their speed of descent. The entire process, running in succession from firing the retro rockets to eventual touch down among the rolling hills, takes about seven minutes.

As the habitat's attitude leveled out, while suspended beneath the three huge parachutes, Carl glanced over at the nearest porthole. Entranced, he witnessed the fiery atmospheric entry of the Falcon 9 booster that had acted as their counterweight for the past six-and-a-half months. As he watched it during the two-to-three seconds it was visible, an ominous thought traversed his mind: 'I trust that was the Falcon 9 booster and not our Earth Return Vehicle turning into a charcoal briquette.'

Tom contemplated a previous historic moment. When Neil Armstrong and Buzz Aldrin touched down on the surface of the moon, Neil announced, "Houston, Tranquility Base here. The Eagle has landed." However, Tom won't be able to make such a proclamation, at least not until he gets the word from Ty that all is a *GO* on his end.

*

Meanwhile, back on Earth: Charlie is very good at what he does; problem solving and making things happen. Like many in his line of work, he is a man of multiple skills. Being a veteran pilot, Charlie can fly pretty much anything that has wings, along with a half-dozen, or more, things without, so he says. Within half-an-hour of Steve's order, he had managed to wrangle up a Leer Jet Challenger 300. This particular craft, which seats eight passengers and a pilot, can make the trip from Charlottesville to Houston in just under two hours with Ty, Steve and five members of his ATAC team onboard. Moments before the 3 a.m. landing, Ty conveyed the necessary message to Tom:

From: Tyler Cody
Subject: Mars Landing Announcement
Date: November 28, 2018 2:55 a.m.
To: Thomas Castle

_____(CLT): 8 min 9.93 sec

Tom,

I assume you have made landing by now. With the time lag, it takes some eight minutes for these communications to travel one-way. By the time you receive this and send a reply, we should be entering the control room of Mission Support. Give us a few minutes to take control of the situation and then feel free to broadcast to the world that you have safely touched down on Mars. I'll make sure that message goes out on all channels and into the history books.

I'm sure you know I'd rather be up there than down here. But since I can't, I'm awfully glad it's you, old friend. Everyone on board Bolo One is like a part of my family. I am eager to be working with each of you again in the coming months and years. Yes, you read it right. I'm going back to active duty status and really looking forward to the challenge. Later, I'll relay more on what has happened.

Your friend and comrade, Ty

< ≡ ♂ ≡ >

After reading the missive from Ty, Tom told Brandon to fire up the communication system and telemetry. "Ladies and gentlemen, it is time to let the good people of Earth know we have arrived. Break out the horns and party favors, and let's make a little noise!" he declared, throwing his arms wide and exhibiting a delighted grin.

"Roger that!" Brandon replied, echoing his smile.

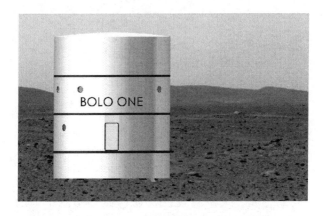

BOLO ONE

*

Once on the ground, it was a short six-minute drive from Ellington Air Force Base to the Johnson Space Center. No one in the ATAC party seemed to be all that concerned, neither with the posted speed limit nor with the traffic signals during the wee hours of the morning.

With having previously been a regular fixture on the base and well known by the Space Center checkpoint personnel, Commander Cody easily gained access to his objective. Known as a man of integrity and honor, his word was good enough for them, as he vouched for Captain Thomas and his men. Had there been any idea of the firepower in the car's trunk, the base would have been locked down tight. Assuming a jovial attitude, Ty informed the guards that he and the others had arrived for the anticipated Mars landing.

Ty had stopped using his cane a little over a month ago, but hadn't done much exercising in nearly a year-and-a-half. As he marched along with his entourage, his leg began aching, but the determination in his gait masked most of his pain, which was only slightly evident in his limp.

In the Mission Support arena, there had been a general murmur over the past three hours, with voices steadily growing louder and more apprehensive. Technicians were frantically trying to redirect additional satellites to search the path which the Hab would have taken after firing the thrusters, while others were busy trying to re-establish contact with Bolo One. As the craft had apparently fallen silent, just as it was firing the thrusters, the team at Mission Support was fearing the worst. So, Mars Observer was directed to scan the Hab's last known co-ordinates as it came round the planet and into range. As the satellite breeched the horizon, it captured an image of multiple objects burning through the atmosphere. It was feared that the crew of six had been lost.

Commander Lewis was also lost, but only deep in his own thoughts: this turn of events was working out better than he could ever have hoped. If the ship and crew had been destroyed in a fiery explosion, he wouldn't have to contend with them and their probing questions during the next twenty months. He was feeling almost giddy at the prospects before him and having a hard time trying to look concerned, fighting to keep his inner satisfaction from emerging on his face. He thought about heading into his office for a celebratory double shot.

Abruptly, there was a sudden intake of breath as the room fell silent. Expressions on the faces of the people at the consoles were fearful and bewildered, as Commander Cody thrust open the door and strode through the entry. He was heeled closely by what appeared to be six soldiers, garbed in black shirts, pants, stocking caps, boots, flack jackets, and holsters. Most still wore black smudge makeup on their faces. Cameramen that had been embedded among the Mission Support technicians rapidly swiveled around, as faces of spectators pressed against the glass in the overhead gallery.

"Commander Cody, what the hell is the meaning of this? Who are these men?" Commander Lewis loudly barked.

Staring stonily at the traitor and conspirator, Ty firmly declared, "Commander Morgan Lewis, I am relieving you of command and placing you under arrest for the crimes of treason, murder, attempted murder, and kidnapping, to start with." Gesturing, Ty ordered Steve to take the Commander into custody.

"What the hell are you talking about? You have no authority to arrest me!" Morgan blustered. "I don't have time for any of this crap! I've got a missing crew to contend with, and you're in the way and need to leave." With that, Commander Lewis tried to sidestep around Ty, but Steve raised his hand, like a waiter intones a guest to wait a moment. That signal was followed by the heart-stopping sound of five automatic pistols being cocked, simultaneously. They were all pointing directly at Commander Lewis' shiny, sweat-slicked forehead.

"Go right ahead, try to escape. Please!" Ty dared, fixing the disgraced turncoat's feet to the floor with an icy stare. Steve stepped around behind Commander Lewis, grabbed a wrist, wrenching it up sharply behind his back, and slipped a heavy-duty nylon zip-strip over it.

"If you're smart, you'll put your other hand in here, too," Steve advised him as he glanced over at Ty and with a wink added, "I'm running low on these cause we've gone through so many in the last couple of hours." But Ty was not feeling amused at this moment. His face was frozen with hatred for the man who had sought his demise and no doubt caused the death of his beloved Claire.

Seconds later, the silence in the cavernous room was broken by a burst of static over the communications system, quickly followed by a flickering image on the super-sized view-screen, mounted high on the wall. A disembodied voice announced, "Houston, this is Commander Thomas Castle from Claire Base. Bolo One has landed, right in line between Penny Bright Crater and FP1 here on the Avernus Colles." As the image snapped into sharp focus, the uniformed figure continued, "I would estimate we are within fifteen meters of our Mars Ascent Vehicle, and oh... about forty-five meters from the edge of the crater. We touched down shortly before sunrise and the sky is just getting clear enough to get a good look at our surroundings."

Gazing into the camera and pointing out a nearby porthole, he continued, "Looking out towards the crater on the east side of the ship, it appears we are not alone on Mars. There is a robotic rover more or less on the edge of the crater's rim. It appears to be collecting shiny mineral aggregate, using two of its arms, and placing them into large piles. I don't recall that task as being in the plans for this particular mission. And, I don't ever recollect any updates mentioning a robotic rover joining the party. This couldn't be that rover from... what was it, 2012?" Tom inquired, as he turned toward Carl.

"Oh, you mean Curiosity?" Carl volunteered from behind Tom, moving into camera view along side and appearing to their distant audience. "No, I'm sure it isn't although, that would have been the closest rover that *we* have. Curiosity landed six years ago in the Gale Crater, about two thousand clicks west of here, and I doubt it could have climbed those crater walls. Besides, I don't remember it looking quite like that. Curiosity was much larger than this one outside, more like the size of a car. This one's only about the size of a quad-runner." he added gesturing toward the porthole.

"Well, whatever the damned thing is," Tom resumed, "we'll get a better look at it in a day or two, after we complete a full systems check on board. Plus, we still need to conduct an exterior damage assessment. There are some external problems we already know about, but we're going to perform a more thorough exam. Our second venture outside will be an EVA to investigate those piles of rock being gathered by the rover."

"We might want to step up that time table, Tom," Brandon said worriedly, staring out the porthole through binoculars. As he passed the binoculars to Tom, he added, "See that large rotary drill bit on the rover's third arm? As the rover changed course, the drill started spinning. The rover is now heading straight toward us and looks like it's going to attack the Hab!"

Tom gave him an unbelieving look, "At this distance you could see the drill start up?"

Brandon replied, "Well, I was watching with the binoculars and when it began spinning, a cloud of dust flew off in all directions. Had it not been for the dust, I probably wouldn't have spotted the drill, at all."

"It might just be re-positioning itself," Carl offered, scoffing at the suggestion. "Why would it attack the Hab? Who would be directing it to do that?"

"I don't know, but it certainly looks like it's been attacking FP1's landing gear," Jackie said, agreeing with Brandon. She directed their eyes to look through the opposing porthole and toward FP1. One and all, they crammed together around the porthole, scrutinizing as best they could what Jackie had been seeing. Upon closer examination with the binoculars, they could see several holes and scratches in a couple of the landing gears, about one meter above the ground.

Carl gazed once again at the slow, but steadily approaching rover. Its rotary drill was, in fact, about one meter above the terrain's surface, and whirling rapidly. The strong vibration of the drill, once recorded by FP1 and transmitted back to JPL, might very well have appeared as minor seismic activity, as reported in a summarily discarded email. "That thing's gone berserk!" Carl exclaimed, now convinced of the danger to them. "It's been drilling holes in anything coming into its radar range, and piling up those shiny rocks around the edge of the crater. And now it's heading our way!"

Something else caught Sally's eye, "That's not all it's been doing. Look at the southern-most side of the lander. It looks like the rover has been piling up rocks over there to possibly use as a ramp. If that thing got up high enough, do you think it could have drilled into the methane and oxygen storage tanks?'

Tom looked worried. "I sure as hell hope not. We'll have to land the FP2 here as well, if it did." Then, looking squarely into the video lens, "Houston, if you have any control at all over this maniacal compilation of nuts and bolts, please direct its attention elsewhere. Granted, our pressure hull is nearly two meters above grade, but if that thing finds a way to raise its drill, prolonged boring into the outer surface of the Hab could be hazardous to our health, to put it mildly. I realize the communication lag for round trip is around sixteen minutes, but it's imperative that you stop this crazy thing, right now. Brandon, what is your best estimate till it reaches our Hab?"

Brandon peered out the porthole, took a sizable step back, closed one eye and stuck up his thumb at arms length, unconsciously mimicking an artist checking for the proper prospective. After a few moments of careful consideration and deliberation, he replied soberly, "If I had to hazard a wild-assed guess, it will reaching the side of the spacecraft's skirt in just around twenty minutes or less."

"OK," Tom thought out loud. "We can't take any chances on that damn thing being directed by someone other than Houston. Let's get our helmets and gloves back on, Bran. You and I are going to take care of that monstrosity before it takes care of us."

*

Back on Earth, Ty enlightened Morgan, "You'd better hope nothing happens to my friends or their ship, or I'm going to be all over you like white on bird shit." Pointing toward the exit he growled at Stave, "Now get this asshole out of my sight. Many thanks to all of you for your assistance in this critically time-sensitive operation. It has been greatly appreciated."

"Anytime, Commander," Steve affirmed, reaching out to firmly pump Ty's hand and clap him on the shoulder in understanding, soldier-to-soldier.

Chapter 16

Wednesday, November 28, 2018 (Wallyday, Aries 30, 0031)

"Bolo One, this is Houston", began a well-modulated voice, with Commander Tyler Cody's countenance suddenly appearing on the craft's monitor. "We received your marvelous transmission. First of all, I want to let you know that Commander Morgan Lewis is now officially relieved of duty. And, I've recently resumed active duty. We send our most heart-felt congratulations on your historic, successful landing on the surface of Mars.

"Secondly, I have just conferred with the staff here in the control room, getting up to speed after my extended absence, and they have assured me that the methane and oxygen tanks are all holding full pressure. Apparently, if the drill penetrated the outer hull, it missed the tanks, and the area containing the tanks was unpressurized anyway, so no harm done. Be sure to plug those leaks before pressurizing that area, if and when you need to do so.

"I can also assure you, we do not have any robotic rovers or other homicidal machines in your area. Therefore, if in your best judgment, you feel the safety of the crew and/or the mission is in jeopardy, feel free to take whatever action you deem necessary to defend yourselves. As the round-trip communication lag time is approaching sixteen-and-a-half minutes, I assume you've already taken such action, and I'm just talking to hear myself speak. Laughter erupted in the control room.

Ty continued, his voice suddenly scratchy and eyes shining with unshed tears, "Claire Base... Thanks for that, Tom.

That particular name means the world to me. And, from the images we are seeing on our monitors, Penny Bright Crater is also aptly named as a tribute to the memory of your beautiful wife. Please give us a read on those rock piles at your earliest convenience. I'm sure there must be some significance to the stockpiling.

"It may take a few days for me to get caught up on the details of the mission at hand, since I have been away from the office for so long. Rest assured, there is no better support team available than we have here at Mission Support and I have the utmost confidence in them. Unless you have more to report, expect our next transmission at 13:00 tomorrow. Check that. It's already after 03:00, so that would be 13:00 this afternoon. Commander Cody, over to you."

Tom and Brandon had indeed dealt with the threat. With the communications lag time working equally well against whomever had been relaying instructions to the rover, the two men were outside more than eight minutes before the machine's remote operator became aware of their presence. This also meant it was nearly an additional eight-plus minutes before the rover received the command to react to the danger. Before it even began responding, Tom and Brandon were outside of the Hab, disarming the threat.

Their first act in setting foot on the Martian surface was to investigate the rover's origin. They examined the machine's composition and manner of assembly, while looking for any telltale markings, such as a U.S. flag. Via Tom's helmet-mounted camera, the rest of the crew onboard was able to see what he was seeing. Markings on the top of the rover appeared to be of an Oriental script and Jackie confirmed, "It says 'LIFT HERE'."

Secondly, Tom pulled out his geologist's rock-hammer, using it to render the rover's camera inoperable by beating the hell out of it. Brandon voiced a comment, while borrowing Tom's rock-hammer, "Like my dad always said: if at first you don't succeed, read the instructions, but when all else fails, get a

bigger hammer." He firmly shoved the hammer's handle into
the spokes of one of the rover's front wheels, as a way of altering
its course roundabout and back towards the crater. Once the
machine was routed toward the precipice, he removed the
hammer handle to straighten out the track and keep it heading in
that direction.

While the enemy was en route to its final resting place,
Tom and Brandon meandered toward the crater's edge. They
passed by the machine during its slow trundling trek, and
approached the piles of stones. Each picked up a few of the
larger specimens, turning them over in their hands. "These are
some of the most unusual pieces I've ever seen," Tom
commented.

"Agreed," Brandon replied. "They give the impression
of raw diamonds, but the colors are amazing, more like fire
opals. In each stone there are at least three or four different
colors. Hold them up to the light and check out their unusual

shimmer," he exclaimed, in wonder.

Sally was on the control deck, monitoring their video and audio transmissions. "Hey, bring some of those in here! I need to see them, right away!" the geologist in her burst forth, in an excited and demanding yelp. "As they are on the edge of a crater, I'm thinking they might be carbonados and we'll probably find microdiamonds in the surrounding soil, too.

"Aye-aye, skipper," Tom shot right back, with a chuckle in his voice and saluting her with exaggerated motions, readily picked up inside the Hab.

Sheepishly, Sally replied, "Sorry Tom." In a more formal tone she requested, "At your earliest convenience, gentlemen, I would appreciate the opportunity to examine some of those specimens collected by the rover."

"Well, since you asked so nicely, we'll be right in," Tom said. Turning to Brandon, he added, "See how many of these rocks you can fit in your pockets. We'll make her sorry that she ever asked for some work to do."

"You got it, boss," Brandon answered back laughing, then added, "Hey Tom, looks like our nemesis is at the edge."

Sixteen minutes after stepping outside Bolo One, the two watched their foe topple over the edge, with great satisfaction. It plummeted ass over applecart some thirty meters to the floor of the crater and finally come to rest upside down in an ochre cloud. Once the dust cleared, it silently remained motionless in a mangled heap.

A quick survey of the vicinity near the crater's rim indicated the Chinese rover had been piling the stones for quite some time. Each mound was nearly a meter high with a base of about one meter in diameter. There were several dozen piles scattered about, if not more. The predecessor craft, FP1, had landed on the small hills of Avernus Colles, over eighteen months ago. The lightweight truck, which was used to deploy the nuclear generator, is mounted with cameras. So, either it was never commanded to drive in the direction of the crater and thereby spot the rover, or the rover arrived after the truck had finished its work.

The crater is to the east of FP1. The truck's duties were performed on the west side of the craft, where the truck is parked. It exhibited non-original exterior adornment, consisting of several holes bored into its body. This mischievous robotic rover had been very busy for quite some time. Fortunately, it never approached the generator or its power cable leading back to FP1. If the rover had bored into the cable, not only would it have been destroyed, but FP1 would have been left powerless and unable to manufacture the much needed fuel.

Though it has been widely suspected for quite some time that there are no viruses or bacteria in the Martian atmosphere, a general decontamination was performed on the specimens, as a precaution. Back onboard, Tom and Brandon placed their samples in the cleansing chamber, where they were bombarded with radiation and sprayed with a disinfectant solution. Both of the men then received this same treatment, before removing their pressure suits. A testing station will be set up just outside of the airlock. If it is determined that there is no danger from contamination, this procedure will be dispensed with in the future.

*

Later that morning, Tom was assisting Sally with the geological evaluation of the highly atypical stones. Brandon's original assessment had been right on the money. These were, indeed, a variety of diamond, but with an intriguing characteristic of colored micro-crystal inclusions embedded within the crystalline lattice. Sally deliberated and drew deeply from her education and lifelong curiosity about the natural world. She had interned with a gemologist in a college elective, and witnessed the way diamond cutters would weigh the stones, assess the clarity, and determine the type of cut to either eliminate the inclusions or accentuate them.

Typically, inclusions are considered to be flaws and detract from the desirability and value of the gemstone. However, these peculiarly colored micro-crystals refract the light in such a way, that even the uncut stones are breathtakingly beautiful, not to mention extraordinarily large. Each of the samples Tom and Brandon brought back to the Hab was of a size between a ping-pong ball and an extra large egg, with one baseball-sized stone in the mix. They were a very remarkable sight to behold, let alone actually hold in the hand.

"Look at the size of this rock!" Sally exclaimed, as she stood at the workbench, placing a 250-gram weight on the scale to properly calibrate to 0.38 of Earth gravity before setting the gem on the scale. "It weighs... 65 grams. On Earth that's..." rapidly punching numbers into the calculator, she read aloud "447'ish, nearly a pound." After punching in a few more quick calculations, "Holy cheese! That's something like 2235 carats. Tom, even with the inclusions, these rocks are going to be worth a fortune. When you and Brandon first brought these in and I saw how big this one was, I did a little digging in the computer. This one here is just about 2/3 the size of the largest gem-quality diamond ever found on Earth, the Cullinan Diamond, at about 621 grams. From it they cut the Great Star and the Lesser Star of Africa on the British Crown Jewels. Those came in at 530 and 317 carats," Sally read from the screen. She quickly stepped over to the porthole to take a look at the mounds of rock, a short distance from the craft.

Tom quietly moved over to the porthole to stand behind Sally, entranced by her enthusiasm and wanting to share in her awe. After a few moments, Sally spun back around saying, "There must be bil... oh!" She found herself face-to-face, and nearly nose-to-nose, with Tom, and stammered out, "billions of dollars in... just a few of those piles..." Tom noticed Sally was feeling flustered at their close proximity, and a similar shyness almost overwhelmed him.

He took a large step back, clearing his throat and saying, "Billions, that's great. Ten or twelve of those piles would pay for the whole damn trip, then. Right?"

Averting her eyes from Tom's features, Sally replied in an uneven voice, "Yes. I imagine the value of this find is most likely the reason why we have been waylaid and our fuel station attacked, to try to prevent us from finding the stones and/or keep us from acquiring them." She glanced up through her lashes to perceive Tom's eyes still on her. She turned away and began to pace the small area, her voice steadying. "The Chinese must have discovered the stones quite some time ago. They've been working against us all along… to keep us from getting here first. I suppose it may have just been a coincidence that this landing site was selected for our mission. Maybe they thought we knew about the diamonds all along and were just trying to stop us."

This time, when she turned back to face him, Tom smiled and his eyes crinkled. "But we did get here and there's nothing they can do about it, now. If that rover had been about two feet taller, it might have done some real damage to the FP1, but boring into the landing gear and the outer hull didn't have any effect on the fuel supply. Even with Commander Lewis feeding them information, they apparently just didn't have the means to inflict any real or lasting damage."

Tom unconsciously reached out and gently enveloped Sally's hand with both of his. "It's sad to consider that this may be the reason Ty was replaced with Jackie, Claire was murdered, and possibly even my Penny. And, they kidnapped Jackie's husband and would have killed him, as well. By turning the tables on the Chinese agents, we will prove that their lives were not just snuffed out, for no good reason. We have the gemstones and now possibly the means to pay for, not only this mission, but also many more to follow in the future.

"Sally, would you like to go on an EVA with me?" Tom asked. "I want to get a better look at the Penny Bright crater."

"I thought you'd never ask," she beamed, delighted at

the prospect of leaving the ship to go exploring. "I'd love to." The touch of his hands was warm and caring, a feeling that both unsettled and excited her at the same time, more than just a little. With her free hand, she clasped his hand, also.

"We can lower our gear over the edge and into the crater first, then rappel down after it. The climb back up should be pretty easy, in this low gravity," Tom observed. "While Brandon and I were out there earlier, I noticed an area of the crater wall that has a bit more gradual slope, and it's not too far from the near rim. I want to get a few soundings at the base of the caldera." Tom suddenly noticed he was holding her hand, but had not even realized he had reached out. Sally's hands were warm and soft, a very comforting feeling. Offering a warm smile to Sally, he squeezed her hand gently, before releasing it from his grasp. She reluctantly let him pull away, while returning the warmth of his smile with one of her own. Tom turned to head up the ladder to the galley.

Puzzled, Sally asked, "Tom, two things. What makes you think it is a caldera and not an impact crater, and two, the EVA Prep is on this deck, so where are you wandering off to?"

He paused with one foot on the ladder and turned back toward Sally. "You don't think this was a volcano?"

"Well, I'll agree there isn't much of an impact rim, but I suspect these stones are not native to Mars. Wind erosion could take down a lot of rim, I suppose. I've been thinking about it since you brought in the samples and I just don't see this as a volcano. More likely, these are carbonados from somewhere else, brought in on either a meteor or comet," Sally told him, seriously.

"Interesting," Tom replied. "So, meteor or comet, you say? Which do you think is the more likely of the two?"

"I think a sounding will tell us that... and where are you going now, if not to the EVA Prep-room?" She asked once more.

"Oh, I just wanted to grab a quick sandwich before heading out. You hungry?"

"Sure, I'll buy," Sally smiled broadly and lightly tossed to him the diamond she had been examining.

Tom laughed out loud, pleased with their friendly bantering, "In that case, I'll have filet mignon smothered in lobster." Oddly, he felt a little like a teenager, going out on a first date. Holding hands with Sally was a nice start. Too bad there was no movie feature in a darkened theatre. He shook his head at himself, amused with his thoughts.

Brandon was seated and reading data on a laptop in the common area, just outside of the galley, noisily munching on a raw carrot. Tom and Sally arrived on the top steps of the Jefferson ladder, laughing together at what appeared to be an inside joke. "And what are you two so giddy about?" he quizzed his crewmates through the open hatch.

"Well," Tom started to answer, but turned to Sally. "Do you want to tell him?"

"OK. Can you keep a secret?" she asked with a devilish twinkle in her eyes.

His curiosity piqued, Brandon replied, "Of course."

Sally snagged her arm through Tom's, "I'm pregnant and Tom and I have decided to stay on Mars, living together in sin!" Brandon started and nearly choked, his hand going to his throat as he gasped and coughed. Tom also had a stunned look on his face indicating that this was not the same information he was anticipating her to announce. "Hey, I'm kidding! Gees-Louise, you guys are so gullible," she ribbed the pair, then went on.

"Actually, you were right about the stones being a form of diamond. The one Tom is holding is about 2200 carats. I think we should re-negotiate our contracts to be... oh, I don't know, perhaps about a tenth of one percent, as a finder's fee.

We'll come out way ahead of the piddling amount they are planning to pay us," she said, referring to the five-to-seven plus million they would each receive. Sally stopped, astounded. "Did you hear what I just said? Who would of thunk it, as my grandmother used to say."

Pausing to regain his composure, but still gazing intently at Sally, Tom inserted, "And, we're going to EVA to the bottom of the crater and conduct soundings to see if we can determine where the heck they came from. The debate is whether they came up from within Mars, volcanically, or hitched a ride with a meteor or comet. Care to make a wager?" he invited, waving the glittering rock lazily before his friend's face.

"No way," Brandon stated, with a snort. "I'm not about to bet on anything having to do with geology, especially with a pair of crazy geologists."

"Smart man," Sally observed, with a quick grin. She and Tom then went about the business of preparing their snack, arguing good-naturedly about the merits of mayo vs. mustard.

Watching the two of them and perceiving how they interacted, always remaining nearby one another, Brandon's mind began mulling over the implications of Sally's somewhat humorless joke. The idea that she and Tom might have contemplated having a child together was not a problem, in his mind. They are two single, consenting adults and what they did was their own affair, so to speak. If they are sharing each other's company... well, why not? Just as long as they are only sharing each other's company (or bed to be more precise) and not planning to actually conceive a child on Mars. That could be problematic and possibly life threatening.

Sally is potentially young enough to becoming pregnant. However, the child would never be able to visit Earth. People visiting Mars from Earth have it easy, going from 1.0 Gee to 0.38 Gee. But, someone born on Mars trying to visit Earth would be going from 1.0 Martian Gee to just over 2.5 Martian Gee. Attempting this would have grave consequences.

A person weighing 70 pounds on Mars would find himself or herself weighing 184 pounds on Earth. This might not sound so bad on Earth, but let's see it from our Earthly prospective. A person weighing 184 pounds on Earth would find himself or herself weighing 484 pounds on a fictional planet, using the same gravity ratios. To take this analogy further, Mars has a very thin and dry atmosphere compared to Earth. So, the atmosphere of that imaginary planet would feel nearly as thick as water, to someone from Earth. He or she would have extreme difficulty moving about or even breathing.

It is anticipated that moving from Earth to Mars will prove to be a one-way trip, primarily due to the human body's inability to adapt quickly. After two or three years of residing on Mars, it could take the body the same number of years to re-acclimate to Earth's gravity and atmospheric pressure. Any children born on Mars would begin exhibiting alterations to their physical structure, within one or two generations. The most obvious change would be in height. It is believed that, under the reduced gravity, heights of seven feet or more will be quite common. However, bone density would decrease and muscle formation would change due to the same reduction of gravity. It could take years of increased gravity exposure, in small increments, to build someone's musculature up to a sufficient strength able to support his own body mass, when arriving on Earth. In addition, the function of the lungs may be impaired due to the differing gravitational loads, atmospheric pressures and weakened muscles, requiring assistance from a breathing apparatus to survive in a thicker and more humid atmosphere. In the end, children born on Mars would be just that: Martians.

*

An hour and forty minutes later, after first eating, donning pressure suits and traversing the treacherous descent, Tom and Sally finally attained the crater floor, near the now deceased and mangled rover. They took the next half hour to roll out the sounding gear and test the apparatus, which appeared to be in good working order. To achieve feedback for the soundings, Tom swung a sledgehammer and struck the terrain several times with great force, each blow causing a small shock wave to ripple downward through the surface. The sensors positioned along the gear's two cables transmitted data back to the nearby computer, being monitored by Sally. As the cables cross in the middle at a 90° angle, this process rendered a three-dimensional view of the subsurface, extending down to a depth of nearly 100 meters.

"Tom! This is amazing! Come take a look at this!" Sally was very excited after viewing the results. In the Martian gravity of 0.38 of Earth's, Tom took a few quick steps as he started moving toward her. He found himself approaching Sally so rapidly that he nearly fell over her, while clumsily trying to come to a halt in the somewhat bulky space suit.

"What is it?" he queried, anxiously.

"Look at the monitor!" she replied, in an unusually high pitch. Tom squinted at the screen for a few moments, then drew back glancing over at Sally.

"Is that really what it appears to be? Can it be what I think it is?" he asked, in astonishment.

Sally adjusted the output on the front of the display, "Are you not seeing what I'm seeing?" she questioned.

"I sure as hell hope so!" he answered, savoring the sight. "Surface looks solid, down about thirty-five meters, then there's about a five meter void above what looks like, HOLY SHIT, WATER! And it's... forty meters down to the pool. From there the depth goes... BELOW THE SOUNDINGS!!" Tom hollered loudly in his elation. "That would put it more than sixty meters in depth! Let's see... that's 100 x 100 x 60 plus... that's a fuckin' lot of water! Plus, we're just on the edge of the crater! This thing must be... what did we figure, eleven and a half kilometers across? Hey! We're sitting on top of a volcanic caldera with a huge subsurface lake!" he finished, with a final fist pump in the air.

"You still think this was a volcano?" Sally backhanded his arm, surprised at his pronouncement of the source.

"You don't?" Tom countered, just as surprised. "What else could it be?"

Sally thought for a moment before responding, "I had originally thought it was a meteor, but all this water means it must have been a comet. Listen," she said. "We both know a comet is basically a large, dirty snowball. So picture a snowball several kilometers in diameter that augered its way into the ground at high speed. The friction of that impact would cause it to start melting, but not before triggered thirty-plus meters of regolith to fall back in on top of it. When it struck Mars, the impact blasted this gigantic crater. Some of its surface material, the ice and hard mineral aggregate gemstone and carbonados got knocked off and landed in the ejecta around the edge of the basin. Then, geothermal heating caused the remainder of the comet to melt and resulted in this enormous underground lake."

Sally could see the glimmer of understanding in Tom's face as she continued with her theory, "I think we will find the perimeter of the lake closely matches the boundary of the crater. There will be more diamond crystals unearthed in the soil between here and the water's surface, but a much larger deposit will be located on the lakebed, assuming the gems were evenly distributed throughout the comet's ice. Plus, the lack of a well-defined impact lip could be due to the melting of the ice in the ejecta near the rim and the surrounding material collapsing back in upon itself, as the water seeped downward, much like sinkholes on a beach in the spring. By contrast, a volcano would, more likely, have a much higher rim and we would see a lot of galvanization and basalt in the surrounding soil," she concluded.

Excellent summation," Tom declared. "But, ya know what? I think the diamonds are going to turn out to be secondary in importance. The real find here is the water! This means that after we land FP2, we won't need to transport any more hydrogen to Mars from Earth. So, not only have we found a way to pay for this mission and the next several launches, we've also discovered a way to make all future missions less expensive! Of course, the location of the crater may just be coincidental to the water below. The comet, if that's what it was, may have just punched a hole in the top of an underground ocean."

"Isn't that a kick in the ass?" Brandon commented over their headsets. "This might just rate right up there with the discovery of the Higgs Boson. It should really make the accountants happy and set the powers that be to dancin' in the aisles," he enthusiastically shouted, leaping up from his seat at the console.

"Brandon, how long have you been monitoring us?" Sally queried.

"Not too long. I tuned in about four or five minutes ago," he replied. "And I'm gonna put a few bottles of the good stuff on ice, so to speak. Oh, by the way, our next uplink to Mission Support is in two hours, nineteen minutes. Do you two think you'll be back in here by then to pass on the good news, or would you rather wait for the following uplink to notify them of your discovery?"

Tom looked over at the crater wall, considered the trek up to the rim, and then glanced at Sally, "What do you think, two hours and nineteen minutes to make it back inside, or a bit longer? There's the slope I spotted," he said, pointing north about a hundred and fifty meters.

In high spirits, Sally jested, "With you climbing up after me and staring at my ass all the way? Yeah, I can make it without breaking a sweat. How about you?" From within her helmet, she favored him with a wink and flashed a smile that could sizzle butter.

"Just don't slow down," Tom warned in return, his own glance warming to her challenge.

Hearing the lighthearted teasing, Brandon again wondered about their future together and commented, "Ok you two, remember that people are listening and innocent ears are a-burnin'."

An hour and fifty-two minutes later, a weary Tom and Sally were slowly starting to remove their suits in the EVA Prep room. As Sally bent over to retrieve a glove she had dropped, Tom's eyes swept down her form and lingered on her trim backside. She glanced around and caught him ogling, "You are staring at my ass, aren't you?" she accused Tom, smiling in amusement and more than a little satisfaction. After all, she was in decent shape and had always maintained her womanly figure, with curves in all of the right places. Plus, she was elated now that Tom was appearing to reciprocate the emotions she had been aware of in herself for the past couple of months.

Tom averted his eyes, blushing furiously, "I'm sorry," he stammered. Sally turned and faced him as she straightened, taking hold of his chin with gentle fingertips and directing his focus into her darkening eyes.

"Don't be," she whispered, as she leaned in, tilted her head, and softly pressed her mouth against his. Tom reached up and grasped Sally's arms at the biceps, with the intent of moving her away, but the smooth silkiness of skin, feminine scent, and moist plumpness of her lips was warm and welcoming. In reflection, it had been oh so long since he had closely held a woman. This time Tom was feeling a bit more receptive to Sally's invitation, his body responding automatically. He slid his hands from her biceps around to her shoulder blades, palms skimming under the sleeveless openings of her tank-top, his fingertips going beneath the fabric to hold her close and his fingertips not finding bra straps. Her breasts had appeared to be supported by a bra, but in the reduced gravity, one was not needed. The firmness of her arms and back felt good against his hands, and the tenderness of her kiss was unexpected. Not hard and fast as during the midst of passion, but soft, like a butterfly landing on a flower. Their torsos were pressed gently together, from chest to groin, and arms entwined. A moment later Tom realized they had been holding their kiss for several pounding heartbeats. Not having been aware they were closed, he opened his eyes. Sally's were still shut. He sighed and reluctantly forced himself to pull away from her warm embrace.

"That was very nice, but I think I'm going to need just a little more time," he said as his thoughts once again traveled back to Penny and the love they had shared. "It's only been a few months." Sally put her hand to her lips and smiled softly at Tom.

"Well, that's not a 'no'," she said, wistfully.

"No, it isn't," Tom smiled back. "Simply a little while to sort out my thoughts." He bowed forward and kissed the tip of her nose, just a tiny peck, conveying affection more than passion.

As they finished dressing, Tom tried to focus his thoughts on baseball, football, or anything else in which he had no particular interest. His encounter with Sally had resulted in a noticeable swelling to his groin and he needed to clear his head. He had a lot to think about and Penny was foremost in his mind. He loved her so very much and missed her, terribly. He was also feeling guilty now about his behavior with Sally and the way he was beginning to care about her. It occurred to him, that if he had died instead of Penny, she had still been young and would most likely have remarried one day. He would have wanted her to be happy and not live her life alone. That revelation abruptly made everything a little bit clearer, tidying his mind. He slipped his shirt on hastily and proceeded out to the control center. Sally followed a short moment later, her cheeks rosy.

"Good timing, you two. Glad you could join us," Carl chided the pair at their late entry. Tom and Sally's eyes darted swiftly at one another, and they tried to act as if nothing had occurred. This pretence made them look guilty of something, but of course no one knew quite what it was. "We should be receiving something very soon from Mission Support," Carl added.

Brandon noticed their looks at each other, as well. Now, more than ever, he realized what a great couple Tom and Sally could be. And, it appeared that they were starting to become conscious of it for themselves. He was in the midst of pouring champagne when the main view screen lit up, and a familiar voice began to address them.

"Greetings from planet Earth, on this lovely second sol during the Occupation of Mars, on the 29th day of November, 2018. This is Commander Tyler Cody, Acting Mission Support Commander, back here in Houston. Once again, I wish to convey our sincere congratulations on yesterday's historically successful landing which transpired within a hose-length of your gas station, no less. Nice bit of piloting on your part, if I do say so." Over the microphone, mild applause and cheering could be heard in the background, but not nearly as exuberant as during the confirmation of their landing.

Ty continued, "To give you an update on the goings on around here: Commander Lewis is on his way to the brig, pending a court-marshal, and my earnest hope for an optional trial and speedy execution. I have it on good authority that prior to his arrival at the appropriate facility, Captain Thomas and his associates were able to convince the commander to give up certain sensitive information regarding his colleagues. Now, it is my understanding that under the 'Domestic Terrorism Act', his court-marshal may have to wait until after the hanging," Ty uttered happily, as he leaned in close to the camera lens for a close-up fisheye wink. Soft laughter could again be heard over the communications system.

He resumed his speechifying, "I should have mentioned earlier, this is a closed session, but the media has been requesting details concerning the landing of the Bolo One, as well as information about its crew and the final mission parameters. Because the communication time lag will prevent a direct question and answer session, we have compiled a list of the questions asked most frequently. Your systems should be downloading the list and we ask that you reply to the questions at your leisure, and send it back to us.

"Next subject: What is the situation there, regarding that crazy run-away rover? Have you been able to do anything about it? And, what about the piles of samples it had been assembling? What are they and what the hell was that all about? Standing by for your reply with bated breath, it's over to you."

Tom turned toward Brandon, "Brandon, please enable the closed communication session, thanks. After a nod from Brandon, Tom began to greet his friend, "Hi Ty." Then, popping up to attention and favoring him with a salute, he added, "I mean Commander Cody, Sir! Glad to hear things are under control, back home." He paused for a moment, then continued, "...after the hanging. Ha! I like that." Tom chuckled heartily, with glee flavoring his tone.

"Well, we have a great deal to report. I only wish I could be there to tell you in person, just so I could see the look on your face when you hear all of what's been going on at this end. In the first place, that robotic rover, which we believe to be of Chinese origin, has been permanently... shall we say, deactivated due to an unfortunate tumble into the crater. We discovered it had attacked the fuel processor and the light truck, damaging them slightly. While Brandon and I were out there on EVA earlier, we checked them out further. The rover had bored several holes into both the truck's chassis and frame, as well as the exhaust nozzles and landing gear of FP1. The punctures in the nozzles were really ineffectual, since the lander is not meant to re-launch from the planet.

When we are ready to deploy the pressurized rover, we will still be able to utilize those nozzles by converting them to wheels for the vehicle. I wish I could thank the guy who came up with that unique idea. And, as the truck is un-pressurized, a few holes in the body won't hurt it either, just so long as it missed the methane and O2 tanks, which I am happy to report, it did.

"Next are the mounds surrounding the Penny Bright Crater," Tom paused for about two beats with reflections of his darling, deceased wife playing in his mind. Then remarked, "By the way, you may have observed that everyone here is in possession of unauthorized champagne flutes. Before launch, we swapped them out for the freeze-dried Green Bean Casserole that we all hate. Originally, we stowed away several bottles of bubbly in advance for celebrating our last day on Mars. But as you can see, we've already popped the cork on day two of our invasion. 'Why?' you may ask. No, we're not ready to head on home just yet. As it turns out, the samples collected by the rover were diamonds in the rough, and that's not a euphemism for anything. They are literally carbonados, or *space diamonds,*" he said, emphasizing the final two words. "But, not just any plain old, ordinary space diamonds." In front of the camera Tom hefted a coarse gem from the bench, the largest of the assortment he and Brandon had fetched on the first EVA. It was the size of a baseball.

"Brandon and I carried quite a few of these onboard yesterday. Well, to be fair, not all of them were this large. But, as you can see from this specimen, there are a myriad of colors shining throughout, much like fire opals. To my knowledge, there are none like this to be found on Earth. In fact, there aren't many diamonds on Earth that can compare to the size of this one. Actually, most of the ones we saw were more around the size of large marbles and ping-pong balls. But, Earth diamonds that are the size of ping-pong balls represent a very small percentage," Tom turned toward Sally, "Did I say that all correctly?" She was sitting just off camera, laughing into her hands as silently as possible, at his put-on slightly fumbling, absentminded professor act.

"Oh, and the piles of diamonds," Tom took a large drink from his glass and went on, "there are close to fifty of them, each about a meter high and a meter in diameter at the base. So, we are estimating that around ten of those piles will pay for this whole fu… fantastic mission. It's a good thing this isn't a live feed going out over the networks. But wait! There's more!" He skewed up his face and took a big gulp, emptying his glass, while everyone onboard hooted at his entertaining parody of a tipsy game show host.

"Earlier today, Sally and I went for a stroll… well, more accurately an EVA, to the floor of the Penny Bright." Tom paused a moment as Brandon refilled his glass. "Thank you. We ran sounding tests and determined that in the top thirty-five meters or so of the ground, there are… a lot… more… diamonds!" Tom intoned his best impression of Captain James T. Kirk and it was dead-on. High on adrenaline rather than alcohol, he was really on a roll and thoroughly enjoying every minute of it.

"But seriously, what did we locate immediately beneath the diamond encrusted dirt?" We found, extended drum-roll please…" Together Brandon and Carl both started beating rhythmically on the console with both hands. "…The source of the diamonds! Hold on! First, let me tell you a little story. Once upon a time, 'a long ago, in a galaxy far, far away…' a huge comet came zipping through our solar system and ran smack into Mars. WHAM!!" he exclaimed and clapped his hands together, with a loud crack to illustrate.

"That collision whacked a few million diamonds off its surface, which then wound up embedded in the soil and now, thanks to the dearly departed robot, many of them are massed all around the impact rim. By the way, it has been proposed that the Sponsors take back their five million dollar per person retainer, in lieu of 1/10 of one percent of the value of the diamonds as a finder's fee. Perhaps you can negotiate that compromise for us," Tom smiled and winked broadly at Ty.

He continued the tale, "The remainder of the comet augered into the terrain and either melted into a huge underground reservoir, or became a part of a much larger reservoir that was already there. Tomorrow, we'll go out and take soundings at ten to fifteen clicks out from the rim in several directions. If we still find water, it's an underground ocean. If not, well this lake appears to be roughly eleven and a half kilometers in diameter and a minimum of ten fathoms deep. That's as much as we could tell from the soundings we took. It could be a lot deeper. What that signifies is: As soon as FP2 has safely landed, we will never need to send hydrogen to Mars again!

Grinning, Tom kept going, "So, to recap, we can now pay for, not only this mission, but most likely all future missions. Plus, from now on, they will all be cheaper to launch by not lugging around 2.6 tons of hydrogen! On a more serious note, the robotic device, which was here, had been collecting diamonds for… well, who knows how long, and they never even had a clue about the water beneath the surface. The Bolo One party is on planet less than twenty-four hours and we have discovered the 'Holy Grail' and it is overflowing with water.

Tom spoke emphatically, "Robotic rovers have their place in the scheme of exploration, working as scouts and general laborers, but nothing can ever beat the human drive to succeed, our passion to explore the unknown and our will to survive against all odds. You can't program any of that into a machine. That which makes us human is what makes us strong; that which does not kill us makes us stronger. No robotic explorer will ever be able to truly realize what it means to be human. A robot can not fall in love, or suffer pain and loss, or thrill to the sight of another sunrise." Tom found himself once again gazing at Sally and beginning to acknowledge his true emotions and awakening yearnings for this amazing woman.

Turning back to face the camera squarely, Tom concluded his discourse with, "Plus, no damn Chinese robot can match good, old fashioned Yankee ingenuity. It all comes down to one simple conclusion: If you're gonna explore Mars, any other planets, or whole star systems, for that matter, ya gotta send humans. From Claire Base on Mars, this has been Commander Thomas Castle reporting, over to you in Houston."

Chapter 17

Afterward: About one month later

From: Emma Devlin
Subject: Happy New Year!
Date: January 01, 2019 10:42 a.m.
To: Brandon Devlin

_____(CLT): 10 min 29.39 sec

Dearest Brandon,

Happy New Year, my darling husband. I'm enclosing
many kisses without benefit of the mistletoe. Wait till you see
the newest calendar photos. For January, I'm decked out as the
New Year's baby, nothing on but a 2019 sash, shiny top hat, and
a fashionable smile. ; p In honor of your arrival on Mars, this
new calendar is made up of the days, weeks, and months
reflecting your time on the planet. Superimposed on the pages
are the usual Earth dates. Surprise! Hope you like it. I used
your Devlinian Mars calendar to put it together. It took a bit of
explaining before the printer got it right. If you want to show
people your Mars calendar, be sure to add a few strategic cover-
ups to the pictures. Hee-hee!

I'm so elated for Tom and Sally. Do you think the
attraction had been building for a long time, or was it kind of
sudden? In your last note you said he was planning to propose
on New Year's Eve. Did he? How did she respond? Are they
both walking on air? Come on now, details are essential here.
Tell me all.

You know, Tom and Penny were dear friends of ours and I was heartsick when her sister called to tell me about the accident. How horrible. The funeral was difficult and everyone was still in disbelief. I almost lost it when I thought of Tom so far away and not able to have closure and grieve with his family.

A lot of men close up and shut down emotionally with loss. I'm really glad you are his friend and have been there to help him through it. From what you said, having other good friends around helped, too. Sally must be a very special person. I had only met her a few times and she seemed like good people. How long was she married? I hope she doesn't end up breaking Tom's heart. You say it's a good match and they obviously adore each other. I trust your judgment when it comes to Tom and won't worry.

Rich says he's having a great time in India. I was able to talk with him on Skype, the other day. He carried his computer around his hotel room and showed me the fancy decorative plaster. He was lucky to get a private bathroom. It was up a small stairs at the side of the room because they were added on to the old buildings. I'm waiting for him to send his blog address so that I can check out the photos.

A friend recommended that he ride the bus to get around, as that would be the only way to really understand the country. So, that's what he's planning to do. Rich said the residents take chickens on the busses and such, and he's looking forward to touring in this way with his group. He's so funny sometimes (kind of like his dad). Can't wait to see the pictures and read about his many adventures.

Speaking of (mis)adventures, I'm still very thankful that everything came out ok after all of what happened on Mars and here on Earth. I got a call from Ty the other day and he filled me in on some of the details you couldn't put in your letters. So much of it was almost unreal. Sweetheart, I'm going to be very, very happy when you are on your way home to me. You're constantly in my thoughts and my heart. I miss you so much that I ache. The calendar can be a reminder of what else, besides my love, is waiting for you. Hurry back, my darling.

Well, I better get off that subject and on to happier thoughts. I have some errands to run, so will head out and about. In a couple of weeks I may go and visit my sister and get another baby fix. He's adorable, loves his Auntie, and his baby kisses are almost as sweet as yours. I'll send more snaps of the baby. You'll see how big he's getting and how much he resembles his daddy. Talk to you soon.

I love you bunches,

Your M

Hope Our Love Lasts And Never Dies (HOLLAND)

< ≡ ♂ ≡ >

From: Tyler Cody
Subject: Big news for the new year
Date: January 01, 2019 11:07 a.m.
To: Brandon Devlin

_____(CLT): 10 min 29.42 sec

It is indeed a happier new year, good friend. I've been promoted to the rank of Captain and they've included a raise in pay retroactive to being 'wounded in the line of duty' (that's what they're calling it now). It goes back to the night of the mission announcement, the nightmarish evening that my dearest Claire was killed. I was placed on the disabled list right after. Maybe it's their way of giving me additional compensation for my loss of Claire, even though they're NOT calling it that. Maybe it was because a foreign power may have caused the injury. No one has claimed responsibility for Claire or the rover. There could never be enough compensation for that sort of loss for anyone, but the extra income will come in mighty handy.

And more first-rate news: The witch doctors have given me a clean bill of health. The shrinks even gave me a pass. In the psychological exam, I showed them that I'm not psycho, but I am logical. (wink) So, I will no longer be the *Acting* Mission Support Commander. They have officially given me the designation of Mission Support Commander. That means you're stuck with me for a while, but not for the duration of the mission. There's an excellent reason: I've been given command of the next mission. While you're heading home, I'll be zipping along on my way to the sunny, southern slopes of Hibes Montes. So, the next time you make a trip over to FP2, stow away a bottle or two of that bubbly for me, will ya. ; ~ p Of course, that means we won't be in the same place, at the same time, until at least May or June, 2023. Good thing we can still get email from Mars.

See you on the flip side,

Ty

< ≡ ♂ ≡ >

From: Steven Thomas
Subject: New Year's Day Greeting
Date: January 01, 2019 11:32 a.m.
To: Dr. Valerie Thomas

_____(CLT): 10 min 29.50 sec

Dear Sweet Val,

Happy New Year, Babe.   Got to bed late last night because of all those revelers making noise outside my window. Hope you were able to sleep in this morning. Well, I gotta tell ya, after that last extraction, I've come a stone cold realization. I'm gettin' too old for this shit! (Since Mike's rescue, everyone, including Mission Support, knows what business he's in, so the emails no longer need to be guarded.) I came so close to catching live fire, this time, that it really got me thinking about my mortality and how death hounds us in this business. Why the hell am I still doing this? It's not like we need the money. In fact, if we lived on Mars, we wouldn't need money at all, for a few years at least. I mean, with all those diamonds to be mined... Ha! We could bank it till we're ready for a vacation back on Earth. What do you think the chances are they'll let me come up there and join ya? That is, if you have any interest in staying there, anymore. In the past couple of months, you've mentioned staying on Mars, and I was wondering if you're still considering that?

Cause, the more I think about what you said, the more I like the idea. How about bringing it up to the powers-that-be and seeing what their reaction is? Tell them I'll work for room & board and a dollar a day, just like a sheriff in the good ole days of the bad ole west. Wouldn't that be a hoot? Maybe I can pin on one of those tin stars, although I probably won't get to carry a gun. In that airtight environment, it wouldn't be a very good idea. Maybe a taser... yeah, that'll do it. Mostly non-lethal, but it'll sure knock 'em on their ass. Zzzzzzttt

But seriously, neither of us has any family left, here on Earth. I really would be willing to move to Mars, to be with you, even if we had to give up everything else we own. Having material goods can't compare to the thrill of holding you close. I love you that much.

Missing you so much more than you'll ever know, Steve

< ≡ ♂ ≡ >

From: Thomas Castle
Subject: New Year's news
Date: Taurus 12, 0031 12:03
To: Tyler Cody

_____(CLT): 10 min 29.57 sec

Hey Ty. Happy New Year from planet Mars. Congrats on the promotion and new mission assignment. Bran shared the news with all of us, just a few moments ago. Well, I guess that changes my plans… I was intending to ask you to be my best man when we get home. But, just about the time we're getting back to the ranch, you'll be arriving here. What a hoot!!

Yeah, Sally and I are getting married. I popped the question last night and she said yes. I'm one lucky guy to be able to marry a girl like Sally. After Penny died, I never thought I could love another woman. I don't have a ring yet, but you should see the pretty little stone I've picked out. Ha, ha. Come to think of it, you have seen it. It's the rock I was holding on day two, when we were sipping Champagne last month. I figure the band will have to fit over her head so she can wear it as a necklace. It's way too big for a ring. : }

Everyone up here knows about the upcoming nuptials and they are OK with it. In fact, Brandon helped us set up private quarters in the Mars Ascent Vehicle. As an apartment, it's a bit cramped, but at least we can have our privacy.

Of course, all of this isn't just for us. Sally and I talked about it and decided we could try to keep our relationship a secret, or be open about it. But, we felt any PDA's (public displays of affection) wouldn't be fair to the rest of the crew, since none of them are having the same sort of intimacy… so far as we know, at least. ; }

Whoa!! Valerie just came down to the lab and told us about a message she just got from Steve. She is wanting to stay on Mars at the end of our tour and Steve is willing to join her. From what I've heard, he sure wouldn't have any trouble passing the physical. If he's allowed to make the trip, one-way, and she stays here, that'll set a precedent for colonization that we didn't think would happen for another 50 years. On the other hand, with all of these diamonds to be mined and setting up livable space for future colonists, I can see how the Sponsors might be anxious to start touting the merits of immigration. They're gonna be needing some slave-laborers. Can you imagine?

Huh!!

TTYL, Tom

< ≡ ♂ ≡ >

From: Jackie Miller
Subject: Happy New Year to You
Date: Taurus 12, 0031 12:12
To: Michael Miller

_____(CLT): 10 min 29.61 sec

Happy New Year, Hon

Looks like it's time to play catch up with you, since I've been away from my email for the past four days. Valerie, Brandon, and I just returned from FP2. Because we had landed so close to FP1 and we had the FP2 following us to Mars, we were able to direct it to land elsewhere. And elsewhere turned out to be almost 400 klicks away to the north-northwest, a place called Hibes Montes. It is a much steeper terrain with mountain peaks and really deep valleys. Definitely not a day trip. With the terrain being so rough and the pressurized rover topping out at about 30 km/h on flat ground, the trip took about a day and a half each way, just for driving.

You may remember, part of the backup plan was to have it launch two weeks after we left. That was just in case we missed the landing site by a distance of 500 klicks or more. (You know, the way we talk is funny isn't it? Why do I type klicks instead of km? One is shorter to say, the other to type. But it feels like I'm talking to you. It's kind of like the way people say vee-double-you instead of Volkswagen. VW is shorter when written, but has more syllables than Volkswagen when spoken.) But, I digress from my catching up.

While we had to remain in orbit for two weeks waiting

for the dust storm to settle, FP2 caught up and was in orbit before we landed. Since we hit right on the mark and were in control of the FP2, we could land it wherever we wanted. With 1000 km roundtrip range, we picked a spot we could drive to, check it out, and drive back on a single tank of fuel. Although, to play it safe we tapped FP2 for several kilos of fuel before we headed back to Bolo One.

The fuel processor is working perfectly and will have made 14 tons of methane and 28 tons of oxygen by the time the next crew arrives. Once they do, they will still need another several tons of oxygen for the proper fuel ratio (3.2 parts O2 to 1 part CH4). But, there's no rush as they will be here for a year-and-a-half and have plenty of time to make oxygen.

On the way over to FP2, we passed several rather unusual looking rock formations and set out flags so that the geologists can inspect them later. They may turn out to be nothing special, but they sure looked interesting to us.

Ok, let's see, what else has been happening? Oh, big news flash!! Tom and Sally are engaged! Do you recall how Tom's wife died and Sally's husband divorced her by way of an email? We've suspected for some time now that Tom and Sally were getting sweet on one another. About two weeks ago they let us all know they were a couple, but the engagement was announced last night. Isn't that exciting!?!? I've always thought New Year's Eve was a magical time, with many a special happening at the stroke of midnight.

Also, Valerie just shared the email message her husband sent. A while back she wistfully mentioned wanting to stay on Mars, if only Steve could join her. Well, come to find out he's all for it! How about them apples! Yeah, he's ready to pack up and immigrate to Mars. Val said if she does stay here, we'd be able to transport the equivalent of her weight in diamonds back to Earth, in fact, we'd just about have to since the fuel in the spacecraft is calculated based on a certain amount of mass. If she stays here and we DON'T haul diamonds, we'll have to haul rocks, just so the weight is right. The Sponsors would go for that, for sure. No doubt in my mind. ;~}

Oh well, I've got to go and work on a few reports before dinner. I'll write more a little later this evening.

Love ya and miss ya, Jackie

< ≡ ♂ ≡ >

From: Richard Devlin
Subject: Christmas break in India
Date: January 01, 2019 12:42 p.m.
To: Brandon Devlin

_____(CLT): 10 min 29.68 sec

Happy New Year Dad,
        Wow, you've already been on Mars for over a month. They say time flies when you're having fun! Speaking of fun, here I am in India for a five-day conference followed by a week of sightseeing. Awesome! Never imagined I'd be able to do something as terrific as this before graduating. I've copied a few pages from my blog about the trip. Hope you'll enjoy the read.

        Starting out, we traveled by charter bus from Western to O'Hare airport. The bus driver was great and funny as hell during the whole trip. I was dictating a 'memo to self' as we were getting ready to head out, and he stood up with his microphone and began reciting this announcement: "Ladies and gentlemen, if I may have your attention for a moment. While we are traveling today, please keep in mind that in the event of an emergency, this bus is equipped with sixteen exits (dramatically pointing toward the exits).

        "The first one is the door where you got on. The next thirteen are the side windows. They are the ones labeled as exits on each side of the bus. If you pull up on the trim and push out at the bottom, they are hinged at the top and will swing open very easily. The last two are those overhead hatches in the aisle with the small red, pointed knobs. If you turn those knobs so that they are pointing either to the left or the right and push on the knob, the hatch will pop open. Now, those hatches are real easy to get to when the bus is lying on its side… I'll try to avoid that." Everyone cracked up. He continued, "Also, in the event of a crash over water, this bus will float… but don't ask me how I know that." And everyone laughed even harder. Woot!!

When we got to the airport, he commenced with another announcement, so I grabbed my phone and recorded that one, too: "Please remain seated until the ride comes to a complete stop. At that time, please check the overhead compartments for anything you may have brought onboard, as well as the floor around your seats to make sure you didn't drop anything of value, such as your cell-phone, car-keys, fast food wrappers… if you dropped any money on the floor, its probably gotten dirty… so feel free to leave it there and I'll make sure it gets disposed of properly." Much more laughter, with me almost splitting a gut. "Please collect your luggage at coach-side to take with you and thank you for riding Indian Trails." Double-Woot!! Maybe we can talk him into working on the Bronco Transit to provide comic relief during finals. What do you think?

As of yesterday, the conference portion has ended for our trip. So now, we begin the fun by following suggestions from some Virginia Beach friends that formerly lived in New Delhi – get out of New Delhi. The Indian state of Rajasthan is our destination, with the city of Jaipur as our centre of operations. But, how to get there…

You can fly to Jaipur, take a slow train, or the slower still, state-run bus service. Or, as suggested by my friend, Bob, "ride a bus with chickens." So, we did. Unfortunately, no chickens on the ride, but I swear I saw some feathers on my seat. So, for 200 Rupees per person (just about $4.44), we took a 35-person bus about 234 km with 60 wonderful people onboard.

The bus was a normal bus, like most others, except that they divided the vertical space in half with a very 'we already

have the spare parts' flair. I had ample clearance sitting down –
there was just someone lying above me. Plus we shared the
same large window across both stories. In fact, that upper berth
had no metal support as the person lay – if he leaned too much
against the Plexiglas, he'd fall out the side.

And we didn't have to worry too much about the safety
glass on the bus's door, as I believe the bus didn't have a door.
No need for air conditioning that way. The bus had a front
mount engine and the driver sat beside it (kinda like some school
buses). Instead of wasting space with the engine, they mounted
a padded carpet shelf over it to allow people to sit, leaving a
small cutout for the gearshift.

Google says it would take 3h 17m for this trip on
National Highway 8. Google assumes things like people driving
in lanes, constant speeds, zero construction, no dodging of
horses, and even pavement. This is an example of a Google fail.

There's no word in Hindi for "expressway". I don't
think there's a word for "freeway" or "turnpike" either. It was a
four-lane road with a divider in the middle most of the way.
Over the length of NH-8, a single bridge was found at what
could be almost described as an interchange. Since there are no
other bridges, there are breaks in the dividers to allow u-turns,
people crossing, and cross streets. Plus, in many of the villages
and small cities, they're starting to build overpasses adding
construction to the mix. Plus we had to pass three elephants.
Google is wrong by about 2h in its calculations.

We hopped on the bus about 10:45 and arrived at 16:00
– so why 2h more than what Google said? This wasn't the
express bus, so there were a bunch of stops. Sometimes, they
included slowing down along a few crowds of people and
shouting "jah-pour, jah-pour, jah-pour" like an auctioneer. For a
few pickups and drop-offs, we didn't even come to a complete
stop; just leap.

There were a few food vendors that got on for a single
stop, selling samosas and other yummy smelling wares. But, on

the advice of a wise sagess, never eat from the street vendors. Plus there were toll-booths and a gas refill.

Then there was the big stop for a snack at a street side hole in the wall. And when in Rome, I decide to partake in a traditional Indian male rite of passage: just take a piss on the side of the road. Don't try to be subtle and hide behind a tree – just stand there and go.

The stop also involved impromptu repair. Some guys crawled under the bus with a large reservoir grease gun to do something with the drive train or axle and hopefully not the brakes.

Was the chicken bus worth it? Yes. I'll admit that I was anxious when I noticed the bus would be making stops. I wasn't sure if the luggage compartment was locked (it was) and if someone would walk off with my bags. I might like to do it again, but without luggage and with a local companion to assist in the adventure (preferably one that speaks Hindi, or better yet, English, also). It's hard to play tourist without a guide.

I have officially concluded that Mom can never visit India. During her rides through the narrow streets of Boston or wide avenues of Manhattan, when we visited the east coast, she made an audible gasp when traveling under the speed limit and with ample clearance – both of which are still uncomfortable to her. Mom's reaction to three motorcycles weaving in the 50cm gap between our taxi and the three wheeled scooter carrying eight passengers may produce a short scream. Add the rule-free traffic circles, roundabouts, and rotaries with the rare (but fun) figure-8 versions and we're moving into the oxycontin & xanax cocktail epi-shots territory.

In Delhi, the taxi ride between the hotel and conference center lasted 15-30 minutes, depending on traffic. Of course, when the commute was bad, it was really bad: one day's was over 90 minutes. We could have gotten out and bought from the street vendors.

The first day, the ride from the airport to hotel was pleasant too: Smokey fog, with 0.25 km visibility, freeway driving, and tractors that don't quite reach freeway speed. And out of all of these journeys, we only saw one accident – in the fog on day one. Looked pretty bad with the car busting off a big truck's wheel and the car's engine compartment now being used as a replacement, but apparently no injuries. And a few seconds later – lost in the fog again.

Well, tomorrow we're off to Agra, to see the Taj Mahal. I'll send pix and write more, later.

Your son, the Globe-hopper, Rich   LOL

< ≡ ♂ ≡ >

From: Mary Croft
Subject: Happy New Year
Date: January 01, 2019 12:54 p.m.
To: Carl Wilson

_____(CLT): 10 min 29.72 sec

Hey Sweetheart,

Happy New Year! I miss you very much and really wish you were here. Last night, I went out with some of the girls to a New Year's Eve party. We had a great time. I only had a little to drink, but Beth Ann got totally wasted. We had to pour her into the car. LOL

At the party I was chatting with a really neat lady from China. I had never met someone from China before, so we talked for hours. I found out we have similar interests. She was very interested to hear about you and your mission and asked lots of questions. Some of them were kind of technical and I wasn't sure of the correct answer, so I told her some of what you had shared with me. She and I made a lunch date for this afternoon and she will be stopping by here soon, to pick me up. So if I have to cut this short, I'll write more, later when I get back and tell you all about it.

I found out she used to be an Olympic gymnast, about ten years ago, or so. Wasn't that about the time that Jackie was in the Olympics? Who knows, maybe they knew each other. Anyway, that must be why she looks so fit. Maybe she can give me some exercise hints. Lord knows I could stand to lose a few pounds. I want to keep looking good so you'll still want me when you get home. (Giggle) Oops, there's the doorbell. Kaiying is here earlier than I thought, gotta go. I should only be gone a couple of hours and will let you know how it all went.

Forever yours, Mary

〈 ≡ ♂ ≡ 〉

52696991R00147

Made in the USA
Lexington, KY
07 June 2016